Where We Began

SERENA CLARKE

FREE
BIRD
BOOKS

Praise for *One Distant Summer*

"What an amazing emotional love story. *One Distant Summer* was my first Serena Clarke book, but it won't be my last. I thoroughly enjoyed reading her writing style, the story flowed flawlessly."
– Mommaleena's Blog

"What an emotional read! I really enjoyed this book—the setting was beautiful and I felt that both Jacinda and Liam were deeply developed characters...the chemistry between them was undeniable."
– Sasha Says

"A story I loved as I read more and more...one that I would also highly recommend!!"
– Cozy Corner Reading Nook

Praise for *A North So True*

"Everything you'd want in a novel. Romance, mystery, suspense, a hero who you fall in love with and a leading lady who you almost wish you could be. A great read that I couldn't put down."
– Amazon reader

"The best book I have read in so long...I was awake until 4am! I couldn't put it down!"
– Amazon reader

"*A North So True* combines the best of so many worlds...from ice skating and snowmobiling to gut-warming shots and hot baths, my senses soaked up every description."
– Random Book Muses

Praise for *The Same But Different*

"A beautiful story about one woman's adventure of a lifetime."
– Written Love

"You can't help but want to keep reading. It's not just romance literature, but also a story about sisterhood, loss and finding yourself. Extremely glad I found this book and *All Over The Place!*"
– Amazon reader

"Plenty of steamy tension...a recommended fun, feel-good story with some unexpected twists and surprises."
– WiLoveBooks

Praise for *All Over the Place*

"One of the best, most romantic, awe-inspiring and awwwww-inspiring happily ever afters I've read in a long time. Brava, Serena Clarke! I plan to read more by you."
– Random Book Muses

"Filled with rich, deep emotion, engaging characters and dialogue, and plenty of intrigue that kept me turning the pages...Ms. Clarke is certainly an author to keep an eye out for!"
– Storm Goddess Book Reviews

"This book reminded me of a great chick-flick kind of movie, only in book form. And everyone knows the book is always better!"
– SMI Book Club

Where We Began

Chapter 1

A very Robinson waved from her front porch as the last guest drove away into the warm Oregon evening, maintaining her smile until the car turned the corner. Then she breathed out for what felt like the first time that day. She pulled all the hairpins from her bun and shook her head, thankful to literally let her hair down at last. Slipping the pins into the pocket of her black dress, she looked down at the big yellow dog sitting at her feet, watching her expectantly.

"You did great today, Ace." His plumy tail thumped on the ground. "Better than me, at least," she added, leaning down and giving him a hug.

Then they went back inside together, through the wide, wood-paneled hallway to the living room. Her aunts were each sitting upright in an armchair, holding a cup of hot tea. With their matching long dark hair and black jackets, they looked like tidy escapees from the Addams family.

Avery plopped down on the sofa, and Ace sat on the rug at her feet. On the coffee table in front of her was an array of baked goods kindly offered by the women of Austen. Apparently funerals called for comfort food— mostly banana bread, apple pie, and sheet cake, but someone had left a giant mac and cheese in the refrigerator too. She had a lot of eating to do before she left.

She sighed and took another slice of banana bread. Ace

licked his chops, but remembered his manners. Avery gave him a corner anyway. He deserved a little culinary comfort just as much as she did. She'd lost her dad, and Ace had lost his human, and saying goodbye was never easy. It had been a confronting day, in more ways than one.

"That was a big day," Aunt Birdie said, seeming to read her mind. "You did well."

"I couldn't have done it without you," Avery said. "Thanks again for organizing everything while I was stuck in Portland."

"We had lots of help," Birdie said. "Your friend Claudia did such a wonderful job with the flowers."

"She did. That was really nice of her." Avery had been glad to have Claudia there. They'd been best friends since kindergarten, in a tight-knit trio with their friend Emma, and Claudia knew more of Avery's history, fears, and secrets than anyone else in the world.

"And wasn't it amazing how many people showed up?" Aunt Cece said. "The Murphys from Spokane, all the cousins from Medford...even Owen's old friend Lyle from when he volunteered in Costa Rica. So many unexpected faces."

Avery picked at the banana bread. "Some were very unexpected."

"Ah," Birdie said. "You saw Logan then."

"I did."

Logan Wagner was the last person she'd expected to see at her father's funeral. Well, maybe third to last, after her own mom, and Logan's dad. She wasn't surprised that *they* hadn't shown up. In fact, she didn't even know where they'd been since they left town together one summer night just over ten years ago.

"He looked so handsome in his suit," Cece said. "Did you talk to him about...anything?" She was clearly itching for details, but decorum kept her from looking too curious.

"Nope. Nothing." Avery found it hard to imagine what they'd have to say to each other. Anyway, he'd stood at the back during the service, not talking to anyone, and hadn't shown up at the house afterward with the other

2

guests. Handsome or not, that was probably for the best. Suddenly exhausted, she leaned back on the sofa and yawned widely behind her hand.

Birdie stood up. "It's time for us to go," she said. "You need some rest. We all do."

Avery stood too, and Ace leaped to attention. "I can keep Ace here tonight," she said to her aunts. "Then you can take him tomorrow, before I go. I'll have to leave before lunch if I want to get back to Portland in time for work."

Cece's blue eyes widened, and she set down her teacup. "Oh, no, honey," she said. "We can't take him."

"Definitely not." Birdie shook her head. Her long hair fell across one eye, and she pushed it aside. "It's out of the question. The girls would never be safe."

Ace leaned in closer to Avery and nudged his wet nose into her hand. She stroked his silky head, and he looked up at her with big dark eyes, as if to say that he would never, ever, even *consider* chasing one of the aunts' pampered ragdoll cats. Avery decided it would be better not to mention the incident earlier that morning, when she'd caught him leaping and scrabbling at the fence, while the neighbor's tabby sat smugly just out of reach. Maybe losing her dad had caused him to be naughtier than usual.

"But he can't come back to Portland with me," she said. "My apartment is way too small, and I couldn't leave him at home while I'm at work. I could try to find somewhere else to live, I guess…but Carter is allergic to dogs."

"We'll have to rehome him then," Birdie said. "I'm sorry, Avery."

Avery sat down again and Ace leaned in, pressing his substantial weight against her legs as if he'd understood the words. She leaned forward and put an arm around him. From the moment he arrived in Austen as a tiny, shaggy puppy of indeterminate breeding, Ace had been by her dad's side, filling the gap left by her mom's abrupt departure with Jeff Wagner. Avery had wanted him to get a dog when she left for college in Portland, but he had

3

resisted, saying he didn't have time for one, being out all the time as a mobile handyman. But when Ace finally came on the scene two years later—thanks to Owen's friend Patrick Brennan, who rescued him from a nearby shelter—he fitted in perfectly, riding shotgun with Owen and charming every homeowner and property manager he met.

For Avery, away at college, it was a relief to know her dad finally had company. He and Ace had quickly become inseparable, filling this big house with warmth, always there to welcome her when she came back from Portland for visits, and take her for walks along the river or the beach, or for hikes in the hills behind town.

Always...until the day her dad's heart suddenly gave out.

Now the silence in the room stretched on as Avery tried to think what to do.

It was hard enough to imagine selling the house—something she was hoping to avoid—but the thought of sending Ace away to people he didn't know was unbearable. And would she even be able to find someone to take a dog his age? At eight, he was well into doggy middle age, even though he was as sprightly as a teenager most of the time.

"You know we do love Ace," Cece finally said. "And he was so special to Owen..." She crumpled, and her sister wordlessly passed her the box of tissues from the side table. Cece plucked out a tissue and pressed it to her face.

Watching them, Avery's heart constricted. "I know."

The unexpected loss of her dad had blindsided her, but it was devastating for his two sisters too. After early romantic disappointments, they'd both stayed single, and Owen had been the man in their life—the big brother, the protector, the handyman who fixed whatever was broken. And now, without him, it felt like everything was broken. But it wasn't something any of them could fix.

Cece rallied a little, straightening her shoulders and giving Avery an apologetic smile. "I'm sorry, honey."

Ace let out a plaintive whine and put a paw on Avery's lap. She held him a little tighter, burying her fingers in his thick, golden coat.

"I have to leave tomorrow," she said.

But even as her words floated in the air, she knew that wasn't going to happen.

Chapter 2

Logan Wagner stopped at the lookout above Austen and checked his smartwatch. Steps taken, heart rate, VO_2 max...not bad. If he kept up with his training—and there was no reason to let himself off the hook—he'd definitely be ready for the Big Sur marathon at the end of summer. He made a mental note to get his assistant to sign him up. Maybe the company could be a sponsor this year—it couldn't hurt to quietly get involved with more community-oriented projects.

Only then did he let himself look at the view. The Pacific Ocean stretched out before him, wide and deep, and as full of possibility as he'd once felt as a teenager stuck in a small town. Below, tucked into the bend of the Austen River where it made one last diversion before heading for the sea, was the town itself. It hadn't changed much in the years he'd been away. The same random network of streets, flung out between the river and the sand dunes like leftover spaghetti noodles, with not a single stoplight. The same stores. The same small-town headlines in the newspaper. The same people.

Even Avery.

For some time he'd been feeling an inexplicable pull back to this place, the kernel of an idea forming in his mind.

And when he heard about Owen Robinson's death, he knew he had to come. He shaded his eyes against the morning sun and squinted down at the town, to where the Robinsons' cedar shingle house sat at the edge of the river. There had been a time he was welcome there…not so much now.

He'd wanted to go to the funeral though. It wouldn't make up for anything, but it was the right thing to do. Even though he hadn't spoken to Avery—he didn't want to create any drama for her on such a hard day—they'd seen each other across the rows of mourners in the church. Time had kaleidoscoped in on itself as he looked at her, ten years twisting and refocusing themselves until he could see seventeen-year-old Avery in his mind, while the grown-up version stood at the front of the church next to her father's coffin. She was beautiful, composed in her grief as she talked about the good man he'd been, her long hair neatly pinned up and her voice steady.

All the while, the teenage Avery remained luminous in his memory—wild-haired, dreamy-eyed, perfectly suited to this unbroken coast. She'd always been in love with the river, and the beach, and the hills—even with the tiny town that had held no secrets for either of them—so he was half surprised when he heard that she'd left Austen for good.

But only half surprised. Because of the two of them, she was the one who deserved—

His watch beeped an alert for him to get moving again, snapping him out of the past. That was no place to linger. He looked beyond Avery's house, over the river to the hills on the other side, a beckoning green landscape swathed in fir and maple and spruce. He was here for another reason too. A piece of that belonged to his family, and he had plans for it. He started back down the hill.

It was time to move again.

Avery speed-walked along the river path, working to keep her breath even as Ace tugged on the leash, pulling her forward even faster. Multitasking this phone call might not have been such a good idea after all.

"I know, Valerie, and I am sorry," she said, trying to sound professional even as she stumbled over a branch on the path. "But it will only be for a couple of days, maybe three. There's more to do here than I expected."

Judging by his overenthusiasm, Ace needed some reminders about manners before she could risk him with a potential new owner. With everything that had happened, she didn't even know when he'd last been walked. And she needed to find him someone special—someone who would love him, and appreciate him, and give him the home he needed and deserved as he headed into his retirement years.

The KXIP operations manager made a disapproving sound at the other end of the line. "This is something we usually only do for our big radio personalities, like Tony Trevino, or Carter Cox."

Avery tried not to be bothered by the implication that she wasn't in their league, despite being a host on the same show as Carter. "Would you do it if I had an alliterative name too?" She laughed, but it was as weak as her joke. She wouldn't even mention their engagement, because that wasn't a factor in why she'd gotten the job.

"Excuse me?" Valerie snapped.

"Never mind." Avery had called Carter last night to update him, and even though he'd seemed preoccupied, he'd promised to talk to Valerie about it. Apparently he'd forgotten. "I spoke to Carter already, and he's happy to have me call in to do the show."

"Don't think that because you're romantically involved with him, you're going to get special treatment," Valerie said.

Avery pulled Ace to a stop, and took a much-needed breath of cool morning air before she replied. "I don't think that at all."

And it was true. After years working behind the scenes in radio, she'd finally gotten the chance to take her place at the microphone at KXIP. Okay, it was a smallish adult contemporary station, and she'd kind of ended up playing backstop for Carter, who portrayed himself as the main star of the show. But it was true that he had more experience on the air, and really, she was just glad to get her big break. Well, her medium-sized break.

Valerie sighed. "Fine. If Carter's okay with it. I'll get Kevin to call you shortly and set up the logistics."

Avery looked down at Ace, who had given up his manic activity and was now standing on her feet as he tried to get closer to her. It didn't seem likely that he'd let her out of his sight—hopefully he'd behave while she was on the air.

"Thank you," she said to Valerie. "I appreciate it. It's been a rough time."

"Just do a good job."

"I will."

Without further comment, Valerie ended the call. Avery stood with her phone to her ear for a few moments, then laughed and shook her head as she put it back in her pocket. What had she been expecting anyway—condolences for her loss? Sympathy? Well, it didn't matter. They would have been token platitudes, coming from Valerie.

She crouched down and put her arms around Ace, and he put his chin over her shoulder, snuggling in. He knew what real support was. She closed her eyes for a moment, resting her head against the dog's sturdy body, letting his warmth soothe her.

Then she heard footfalls on the leafy path, and looked up. A man was rounding the corner at a run, wearing athletic shorts, a T-shirt, ear buds, and a look of slightly sweaty determination. He was almost upon them before he realized they were there and stopped suddenly, his expression changing to surprise.

Ace went straight to the man, his tail flailing wildly as he danced around in excitement. Avery dropped the leash and stood up, stepping back as the man took out his ear buds and ducked down to return Ace's greeting.

When the canine flurry started to subside, the man stood up again, and Ace looked between them, one to the other then back again, seemingly delighted with the trio they formed.

Avery was less delighted.

"Hi," Logan said.

And at the sound of his voice—deeper, with a touch of gravel that never used to be there, but still Logan through and through—she was seventeen all over again.

Chapter 3

A very called Ace to her, but the yellow dog just sat where he was next to Logan, happily smiling at them both. The big furry traitor.

"Hello," she said, because she wasn't completely without manners.

Logan nodded to Ace. "Who's this guy?"

"This is Ace," she said. "He was my dad's dog."

Logan hesitated, then said, "I'm really sorry for your loss."

"Thank you," she replied cautiously.

"I was glad I could be there yesterday."

"Were you?" It came out more accusing than she'd intended, and she saw his jaw briefly tense.

"Of course. Your dad was one of the good ones."

His words didn't sound token. They sounded genuine. And it was only slight, but she didn't miss the emphasis he put on *your*. "He was," she said.

Even from across the church yesterday it had been obvious that Logan had grown into a striking man. But now, up close, she was extra aware of how much he'd changed. He'd always been tall, but he'd filled out. His T-shirt clung to broad shoulders and a strong chest, and as he reached out to stroke Ace's head, the defined muscles in his arm flexed. She tore her eyes away.

"So you came back for his funeral, after all this time," she said, focusing on his face in an attempt to distract herself. It was strange to see him as an adult, still so much like the teenage Logan but with a rugged, masculine edge. Judging by the shadow of stubble across his jaw, he hadn't shaved yet this morning. But despite all the ways he was different, his eyes were still the same shade of golden brown, and he still looked at her in that curious way, as though he wanted to know everything about her.

"I wanted to pay my respects." He bent over and used the hem of his shirt to wipe his forehead, revealing a brief flash of taut, tanned stomach.

She pulled herself together and reached down for Ace's leash. Time to go. "Okay, well, have a good stay."

"Avery…"

His voice was low, magnetic. She stood up, her heartbeat doing a jittery skippity-skip. "What?"

"About…everything."

Oh, no. She did not want to go there, with him of all people. "I don't think there's anything to say. Your dad and my mom supposedly fell in love. They left us. Then you followed them out of town."

He frowned. "I didn't follow them. I went to live in Oakland and…never mind. The point is, there was nothing for me to stay for. You know that."

His intonation set her on edge. "Wait, are you saying it's my fault you left?"

"No, I'm saying…" He blew out a breath. "I'm saying it was a long time ago, and maybe we could let it go now."

She stared at him for a moment. Her once-upon-a-time childhood sweetheart. He'd already walked away once, and now he was telling her to let it go. The finality of it, coming on the heels of her father's death, was a hard, sharp slice of reality. She laughed, even though inside she wanted to cry. "It *was* a long time ago. Don't think I'm still fretting over you, because I'm not. I'm fine—I'm getting married." She waggled her left hand at him, the big diamond flashing in the light.

Something shuttered in his face, and she made herself be glad. She had moved on, after all, and ten years of silence proved he had too. There was nothing to hold onto anymore, nothing to let go of.

"Okay, then," he said. "I guess I'll..." He gestured to the path, and she nodded.

He put his ear buds back in and pushed a button on his watch, making it beep. Then he set off at a steady pace. She made herself turn around and start walking in the opposite direction. Ace whined a little, but she urged him on.

Just keep walking. Just keep walking.

As she came to the bend in the path, curiosity overcame her and she looked back over her shoulder. At that exact moment, Logan did the same, and their eyes met. She was about to look away when he suddenly jolted off course and stumbled on the path, holding his head. She couldn't help her snort of laughter when she realized he'd jogged into an overhanging branch—the same one she'd just passed underneath without incident. Served him right.

Without meeting her eye, he gathered his dignity and continued on with a determined, nothing-to-see-here stride.

And she let him go.

Logan pushed open the door of the vacation rental he was staying at and kicked off his running shoes. His head pounded from where he'd run straight into a branch like some distracted, lovestruck kid.

Which he had been, way back when—but not anymore.

He went into the big marble-clad kitchen and grabbed a bottle of water from the extra-large French door refrigerator, noting that it had been newly restocked with food for the day. Suddenly starving, he pulled out a bowl of freshly sliced tropical fruit, some eggs, and a packet of bacon. The owner of the house, Barbara, had offered to cook for him as she usually did for guests, but he liked his privacy too much to have someone coming in and out while he was there.

His assistant Lisa always booked his accommodation when he traveled, and he trusted her to choose somewhere he'd like. But he'd been surprised to arrive and find himself somewhere so high-end. Austen had never had anything this fancy when he was a kid. Barbara had told him that tourism was growing in the area, and the visitors were providing a steadier income for many of the businesses that had been in danger of closing. Her property catered for tourists who wanted somewhere more luxurious to stay, but there was a shortage of all kinds of vacation accommodation.

He wasn't surprised that people were finally discovering the town. It was in the perfect location—close enough to Portland for an easy weekend getaway, with stunning views of the river and the hills. Sheltered from the coastal winds, but just a short walk to the long, wild curve of beach. And the influx of tourists suited his plans perfectly.

There was hot coffee in the machine, so he poured himself a cup, dark and strong, to have while he was cooking. Then he fixed himself bacon and eggs and took his plate, and the bowl of fruit, out to the wide deck overlooking the river.

It was still early enough that there was a gentle chill in the air and the light was soft. The deck was edged with clear glass panels, so he had an unobstructed view of the slow-flowing river, wooded hills, and clear Oregon sky. Avery's house was on the same side of the river, farther along toward town. He wondered if she was in her backyard looking at this same view, just from a slightly different perspective. A wry laugh escaped him. Their perspectives were different, that was for sure. He took another bracing mouthful of coffee, then ground plenty of salt and pepper onto his breakfast and dug in. He wouldn't say he was fussy, but he liked his eggs just so. No one else could make them exactly the way he liked.

Okay, maybe he was fussy. But you didn't achieve a certain level of success without being particular about things—everything from eggs, to accommodation, to investment strategies.

After he'd eaten, he took a shower then went back to the outside table to call into his office in San Francisco. Talking through the day's priorities with Lisa, he flicked between his calendar and the app he used to manage his projects.

"Have you made any progress with the Austen development?" Lisa asked once they'd gone through the most pressing questions.

He sat back in his chair and considered the view in front of him. Part of that scenery was Wagner land, but he might need more if he was going to do anything substantial with it. Although there was a baseline return needed on any investment, he always aimed higher.

"Not yet," he said. An image of Avery flashed into his mind, cranky and beautiful on the riverside path. "I think I'll stay a bit longer. Can you cancel the New York trip for now? Tell them I'll reschedule when I'm in the clear."

"Sure," Lisa said. "Oh, and the reporter from Finance Today magazine called again. She wants to include comments from you in the article, but she said they'll run with what they have if you're not available."

He knew the reporter was already profiling several other people in the piece she was writing about self-made millionaires under thirty, so he'd hoped that if he maintained a firm "no comment" stance, she would move on to an easier subject and leave him out of it. He had no interest in becoming a personality in the financial media, or anywhere else. But she was obviously too good at her job to be put off by his passive obstruction.

"They can publish without anything from me," he said. "Commenting will only give it oxygen."

"Okay." There was a pause, and he imagined Lisa making a note in the tracking app she used to manage her day. "Have you got everything you need there?"

Did he have everything he needed?

Until yesterday, he would have insisted that he did. But now, back in his hometown, sitting by himself in this palatial house just along the river from the girl he'd left behind, he wasn't so sure.

Chapter 4

A very was pinning up the last blanket in the closet under the stairs when there was a knock at the door. She ducked a little as she came out, to avoid hitting her head, and went to see who it was.

She opened the door to find Cece and Birdie dressed like extras in a BBC production, both in empire-silhouette dresses accessorized with gloves and bonnets. Birdie's was pale blue, and Cece's was white with tiny sprigs of flowers.

"Oh, my. You look very…authentic."

It was exactly the right thing to say. They glowed with pleasure.

"How very kind of you to say so," Cece said demurely as they came in. "We're on our way to book club."

Avery thought she detected a certain Britishness in her aunt's pronunciation. "You're still Jane Austen fans then?"

It seemed inevitable that there'd be a Jane Austen book club in a place that shared a name with the legendary author. According to the local historical society, the town's founder, George Bunzel, had been determined to name it after himself. Fortunately, his wife Ida—who was a Jane Austen fan herself—convinced him otherwise. If not for George's devotion to Ida, they might now be living in Bunzel, Oregon. Which didn't have quite the same ring to it.

"Oh, yes." Cece produced a fan out of nowhere and flipped it open coquettishly. "We're even having our first ever Austen festival here in town next weekend, and showing Pride and Prejudice on an outdoor movie screen. We've been planning it with our book club and the chamber of commerce for ages."

"It's going to be called 'Austen in Austen,'" Birdie said. "That was Lila's idea. Even though she's not here, we keep her up to date with book club news."

"Oh, Lila. How is she?" Avery asked. Lila Marshall was the founder of the book club. Everyone in town knew she'd had ups and downs in life, and the local bookstore, Pemberley Books, had been her retreat and comfort. But when Theo Rutherford arrived in Austen—*Professor* Theo Rutherford, complete with velvety English accent and gentlemanly manners—bookish Lila found her life turned upside down again. In a very good way.

"She and Theo are in Vermont now," Cece said. "And they just had a baby!"

"A little boy," Birdie added. "Isn't that lovely?"

"It really is." Avery smiled at their enthusiasm, and at the thought of Lila finding such happiness. "And the festival sounds like fun. Maybe I'll come back to visit for that. I have to sort out Dad's things anyway."

She hadn't made any kind of start, so the house still felt like he might walk back in at any moment. And she still needed to deal with all the legal stuff—the will, and the financial details. It felt like too much right now, but she knew it had to be faced.

"We'll help you with all that," Birdie said. "Don't worry."

"Thank you," Avery said. Then she had a thought. "Is the store not open today?"

Her aunts had run a small store—named Persuasions, as a nod to another of Jane Austen's books—on the main street for as long as she could remember. It stocked an eclectic collection of gifts and home decor, and it was very popular with locals and visitors alike despite the aunts' slightly haphazard approach to opening hours.

"Our part-time sales assistant is looking after things while we go to morning tea with the book club," Cece said. "We're reading Pride and Prejudice again, in preparation for the festival."

"She only wrote six books, so we've been rereading for a few years now," Birdie explained. "Thank goodness we got Mansfield Park out of the way last month. It's not my favorite," she confessed.

"Ah," Avery said. "I see the difficulty. So you still only read Jane Austen?"

Cece shook her head behind her fan. "No, not at all. We also read Austen-related books. Maeve at the bookstore—you know, your friend Emma's aunt—gets them for us. Reimaginings, sequels, fan fiction, biographies…" Her voice trailed off as she looked over the fan at something behind Avery. "What are you doing there?"

Avery turned to see Ace grinning at them from the closet, sitting comfortably on the blanket she'd just pinned up. "Oh, Ace." She tugged at the blanket and he reluctantly moved off it. "I'm trying to make a soundproof studio where I can call in for the radio show. It's lucky the stairs are so steep."

Her aunts looked impressed. "Well, isn't that fancy," said Birdie. "When you called this morning to say you were staying longer in town, I didn't know you'd need a special room and everything."

Avery shook yellow dog hair off the blanket and draped it over her arm. "It's pretty low tech, but the blankets should keep it quiet and dull any echo."

"Will you take the phone in there?" Cece asked.

"No, I can call in via my computer, using a headpiece, so I'll take that in with me. And Ace, probably. Hopefully we'll be able to squeeze in okay."

The canine in question was leaning against her, one paw on her foot as he listened attentively.

"He's very fond of you," Birdie remarked.

Avery ran a hand over one of his soft ears and hugged him closer. "I guess he's missing Dad. It's going to be tough on him to leave this house and go to someone he doesn't know."

All three of them looked at him. The aunts said nothing, but Avery could feel the tension in the air. She sighed. It wasn't their fault they couldn't take on a dog. She could potentially find a way to have Ace in Portland, but she couldn't imagine life there making him happy. There was doggy daycare, but that was expensive. And after being used to life in Austen, with the big yard, and the freedom of the beach, river, and hills, she knew that city life wouldn't measure up. Plus, Carter had been easily annoyed at the best of times lately. She couldn't see him being willing to put up with allergies every time he came to her apartment. And when they got married—if they ever actually set a date—that wouldn't work at all.

She plastered on a smile for her Regency-clad relatives. "Anyway, it's good the station's operations manager agreed to let me do this." *No thanks to Carter,* she didn't add. "Now I can stay on for the rest of the week."

"It's wonderful," Birdie said. "That's why we stopped by—to let you know what's happening today."

"*Everyone* is planning to listen to your show, now we know we can string it," Cece said, suddenly looking more cheerful.

Avery suppressed a laugh. "Stream it, you mean?"

"Oh yes, stream it. You're a celebrity in town now. Just like..." She cast around for a comparison. "Ryan Seacrest!"

At that, Avery's laugh escaped. "Not really. But thank you."

"Everyone's going to meet up and listen at the Clover," Birdie said.

"Oh...okay." Avery's nerves spiked as she imagined half the town jammed into the Irish pub listening to her do her thing. Never mind that thousands of people heard her and Carter every weekday—for some reason the thought of the hometown crowd was more daunting.

"Three till seven, right?" When Avery nodded, Birdie continued, "And afterward, Cece and I are buying a drink for everyone who helped with Owen's funeral. So you have to come. I know you didn't get to talk to everyone yesterday."

"It'll be quite the occasion," Cece added. "Patrick told us he asked Logan to come in and help set everything up."

Avery felt her tension go up another notch at Cece's words. "Logan?"

"Yes. He knows all about that kind of thing apparently. *Streaming* and such." She smiled proudly at getting the word right.

"Huh. He didn't mention it when I saw him this morning."

That caught their attention.

"You saw him today?" Birdie asked.

"Briefly. He was out running when I took Ace for a walk before breakfast."

"Oh, then that was before Patrick spoke to him. We didn't tell Patrick about you staying until after I talked to you."

Avery should have remembered that any piece of news, no matter how small, would make its way around town in the blink of an eye.

"Did you and Logan have a chat?" Cece asked.

Avery reached for Ace's brush, which was sitting on the console table near the front door. "We talked. You know…small talk."

Cece tapped her fan thoughtfully against her chin. "Didn't you go to prom together?"

"Sit," Avery said, and Ace obeyed. She kneeled down next to him. "I didn't go to prom. That was the year Mom left." She started to brush Ace's coat, in long, firm strokes.

Cece put a hand to her chest. "Oh. That's right."

Avery didn't want to revisit any of that right now. She concentrated on the task at hand. Brush. Brush. Brush.

"Well," Birdie said. "Look how everything turned out though. You went to college like you planned, and you have a great job, and now you're engaged to a successful, good-looking man. Your dad was very proud of you. And we are too."

Avery smiled at her aunt's determined encouragement.

"Thank you." She had no idea if her mom would be proud of her too, but she wasn't ever likely to find out. And why would she care, anyway?

Birdie hitched up her long white gloves. "Now, we'd better go."

"Okay." Avery tried not to look too relieved as she stood back up.

"We can't be late," Cece said. "Ruth is bringing her special secret-recipe red velvet cake." She leaned closer to Avery and lowered her voice. "She makes it with instant chocolate pudding mix."

"Huh. That's interesting."

"I would offer to bring you a slice, but with Lori and Debra-Ann there, there'll be nothing left." She pursed her lips.

Avery laughed. "That's okay—I'll probably have to give you some of the home baking from the funeral anyway."

"Oh, goodness no." Cece smoothed her hands down the front of her dress, over her gently rounded stomach. "If I eat too much more I'll grow right out of this little number."

Birdie gave her sister an impatient nudge. "Let's go. We'll see you later at the Clover, Avery."

"Okay. Have fun."

She saw them out, then stayed on the front porch with Ace to watch them walk down the path and along the street, looking like a pair of time travelers transported to current-day Oregon. She wondered if they'd wear their Jane Austen outfits to the Clover. It seemed like something they'd do.

That thought reminded her of who else would be there. She'd rather not see Logan again, but there was no escaping it—she had to go. And anyway, she *wanted* to go, to thank the people she'd grown up with for their help in farewelling her dad. Plus, it was the perfect chance to start looking for someone to take Ace.

If Logan was still there when she arrived, fine. She had more important things to focus on.

Chapter 5

"This is Carter Cox, taking you home."

The snappy jingle that always accompanied Carter's catchphrase blasted through Avery's headphones, and she visualized him pressing the button on the console with his usual flourish. She loved to tease him about how cheesy the whole thing was—cheesy with a dose of innuendo—but he embraced it. "Cheesy sells," was his standard reply, usually accompanied by his megawatt smile that was wasted on radio.

Even shut in a closet under the stairs, miles from the studio in the center of Portland, Avery could feel the charisma of that smile. No wonder he was pushing the station to do more filming in the studio. He loved performing, and was confident on camera in a way that she wasn't. After all, that was why she'd chosen radio, not TV—but even on their midsize station it seemed like the cameras were catching up.

Carter's jingle was followed by the start of a song, and she relaxed a little. Almost two hours in, and the show was going fine.

"How're you doing, Ave?" Carter asked her.

"Great," she said. "I mean, apart from having pins and needles from working with a giant dog lying on my legs."

She laughed and gave Ace a scratch, and he yawned then went back to his nap.

"Just hearing you say that makes my nose itch," Carter said. "Have you figured out what to do with him yet?"

Avery fought down the annoyance that sprang up at his words. No one *chose* to be allergic to dogs. She should feel sorry for him, not irritated that he seemed so focused on getting rid of Ace.

"No," she said. "But it hasn't even been a day since I found out that the aunts can't take him."

"Right, right." Carter sounded distracted, and she could imagine him doing the usual tasks there in the studio—running through the schedule, checking traffic reports, noting down one-liners that occurred to him, all with one eye on the time. Even though everything was going smoothly, she felt at a disadvantage not being on the spot.

"What's up next?" she asked him.

"We've got a couple more callers waiting. I'll take the next one after this song."

"Okay, sounds good."

The running theme for the hour was funny mishaps with kids, and they'd already had people call in with hilarious stories. When the song ended, Carter was straight into performance mode again, with a joke about Avery broadcasting with a hellhound on her lap. After some of the usual teasing back and forth, with cheeky interjections from Roger, who read the news and weather, Carter went to the caller.

"You're on the air," he said. "Go ahead and entertain us!"

There was a silence just long enough that Avery wondered whether the person had lost their nerve, then the sound of someone clearing their throat.

"Hello," the caller said, her voice high but determined. "I'm...uh...calling about a mishap."

Avery expected Carter to steam right ahead as usual, but he seemed to hesitate for a beat, so she replied herself.

"Hey, thanks for calling! What's your name?"

"I...actually, I'd rather not say." The caller barked out a laugh.

"Ah, okay," Avery said, trying to infuse her words with enough warmth to reassure the caller. "Protecting the innocent, huh?" She laughed too, making sure it sounded like she was laughing *with* the woman, not at her. It was common for callers to suddenly be overcome with nerves.

"Ha-ha, sure." The woman paused. "Well, not really."

Avery felt caution creeping in. You could never guarantee that people would keep it seemly once they got on the air. But the staffer who initially answered the phone would usually screen out anyone who called in drunk, or just sounded like trouble, so she carried on. "Okay, well, tell us your story...assuming it's suitable for the airwaves!"

"I don't know what's suitable. I just know what I need to say. Is Carter still there? He needs to hear this."

"Hey, Carter," Avery said. "You still on board there?" What was he doing? It wasn't like him to go radio silent, even for a minute.

"Sure, I'm here," he said. "Let's get this over with."

That was a weird way to put it. Avery wriggled uncomfortably under Ace's weight. Tomorrow she'd make sure to bring in a low camping chair or something. There were probably some in the basement.

"Get this over with?" the caller said. "That wasn't what you said last night."

Avery stopped wriggling. That sounded bad, but people loved to go the innuendo route with Carter...especially female callers. Avery had fallen for him herself, with his teasing grin and his bold charisma, so she could hardly blame their listeners for appreciating the same attributes that made her weak at the knees.

"Okay, so, tell us your story," she said lightly, trying to keep things on track. "What's your kid-related mishap?"

The woman snorted. "My *kid-related mishap* is that your Carter Cox knocked me up. And now I'm going to have a kid. Which is a pretty damn big mishap, don't you think?"

Avery's heart seized, and all the breath stopped in her lungs. But she forced herself to breathe out, then in again.

The first rule of broadcasting was *no dead air*. They had to keep going. She waited for Carter to say something, but he was uncharacteristically silent. What in the name of Casey Kasem would she say now?

"Are you...are you sure you have the right person?"

She knew it was a ridiculous question the moment she said it. As if a person could be confused about something like that.

The woman ignored her. "Carter, I've given you the chance to make things right in your own time, and you haven't. So now I'm forcing you to man up."

Suddenly Avery remembered the broadcast delay function. There was no need to have this going out live on the air. Stuck in her airless makeshift studio under the stairs, she felt sick with powerlessness. Why hadn't anyone activated the delay? There was technology to handle this kind of situation.

And yet it continued.

"I was going to," Carter said. "I just wanted to do it right. It was bad timing."

Avery held tight to her laptop. What did he mean?

"Bad timing?" the woman replied. "Bad *timing*? Yes, this is the worst possible timing—for me. And you are handling it in the worst possible way."

Something stirred in Avery's memory. The woman's voice was vaguely familiar. And something wasn't adding up.

"Uh...can I just clarify one thing?" Blessedly, her voice was steadier than she felt inside. "You said *last night*, so how can you know you're pregnant already?"

Carter jumped in, a warning note in his voice. "Karen—"

"Oh, honey," she said to Avery. "You need to talk to this guy off the air."

At that, Carter's jingle burst into life, cutting off the conversation, and Avery's connection went dead.

Silently, she closed her laptop and pulled off the headphones. In the muffled quiet of the closet, the only sound she could hear was Ace's breathing, and the thudding of her heart in her ears.

Karen. Karen…

Then it clicked. Karen Frazier. The glamorous anchor of a local entertainment news TV show, who they'd met at a media awards dinner earlier in the year. Carter had abandoned his radio colleagues to hang with the TV crowd that night, dragging Avery along with him to "network" and "make connections." He'd obviously gone on to make more connections with one person in particular.

This is Carter Cox, taking you home. Suddenly his catchphrase rang with more truth than innuendo.

Her phone vibrated on the floor next to her. She looked at the screen—Carter. For a moment she was tempted to let it go to voicemail, but decided against it. There were things she wanted to say…questions she wanted answered. She picked up the phone and accepted the call.

"Just tell me," she said, before he could start trying to talk her around in circles. "Tell me the truth."

"She told me the day your dad died. I didn't want to upset you."

Upset her? She didn't even know where to begin. Now his decision to stay in Portland supposedly for work, instead of coming to the funeral, made more sense. Not to mention his distracted demeanor on the phone last night.

"It started after the media awards, didn't it." It was a statement, not a question. He hesitated, and she felt her emotion heat up another notch. "Seriously, Carter, there's no point in trying to sugarcoat it. The mother of your child just broke the news to approximately fourteen percent of greater Portland's twenty-five to fifty-four radio demographic." The station had lost a few percentage points in the last audience demographics survey. Maybe this little scandal would boost them back up again. "And the rest of Portland will be finding out soon enough."

She suddenly remembered who else had been listening to Karen's revelation—a significant percentage of the Austen population, currently assembled in the Clover.

And one visitor in particular. Oh, no.

"Carter…why? Why do that behind my back?"

"It's nothing personal," he said. "I just...liked her better."

With that simple, brutal answer, she realized exactly how little regard he had for her. That the relationship they'd had was more one-sided than she could have guessed. More fool her for thinking it had been something real. For having faith in someone who was so obviously not worthy of it. Then she remembered one more thing.

"I *cannot believe* I was going to give Ace away, for your sake. And you would have let me."

What in the world had she been thinking? She gathered the yellow dog in close and he snuffle-licked her cheek, always ready for some love.

"I would have told you before you did anything permanent," Carter said impatiently. "And Avery, it was time for us to move on anyway. Greener pastures, you know."

"Greener pastures? What are you even talking about? We were going to get *married*." And then her puzzlement cleared away as something else fell into place. "Oh...I get it now. You always were ambitious, but I never thought you'd use a woman as your ticket into TV."

"Why not?" he shot back. "You used me as your ticket into radio."

She sat upright, choking on a white-hot bolt of hurt and anger. "I did *not*. I paid my dues, I did my time behind the scenes, and I deserve my place in the studio. You know that."

In reaction to her raised voice, Ace stiffened and let out a loud bark, almost deafening her in the tiny space. She reached for the closet handle and shoved the door open, and they both burst out into the fresh air of the hallway.

"Avery, calm down. Maybe you'd rather not continue on the show, if it's going to be awkward."

Carter's attempt at a placating tone had the opposite effect. "Awkward? Oh, no," she said, one thing perfectly clear in the turmoil as she stood up. "You don't get to use this as a way to push me out."

He started to protest, but she wasn't falling for his

performance skills anymore.

"I'm not going to call in for the show tomorrow, but I'll be talking to Valerie, and you can bet I'll be back on Monday. So you'd better bring your A game."

"Avery, let's just—"

"Let's not. Really." She was almost done, but there was one more thing to say. "And Carter? Be a good father to that kid. Karen is right—you need to man up."

With that, she ended the call.

Chapter 6

A very dragged her feet on the walk from her house to Main Street. The last thing she wanted to do after that live humiliation was step into the Clover and see the sympathy and embarrassment of the town. She had just reached the corner of Main Street when Claudia appeared, looking flustered.

"Avery!" she said, pulling her into a hug. "I was in the Clover. I heard what happened. On top of everything you're going through with losing your dad..." She squeezed even harder.

Avery sank into the embrace, Claudia's long dark hair tickling her nose. A little boost from her best friend before facing everyone wouldn't go astray.

"I guess everyone else heard too," Avery said as they parted.

"Yes." Claudia looked apologetic. "It was really full for a weekday afternoon."

Avery sighed and leaned against the brick wall of the antique store, warm in the late afternoon sun. "I was hoping someone might have turned it off as soon as things went off script."

"Ugh, I'm so sorry. Everyone was kind of paralyzed with shock. Even me." Claudia paused, looking remorseful.

"Except for one person. Logan was over the other side of the room, but when he realized what was happening he got up and headed for his phone by the sound system. But it was all over by the time he got there."

"Really?" Avery didn't know what to make of that.

"Yeah, it was kind of heroic. Or it would have been, if he hadn't tripped over Debra-Ann's bichon frise and knocked her drink straight into Ruth's lap."

Avery had to laugh along with her. Knowing Ruth's disposition, that wouldn't have gone down well.

"So...what are you going to do?" Claudia asked.

"Well, I'm not walking away from my job over this," Avery said. "But I am walking away from Carter." For a moment she felt tears threatening as she thought about all the plans they'd made for their life together. Then she remembered that it had only been her making the plans, and anger got the upper hand again. "Obviously."

Claudia nodded. "Good for you. You don't need him in your life. Not in your personal life, anyway." She hesitated. "You know, I've never understood why the catchphrase is 'Carter Cox, taking you home.' Shouldn't it be 'Carter Cox and Avery Robinson, taking you home'?"

Carter's words echoed in Avery's head. *You used me as your ticket into radio.* "Maybe because everyone thought I was only there because of him. He obviously did."

"No. You know that's not true. You had to audition along with everyone else. You went through the whole interview process. And you guys had only just started dating then. Did anyone at the station even know?"

"I didn't mention it, because I didn't want it to look like I was using the relationship to my advantage. But Carter told the station management—he said it would look like a conflict of interest if we didn't declare it. I never thought that made any difference, but maybe it did."

"They were lucky to have you," Claudia declared, then realized what she'd said. "I mean, *are* lucky to have you."

"I guess." Avery wasn't looking forward to the conversation she'd have to have with Valerie, and the station's senior management. And she *really* wasn't looking forward to Monday, when she'd have to go into the station and carry on, with her chin up. In the meantime, though, there was her hometown to deal with.

Claudia was watching her. "Do you still want to go to the Clover?"

She thought of everyone in there waiting for her. All the people who'd helped with her dad's funeral. The same people who'd already helped to see her through one emotional crisis, when her mom left. Then she thought of Logan, and wavered. But Austen was her home, the place that she'd protect as fiercely as they protected her. There was no reason to hide away here. Plus, she wanted to acknowledge everyone's help—and their loss, too. She'd been living somewhere else for a long time now, but her father had remained a vital part of the community. At the funeral yesterday, she'd realized that there were a lot of people feeling the impact of his death.

She pushed off the wall and stood up straight. "Yes. Let's go."

Logan rubbed his knee where it had connected with the edge of Debra-Ann Dixon's chair. Why people had to take those purse dogs everywhere, he didn't know. At least they should be on their owner's lap, or stowed under the seat like on an airplane, not wandering around causing a safety hazard.

In the crowded pub, he'd found himself entrenched at a table with an insurance broker, a piano teacher, and a local businessman who was deeply involved with the chamber of commerce. Although he'd made an effort at first, his mind had wandered since the startling developments on Avery's radio show and his incident with the white furball of death. Until he saw her on the path yesterday, with her engagement ring, he hadn't known that she was involved with anyone. Hadn't known much about her life now at all. There was a reason for that, but—

"Tell me," the businessman said, interrupting his thoughts. "Are you from around here?"

Logan forced himself to be polite. "I was, but I left a long time ago."

"I'm new here myself," the man replied confidingly. "Came on board with the chamber about two years ago, when we opened the new grocery store." He held out his hand. "Name's Phil. Phil Bagley."

Logan shook his hand. "Logan Wagner."

"Pleasure to meet you. Great little town here, great little town." He grinned. "You here on business? Visiting family? Friends?"

Logan chose his words carefully. "Well, Phil, as you know yourself, even a trip somewhere for pleasure can bring the opportunity to do business."

"Ah, you're a man after my own heart," Phil said. "I like the way you think."

Logan had suspected as much. "Thanks."

Then Phil turned to talk to the insurance broker, and the piano teacher leaned toward Logan. "I was surprised to see you yesterday at Owen's funeral," she said. "There hasn't been a Wagner in this town for a long time."

"Just wanted to pay my respects," he replied, suddenly on edge.

"Is that so," she said dryly. "Didn't see you at the house afterward though."

He hadn't expected her to be so direct. Then again, a lifetime of dealing with kids forced to practice piano against their will might do that to a person. He'd never taken piano as a kid in Austen—something he was now grateful for, if this was the person who would have been teaching him.

"I'm sorry, I didn't catch your name," he said to her.

"Ellen," she said. "Ellen Allsopp."

"Well, Ellen," he said, modulating the impatience out of his tone, "I wanted to pay my respects, but I didn't want to make anything difficult for Avery. Under the circumstances. It was a very nice service though."

He wouldn't mention that he hadn't stayed to speak to anyone because he didn't know how he'd be received. Since he left, he hadn't kept in touch with anyone in Austen. Owen and Avery hadn't needed one last Wagner hanging around, reminding them of what his dad had done. And although he'd thought about Avery often over the years— more often than was wise—he'd always decided against looking her up on social media, or trying to find out anything about her. For his own sake as much as hers. She wouldn't want him around, and holding onto the past would only stop him from concentrating on the now, and planning for the future. His laser-like focus hadn't come naturally, but he'd sharpened and honed it over the years, and it was one of the major reasons for his success in business.

His personal life had been less successful. The single-minded pursuit of business at the expense of a well-rounded lifestyle wasn't the kind of thing that women found attractive. At least not when the reality of that kind of life sank in. His previous girlfriend had told him exactly what she thought of his dedication to his business, right before she walked out the door. Since then, he'd decided it was better not to disappoint anyone else.

He glanced toward the pub's entrance. Avery had been off air for a while now. Maybe she wouldn't come to the Clover after all. After what had happened, he'd understand if she didn't. Not that he was waiting for her—he could go back to the vacation rental at any time. Any time at all.

He realized Ellen was watching him. "You didn't want to make anything difficult," she said thoughtfully. "But you're still here now. I wonder why that is?" She tipped her head and gave him a smile that he knew she didn't mean.

"Patrick asked me to come," he said. Thanks to the gregarious Irishman turning up at the door of the vacation rental—apparently news still traveled fast in Austen—and despite his misgivings, Logan had ended up seeing a whole lot of locals today. But so far Ellen was the only one who'd given him attitude.

"Of course." She lifted one drawn-on eyebrow and sipped her wine.

"If you'll excuse me..." he said, indicating toward the bar. She added a nod to her thin smile.

He extricated himself from the table with relief and

headed for the bar. Maybe it was time to switch up his drink to something stronger. He looked at his watch. Five forty-five. Something harder wouldn't be out of the question. Just one, and then he'd go. For some reason he'd been a complete klutz since he came back here—probably safer to quit while he was somewhat ahead.

The hum of conversation in the pub paused briefly, stopping him in his tracks. Avery was standing in the doorway, with Claudia beside her. He watched her face go pink as everyone looked in her direction, then the hum started up again. People had obviously decided to give her space. Her eyes scanned the room and found his, but she quickly looked away. Within a moment Cece and Birdie and a few other women were upon her, fussing and exclaiming, along with Patrick. From this distance he couldn't hear what they were saying, but he could make a pretty good guess. For some reason the aunts were wearing old-fashioned dresses and gloves, topped off with bonnets tied under their chins with ribbons. He'd always remembered them being eccentric, but that seemed to be taking it up a level.

He continued to the bar, taking the long way to avoid going past the dog woman and her friends. All the same, he felt the heat of their glares as he crossed the room.

"What can I get you?" the bartender asked.

He thought for a moment. It was still tempting to go for something top shelf, but then again, he wasn't here on vacation. "Just a beer, thanks," he said. "Can you recommend something local?"

She thought for a moment. "There's a nice pale ale made not far from here."

"Perfect." Wherever he went, he always tried to support businesses and startups in the area. Some of those local entrepreneurs could be the next national—or international—high fliers. Maybe even a business he'd want to invest in himself. Property development had taken him far, but lately he'd been thinking about dabbling in something smaller, more boutique.

"Hey."

He turned to find Avery standing next to him. Claudia and the aunts were on her other side, all watching warily. He involuntarily stood a little straighter, and held tight to the glass the bartender passed him.

"Hi," he said. He waved cautiously along the line of women. They looked like a row of oddly-dressed bodyguards. "Hello." Then he returned his attention to Avery. Her blonde hair was in a loose plait, and her cheeks were still slightly pink. Was it his imagination, or did they warm even more as he looked at her? "I'm sorry about what happened on the show."

"Don't," she said, shaking her head. "Just...no." She waved a hand as if dismissing him.

"Okay." He knew her well enough to know that no meant no. As the bartender started taking the women's orders, he turned to go.

"Thanks, though," Avery said.

He paused. "For what?"

"Claudia said you were the only person who tried to stop the broadcast playing through the speakers."

"Oh." He shrugged, but he could feel unwarranted pride bloom in his chest. "If I'd kept my phone with me I could have done it straight away." And if he hadn't been frozen with fascination at the unfolding drama, he might have shifted himself quickly enough to cut the connection between phone and speaker before the moment of the revelation.

She nodded. "Well, thanks anyway."

Looking at her standing there, radiant despite the grim week she'd had, a rash impulse forced him into action. He'd messed up their unexpected meeting on the river path earlier—*maybe we could let it go* was completely the wrong way to say what he'd intended—but maybe he could smooth things over now. It would be better to have it settled before he left.

"Would you like to..." He gestured with his glass toward an empty table nearby.

"No," she said, without hesitation.

In that instant, he was back on her doorstep that spring

night in senior year, as she told him she wouldn't go to prom with him after all. In fact, she thought it would be better if they didn't see each other at all. She'd meant it—they had barely exchanged a word between then and the end of school, when he left Austen. He still remembered the weight in his chest as he went down the porch steps, knowing this was too big for him to fix. He'd stopped under the maple tree in the front yard and turned around. She was still there, watching him go, her expression unreadable. He raised his hand, and regret briefly crossed her face. Then she turned and went inside, into the house that no longer held a family—just Avery and her dad.

"See you later, Logan," Claudia said now, and the women started toward a table in the center of the room. Avery lifted her hand in a half-wave, an echo of his attempt to connect all those years ago. But her "no" was as firm now as it had been then.

He stood with his drink in hand, watching them go, feeling that weight in his chest all over again. Avery's mom and his dad had claimed their love, regardless of the consequences, but their action had cost him the love of his young life. He'd never felt the same about anyone since. For a long time he'd told himself he was being unrealistic, comparing adult relationships with heightened teenage emotions. The rational, logical part of his brain insisted that they were nothing more than rose-tinted memories of the past that wouldn't survive the clear light of reality.

But now that he'd seen Avery again, he knew that he'd been wrong. Despite all the years that had passed, his desire for her was as real as ever.

He hated being wrong.

And she still hated him.

Which left him with one question: what was he going to do about it?

Chapter 7

A very woke with a start early on Friday morning. It was very quiet. Well, if she didn't count the sound of Ace snoring gently on the floor. He'd tried to get in with her the night before, but her childhood bed was too small for the two of them. Now she lay still for a minute as the events of the last few days unrolled in her head, trying to get a grip on all the pieces. Only a week ago, she'd been living in blissful ignorance of how her life was about to change. What she wouldn't do to go back to that time.

Or maybe not, in one way at least. Because all that time, Carter had been "connecting" with Karen Frazier.

She got out of bed and pulled on her dad's robe. It was made of a scratchy, tweedy material, but it was comforting to feel close to him. Ace got up then, and came for a morning scratch behind the ears. He snuffled in the robe, which still smelled like her dad—a mixture of wood chips, Vitalis hair tonic, and scotch whisky. Actually, maybe that was her imagination. Either way, Avery's heart ached for Ace...for both of them.

She tied the robe's cord tightly around her waist and went downstairs, the long sleeves flapping around her hands. Ace followed, closer than a midday shadow. In the kitchen, she rolled up the sleeves and made coffee. Her phone was sitting on the counter, still turned off after her call with Carter yesterday. She avoided looking at it as she opened the back door to let Ace out, then pulled a box of Cap'n Crunch from the pantry. It wasn't her favorite, but her dad had loved it, and there were two more boxes waiting after this one. He'd hate to see them go to waste.

She grabbed milk from the fridge, then sat down to her cereal breakfast. After a while Ace came back in, his nails clickity-clicking on the hardwood floor.

"No cat today?" she asked him. He tilted his head, then looked to the door as though intending to race back outside, and she laughed. "Don't even think about it, buddy."

She gave him some breakfast, trying not to dwell on how he was also in blissful ignorance about how his life was about to change. She'd asked around at the Clover last night, after Logan left, but no one had volunteered to take him. It was short notice, she knew, but surely someone in town would have a place for such a sweet dog.

Finally, after putting her breakfast things in the dishwasher, taking a shower, and standing in the doorway of her dad's room for a while, trying not to think about how much cleaning out would have to be done, she went back into the kitchen and picked up her phone. When she turned it on, texts and message notifications started coming up on the screen—one, and another, and another, and another, until she wanted to throw the phone into Ace's water bowl. She sat down at the big table, with Ace at her feet, and scrolled through them. Portland friends, colleagues from the station, journalists, her friend Emma, who was a librarian in Nebraska now...even her hairdresser. None from Carter.

She looked at the diamond on her ring finger, then slid it off and put it on the table. It sat there alone, pretty and unwanted. She'd have to give it back to Carter, but she'd think about that later.

As she picked up her phone again to reply to Emma, it rang in her hand, making her jump. When she saw who it was, her stomach did a somersault. Valerie. Well, no more putting off that conversation. She answered the call.

"Hi, Valerie."

"Good morning, Avery."

Her voice gave nothing away, so Avery got straight to the point. "We need to talk about what's happened."

"We do."

"I think Carter should do the show himself today, to let things settle down, but I'll be back on Monday as planned."

"Avery." There was a long-suffering tone in Valerie's voice. "Nothing is as planned right now."

Avery let out a dark laugh. "You're telling me."

Valerie sighed. "You know, I've been around a while now. I've seen more scandals than you even want to know. And the truth is, everything blows over eventually."

"That's good to know." Avery felt her tension start to lift. "Yesterday's news, right?"

"Exactly right," Valerie said. "Yesterday's news."

"So...I'll see you on Monday?"

"Sure. You can come clear out your desk."

Shock drove Avery to her feet. "What? I thought you said—"

"I said everything blows over eventually. The biggest scandals become yesterday's news. That doesn't mean you get to stay."

"But...it wasn't my fault. I'm not the one who cheated and got someone else pregnant. Why are you firing *me*?"

Now it was Valerie's turn to laugh. "Oh, we're not just firing you. Carter is clearing out his desk today. The weekend hosts are taking over your slot until we find permanent replacements."

Avery stood in the kitchen, her head spinning. "Carter is fired too?"

"We have standards to uphold," Valerie said. "Our audience wants to know that they're listening to radio personalities with integrity."

"I have integrity," Avery protested.

"You two came as a package," Valerie told her. "We wouldn't have hired you if it wasn't for Carter. It's simple—

if Carter goes, you go."

They came as a package. She hadn't gotten the job on her own merits.

"And now I have to go," Valerie said. "You'll be receiving an email with confirmation of your severance package. I'll see you on Monday." The call ended.

Avery looked down at Ace. "I guess you'll have me here for a little longer after all."

Seemed like she had her own catchphrase now. *Avery and Ace, staying at home.*

Chapter 8

H is boots were too new. Logan cursed his uncharacteristic lack of planning as he felt the steady burn of a blister starting to form on his left heel. As a kid he'd never bothered with special hiking boots, anyway. He'd come out here, to the hills over the river, and run around in tennis shoes like every other Austen kid.

Patrick stopped and turned back to check on him. "Are you not very fit then?"

"My fitness isn't a problem," Logan said tersely, catching up. "It's my boots."

"Ah. You should've broken 'em in properly," he said, just the trace of an accent coloring his words.

Logan gritted his teeth at this statement of the blindingly obvious. He'd had no intention of coming out here with anyone else, but the Irishman had happened upon him as he was about to cross the narrow footbridge over the river, and then there'd been no shaking him. And this was a person Logan would never disrespect, in any case. Patrick had been one of his dad's best friends, and Logan had fond memories of fishing trips and football games and hours in his dad's workshop with him and Owen Robinson for company.

Now Patrick adjusted his Oregon Ducks cap and

scratched his bearded cheek, looking around at the trees. "What are we doing over here, anyway?"

It was a good question. "I just wanted to have a look. I haven't been here since I left town." He could have sent a team of surveyors to assess the land's suitability for development, but something had called him back to see it for himself first, and Owen's funeral was the final impetus to come. But now he was starting to wish he'd kept a more professional distance. He started along the path again, and Patrick kept pace with him.

"It's nice having you back," Patrick said. "Been strange having no Wagners in town."

There was a wistful tone in his voice, and it made Logan wonder something. "Do you ever hear from my father?"

"No. I never did." They continued on in silence for a minute, the only sound birdsong and their footfalls on the path, then Patrick added, "You?"

"No." Logan had never gone looking for him either. And he'd done just fine without him, so far.

Patrick sighed. "Never could understand your dad's thinking. Everyone felt for him when your mom passed, when you were so tiny—felt for you too, of course. But to do what he did, breaking up a family, and walking away from everything here…"

Logan kept walking, the familiar fragrance of fir and damp soil pulling him back to the past along with Patrick's words. The absence of his mom had been a constant in his life, but she passed when he was a toddler so he'd never known anything different. And he'd always known she would have been there with him if she could. His dad's deliberate departure was something else entirely. "He made his choice."

"True enough," Patrick said. "That's what we all do, for better or worse."

Something in his tone made Logan glance sideways, but the older man said nothing more, just kept striding along the path.

After a few more minutes they came down to the

river's edge, where the trees opened to the sky and the water was clear enough to see the rocks in the riverbed. Logan sat on a fallen log and unlaced his boots, letting out a breath of relief when the pressure came off his heels.

"Shouldn't take them off," Patrick said as he sat next to him. "It'll be hell getting them back on."

With annoyance, Logan realized he was right. Ignoring the niggle of pain, he rested his elbows on his knees and surveyed the view. "I'd almost forgotten how nice it is here."

The town was partly obscured by trees on the other side of the river, but he could clearly see the hill with the lookout, standing between there and the ocean. The path where he'd met Avery and Ace yesterday morning ran along the opposite riverbank, winding in and out of the trees. There were houses dotted along the river, but fewer than you might expect. Years ago the town had purchased the remaining riverfront land and designated it as public parks, preserving access for all residents. That had also instantly raised the value of the existing homes on the river. The Robinsons' house was almost directly opposite where he and Patrick were sitting, but the big house where he was staying was farther upriver.

"This is special country alright," Patrick said, taking off his cap and running a hand through his salt-and-pepper hair. "You're lucky to have a piece of it in your family."

"Yeah." He was, and he intended to make the most of it. A sympathetic development here, with luxury dwellings, would be snapped up by people wanting a retreat from city life. There was no immediate road access, but that could be a selling point that added to the charm of the location—a feature, not a bug. Here at the meeting place of the river, the beach, and the hills, there was a little bit of magic in the air. But it was close enough to town for the owners to reach all the amenities they'd need. And when Barbara had mentioned the positive impact of increasing tourism in Austen, it brought home to him the potential economic benefit to the town.

But there were a few things to work through before

he'd know if the project had legs, and one complication in particular. One *person* in particular…his father.

"Well, I'd better get back," Patrick said, standing up and putting his cap back on. "Need to get ready for the lunch rush. Fridays are always busy."

"I'll come with you." Logan retied his laces, flinching a little as the boots tightened against his heels. When he stood up, they both paused for a moment, looking at the scene in front of them.

"I wonder if he ever thinks about coming back," Patrick mused.

Logan shook his head. "I have no idea."

Then Patrick slapped his hands on his thighs, snapping them out of the moment. "Alright. Let's get moving."

"Sounds good," Logan said.

If in doubt, keep moving. It was his fail-safe strategy, the mindset that had taken him from assistant carpenter, to building contractor, to nationwide property developer. To trading in futures and options with a fearless hand. To more financial success than he'd ever expected.

Keep moving. Do the next thing. Don't look back.

But this time, in order to move forward, he'd *have* to look back.

Chapter 9

A very sat on a stool by the counter in Claudia's store, Beach & Bloom, twirling white florist's ribbon around her fingers as she watched her friend put together a stunning arrangement. Claudia added one flower after another to the bunch in her hands, the long stems sticking out below. She seemed to know without hesitation where to put each flower for best effect.

"So...I talked to Valerie."

"Good," Claudia said, her agile fingers turning and adjusting the flowers. "How do you think the show will go on Monday?"

Avery picked up a white rose from the counter and automatically put it to her nose. It didn't smell like anything. "Actually, I won't be doing the show on Monday."

Claudia looked up from the bouquet. "What? Why?" She held out her hand for the flower and Avery passed it over.

"Valerie fired me."

The rose fell to the counter. "How could she fire *you*? You weren't the one doing the dirty."

"Yeah, that was pretty much what I said." Avery reached down and stroked Ace's warm, velvety ears. There was no comfort like canine comfort.

"Oh, that's just great." Claudia picked up the rose and shoved it into the arrangement. "So Carter gets to carry on like nothing at all has happened."

"Not exactly," Avery said. "He's fired too."

"Oh! Well, good." Claudia nodded emphatically. "But it's still not right that you have to go. What will you do?"

"I haven't had time to think about that. I mean, I'll have to go back and clear out my desk, but after that...I don't know. They're offering severance pay, so I'll be okay for a while." The email had come through moments after she spoke to Valerie, which was impressive in its efficiency, but kind of depressing in its finality. They'd obviously prepared it yesterday, right after the show.

"That's something, I guess," Claudia said, adding greenery around the outside of the bouquet. "But I wouldn't want to go back after something like that. Why don't you ask someone else to clear out your desk for you?"

Avery thought for a minute. "I guess I could." There wasn't much personal stuff there that she wanted to keep, just the usual office things—hand lotion, a potted plant, her favorite coffee mug...which Carter had given her. That could stay. Ugh, and a framed photo of her and Carter—taken, she realized with a sting, at the media awards where they'd met Karen Frazier. "Actually," she said, "I don't need any of it."

"Will you stay in Austen for a while then?" Claudia asked. "Oh, and does this mean Ace can stay with you?" Hearing his name, Ace sat upright, his tail quivering, and gave a small yelp to let them know he was ready for anything.

Avery had to laugh at his endearing eagerness. "For now. Until I figure out my next step."

"We've missed having you in town." Claudia smiled at Avery over the top of the now-finished bouquet. "*I've* missed you."

"I've missed you too."

She leaned a hip against the counter, considering. "I think we probably saw each other every single day from the time we started kindergarten. And Emma too. Right up until we left for college."

"A lot happened in those years," Avery said.

"It did. Good and bad."

They were silent for a moment, and Avery knew Claudia was thinking about the same things she was—her mom and Jeff Wagner, and Logan.

"But there was lots of good," Avery pointed out. "Remember how we used to go over the river in summer, and just disappear for the day?"

Claudia laughed. "I remember."

"And my dad would open the gate at the bottom of our backyard and yell across for us to come home."

"He sure could project his voice." Claudia sighed as she finished securing the stems with florist's tape, then wrapped them in ribbon. "I used to love going over there— it was so magical."

"Like a whole other world," Avery agreed. "I'm glad it's there, still beautiful and untouched. Some things are too special to lose."

"They are." Claudia pushed a pin into the ribbon to secure it. "I need to get over there, instead of just looking at it from this side of the river. Fill up on wilderness again."

"You've been working too hard," Avery told her.

"Comes with the territory when you're running a business," she replied. "But we should go now you're back, for old times' sake." She gestured to some heavy-duty floral cutters sitting by Avery on the counter. "You know, I always thought our kids would get to do the same thing together."

Avery handed her the cutters. "Kids? I can't see that happening any time soon. You're talking to the woman who just got dumped on air, remember."

Claudia winced. "Sorry." She snipped off the ends of the stems, wielding the cutters with a dangerous flourish. "I could just kill that Carter Cox."

"You'd better not," Avery said. "He's the one having kids now. Or *a* kid, anyway. And for that kid's sake, I have to wish him well."

"You're a better woman than I am, Avery Robinson."

Her friend might not say that if she knew the thoughts that had run through Avery's head since last night. "I doubt that very much, Claudia Larsen."

Claudia pointed the bouquet at her. "You're a better woman than he deserves. And don't you forget it."

Avery wanted to go around the counter and give her a hug, but at that moment the bell over the door rang, and a customer came in.

"Good morning, Freya," Claudia said. "I just finished your order."

Freya Blackwood came over to the counter, one hand to her mouth. "It's gorgeous, thank you. My mom will love it."

"You're welcome. All old-fashioned pink and white, as requested—roses, alstroemeria, and bouvardia. And myrtle and bells of Ireland for greenery."

Freya laughed. "That means nothing to me, but Mom will know every one. Thank you." She took the bouquet from Claudia and paid with her card, then turned to Avery. "Hi, Avery. Sorry to interrupt your conversation." She leaned down and gave Ace a tickle, and his tail thumped on the floor.

"That's okay," Avery said. Freya had gone to school with them, but was a couple of years younger. Her older brother Daniel had been best friends with Logan.

Freya hesitated. "I'm so sorry about your dad. And about...the radio thing." She made an awkward gesture.

"Thank you," Avery said. "It's been..." She made her own awkward gesture. Her heart, already aching from the loss of her dad, was still getting to grips with this latest twist.

There was a moment's silence as all three of them looked at Ace, who continued his merry tail-thumping. Then Avery rallied.

"I'm sorry I didn't get the chance to talk to you at the funeral. How are things?"

Freya smiled. "Pretty good, actually. I'm loving my new job."

"Oh, what are you doing?" Avery asked.

"I work at the chamber of commerce, doing events and promotions for the town. It's a new role, so I've been able to make it my own. I'm looking after the beach cleanup, and the farmers market, and I'm thinking about some kind of hummingbird celebration, although that might have to wait until next year. Oh, and we have a big Jane Austen festival coming up. That was your aunts' idea."

"They mentioned that," Avery said. "It all sounds great. And my dad would have loved a hummingbird celebration. Congratulations on doing so well."

"Thanks. The truth is, the way tourism is growing here, there's probably going to be more work than I can handle this summer. But don't tell anyone I said that." She laughed. "What about you, though? When are you going back to Portland?"

Avery exchanged glances with Claudia, who raised an eyebrow. There was no point in keeping it a secret—everyone would know soon enough. "I'm not really sure. I won't be doing the radio show anymore."

Freya looked sympathetic. "I don't blame you. I wouldn't want to work with him either."

At that moment, Avery realized that everyone would probably assume the same thing—that the embarrassment had made her quit. But she wouldn't walk away because of a man, no matter how much of a jerk he was.

"I didn't quit," she said firmly.

"Oh." Freya looked puzzled. "So you are going back to the station then?"

"Uh...no." A deflated feeling came over her. Her last shreds of pride couldn't disguise the fact that she'd been fired. "They let me and Carter go."

Freya's eyes widened. "They fired *you*? No way."

"Yeah."

"That's insane," Freya said, her voice getting louder. "You should sue. You should sue them, and Carter."

"Maybe," Avery said. "Thanks for your support. I appreciate it."

"No problem. We're all behind you." She held up a fist

in solidarity. "Oh, will we see you at the beach cleanup tomorrow? All the kids from Austen Elementary are coming, and there'll be spot prizes, and food trucks so we can all eat when we're done."

Avery wasn't sure she'd feel like all that socializing, but cleaning up the beach was something worth doing. Plus, Ace would love it, and he deserved all the fun she could give him. "Sure, I'll come. That sounds fun."

"Great! We're having a birthday dinner tonight for Mom, so I'll tell Daniel you're coming. He'll be pleased to see you while he's in town, and Logan too. It'll be like a reunion." She beamed, then seemed to remember that it might not be a *happy* reunion. "I mean…I don't suppose Logan will come anyway, so it won't be a reunion at all." She backed away. "Thanks again for the flowers, Claudia."

"You're welcome," Claudia said. "Say happy birthday to your mom from me. I'll see you tomorrow."

When Freya was gone, Claudia turned to Avery. "What kind of reunion *are* you having with Logan?"

"No reunion at all."

"Really?" Claudia had a glint in her eye. "Because in the Clover last night, he was looking at you like he had something on his mind."

"No." Avery worked to erase the image of him in running gear from her mind. "He wasn't looking at me any way at all."

"Okay. If you insist." Claudia shrugged and started sweeping off the counter. "Did you find out why he's in town? Did he come for your dad's funeral?"

"That's what he said." She hadn't thought to ask if there was some other reason why he was here.

"It is kind of momentous having you both in town again at the same time, after all these years."

"There's nothing momentous about a person attending a funeral," Avery said. "It's commonplace."

Claudia tipped the flower stems and clippings into a green waste bin. "There's nothing commonplace about you two. Everyone knew you were meant to fall in love."

Avery shook her head. "That's all in the past."

"Right." Claudia nodded. "The past."

"Yes. And now I'm going. Because I have to do some thinking about the *future*."

But as she walked home through the long-familiar streets of Austen, with Ace sniffing at every corner, Avery could feel the past right over her shoulder.

Chapter 10

B ack in Austen, the streets were busier than when Logan had passed through earlier. Obviously Patrick had been right about the lunchtime rush. With his feet hurting, Logan abandoned his plan to get a double espresso from the coffee cart on Main Street and decided to detour through the quieter riverside streets on his way back to the vacation rental. First, though, he stopped and took off his boots and socks. He'd rather walk back barefoot than aggravate the blisters any further.

He set off, the sidewalk warm under his feet. Then, as he turned a corner, he saw a familiar figure ahead, accompanied by a big yellow dog.

"Avery," he called.

She jumped, as though he'd given her a fright, and turned to look over her shoulder. As she did, her expression changed from surprise to a discouraging look.

He hesitated. Her name had burst out before he could stop it, or think what he was going to say next.

As he caught up to her, she looked down to where he was carrying his boots in one hand, then to his bare feet. "Hello," she said. There was zero encouragement in the word.

Luckily Ace seemed to feel more warmly toward him.

The dog strained on his leash as he tried to get closer, wiggling in welcome, his tail flailing.

"Ace, sit," Avery said firmly, but the dog paid no attention, continuing to wriggle and grin as he tried to get closer to Logan.

Logan didn't know what he'd done to deserve the dog's enthusiasm, but he decided to take advantage of it. Ignoring Avery's apparent disapproval of both his bare feet and his very presence, he bent down and reached out one hand, shamelessly adopting an encouraging tone. "Hey, Ace. Hey, buddy. Good to see you again. What a good boy. Yes, you are a good boy."

At that, Ace tugged on his leash so hard that Avery gave in and came closer, letting him reach Logan. There was a flurry of tail wagging and mutual appreciation, then Logan stood up and looked at Avery. The flush in her cheeks was obviously from annoyance, but it only accentuated her pretty features.

"What a great dog," he said, figuring that any kind of canine talk would break the ice with a dog lover.

It almost worked. A flicker of warmth crossed her face as she glanced down at Ace, but it was gone by the time she met Logan's eyes again.

"He is."

Nothing else was forthcoming, and she looked ready to leave, so he said, "You guys just out for a walk?"

He immediately cringed inside at the inanity. Usually he knew exactly what to say in any situation. Well, any *business* situation.

"Yes." A strand of flaxen hair had come loose from her ponytail, and she pushed it off her cheek. "You too?" She glanced down at Logan's feet again, and he resisted the urge to curl his toes.

"Yeah." He held up his boots. "They're brand new. They were giving me blisters, so..." He shrugged. Ace snuffled at the boots, and he lifted them out of the dog's reach. "Not so fast, buddy. These weren't cheap."

Avery looked like she couldn't care less about his blisters, or his boots, or him. "Okay, well, we're going to keep moving. Good luck with your walk."

She turned to go, and Logan knew the encounter was over.

But then Ace lunged forward, grabbing at the boots. In a flash, one was in the dog's mouth, and he turned and made a break for it. Whether she'd been taken by surprise, or because she was secretly on Ace's side, the leash slipped from Avery's hand, and Ace was off.

For a heartbeat they both stood frozen in surprise, watching as he galloped gaily down the street, his feathery tail held high.

"He's pretty fast," Logan commented.

That seemed to jolt Avery out of her shock, and she sprang into action. "Ace!" she yelled, starting after him at a run. "Ace!"

Apparently she wasn't completely on the dog's side. Logan allowed himself a moment to watch her run, her bottom shapely in denim shorts. Then he took off after her and Ace, one boot in hand.

Maybe this town still held some surprises for him after all.

Avery would never have guessed Ace could run so fast. Evidently Logan brought out the worst in him. She had no idea why he'd taken such a shine to the man, but it was irritating to say the least.

She finally caught up with the runaway rogue at their gate, where he danced around proudly with his prize. She made a grab for it, but he scampered away, thoroughly enjoying himself. After some oh-so-hilarious chasing around the garden, he found a spot at the side of the porch and settled in for some boot chewing, keeping a wary eye on her in case she came after him again.

She stood for a moment in near-defeat under the maple tree, panting a little, watching as he dismembered what did indeed look like very expensive leather footwear. Then she dived in once more, determined not to be beaten.

She managed to capture the boot from Ace just as

Logan arrived. In contrast to her own flustered state, he looked like he hadn't even broken a sweat. That was also irritating.

"I'm sorry," she said, holding out the drool-covered remains. "I don't know what came over him."

Logan regarded the sorry offering, then looked wordlessly down at Ace, who appeared very pleased to see him. Avery was pretty sure the feeling wasn't mutual.

"I'll pay for a new pair, of course," she added hurriedly.

At last Logan took the boot from her, letting it dangle from its soggy laces. "That's okay," he said. "I don't want you to pay for anything."

She decided not to argue. She was unemployed now, after all.

"Actually, he can have it." Logan started to give the boot back to Ace.

"No!" she said, more loudly than she intended. "That's like rewarding him for bad behavior."

Logan sighed and stood upright again. "I don't really want it myself."

She held out a hand, and he passed the mangled boot back to her. Ace sprang up hopefully, but she gave him a steely glare, and, surprisingly, he sat back down.

"He's never usually this naughty," she said. "I think he's feeling lost without my dad."

"That makes sense." Logan's voice was understanding. "You must be lost too."

His sympathetic words cut way too close, and she waved them away. "I'm doing fine."

He nodded, even though the sudden quiver in her voice had made it obvious that she wasn't really. "Well, if there's anything I can do..."

Anything *he* could do? Please. "I don't think I'll be asking you for help," she said. "We've let it go, remember? Just like the song."

His brow creased. "What song?"

She stared at him for a moment. Everyone knew that Frozen song. Where had he been for the last who-knows-how-many years? Oh, right. He'd been gone. Just like his dad, and her mom.

"Never mind," she said, losing patience all of a sudden. "Why are you even here?"

He hesitated. "I told you—I came for the funeral."

"Okay, but that was two days ago. Why are you still here? You don't care about this town, or the people in it."

"I do."

"Oh, come on," she said. "We both know that's not true. You left, and you never looked back." She went up the steps to the porch, Ace at her heels.

"You left too," he pointed out.

She turned around. Seeing him standing there on the path, she was struck by a flashback to the spring night he'd stood hopefully in her front yard, so many years before. After everything that had happened, she couldn't face going to prom at all, let alone going with Logan, whose dad had just skipped town with her mom. It was all the town could talk about, behind her back—and behind her dad's back. What would it have done to him, if she'd carried on dating a Wagner? She and Logan had grown up together, and their childhood friendship had slowly turned into a sweet love connection, something that felt meant to be, full of possibility. It had broken her heart to say no that night, and watch Logan walk away in the moonlight. But she'd had no choice. Now she blinked, and in place of the lean, eager teenage boy stood a broad-shouldered, unknown man. Unknown, because he hadn't just walked away—he'd kept going right out of town, and right out of her life.

"You left first," she said.

He frowned. "Is it some kind of competition? We both left. That doesn't mean we don't care about Austen."

"I didn't stay away for ten years," she said. "I came back to visit."

"I've been busy."

"Busy?" She snorted. "Alright, if you care so much, then prove it."

"I will," he said emphatically. "And what counts as proof, if you're standing in judgment?"

She ignored his tone. "Spend the day helping at the beach tomorrow. Freya Blackwood is organizing a community cleanup."

"Fine," he said. "I'll see you there."

She rolled her eyes. "Fine."

She herded Ace inside then went through the door herself, still carrying the dead boot. But before she closed it, she looked outside once more. Logan was standing under the maple tree with his other boot, a thoughtful look on his face. Then he turned and went out the gate and down the street, walking slightly tentatively on his bare feet.

She closed the door, regretting her rash challenge. Now she'd have to see him again at the beach, along with half of Austen, including Daniel Blackwood. Thanks to her impulsiveness, it looked like Freya and Claudia would get their reunion after all.

Chapter 11

L ogan walked to the beach the next morning in tennis shoes, with Band-Aids stuck on each heel. He avoided the town, taking a narrow track that started near the vacation rental and went through the sand dunes before emerging at the bay. He could see a large group of people gathered close to where the road from town met the coast. Multicolored flags were planted in the sand, kids were running everywhere, and a banner announced *The Awesome Austen Cleanup*. The long, wild sweep of beach curved into cliffs at its northernmost point, punctuated by three towering sea stacks.

Laughter and snatches of conversation floated to him on the fresh ocean breeze. He put up a hand to shade his eyes and scanned the crowd, looking for familiar faces. First the funeral, then the Clover, and now the beach. He hadn't intended to get drawn back into Austen like this, but here he still was. Proving something he'd never felt the need to prove. He shook his head and started toward the gathering.

As he came closer, he could see a registration table. That seemed like the obvious first stop. He went over to the table, where Freya Blackwood appeared to be in charge. He waited while she gave instructions to some kids and handed over gloves and garbage bags.

"Hi," he said when she was done.

She looked at him, and her face lit up. "Logan? No way! We didn't expect to see you here." Then she turned and yelled to a group of people standing nearby. "Daniel! Come see who's here!"

A tall figure left the group and came toward them—Daniel, walking with that same slow, easy gait like he always had, a grin plastered across his face. "Logan Wagner," he said. "Unbelievable."

Logan took his outstretched hand, but instead of shaking it Daniel pulled him into a half hug complete with back slaps that reverberated in his chest.

"It's been way too long," Daniel said, letting him go. "Where the hell have you been?"

Logan shrugged, laughing. "Here and there. Working. You know."

"This town was never the same after you left," Daniel said. "Right, Freya?"

She nodded. "We sure missed you. Some of us more than others." She pointed at Daniel, and he laughed.

"Alright, alright. I'm not going to get all gushy now. But seriously, we need to catch up. How long are you in town?"

Logan hesitated. "I'm not sure. I hadn't planned to stay more than a day or two, but..." He gestured around. "I'm still here."

"Be careful," Daniel said. "You might never get out. Look at me—I do my best to stay away, but I keep ending up back here." He held out his hands to take in the surroundings—the white-capped sea, the wide ribbon of beach, a cloud-studded sky—and laughed, apparently untroubled by his fate.

"Business will call eventually," Logan said.

Daniel nodded. "Right. I heard a whisper that you're doing very well."

"Don't believe everything you hear," Logan said lightly. For some reason he didn't feel inclined to share any details about his success. It would set him apart in a way that he didn't feel comfortable with in his hometown. Plus, he'd found that once people knew how wealthy he was, it changed things. The money hung over everything, either making people uncomfortable or bringing out the worst in them, the temptation to somehow get a piece for themselves too much. He was still figuring out how to manage that, and he didn't want to bring it to his friendships in Austen. Friendships that he was surprised to discover he still had.

Changing the subject, he turned to Freya. "So how does this cleanup work?"

"O-*kay*." She passed gloves and a garbage bag over the table, swinging into official mode again. "Everyone is allocated a teammate, and you'll be responsible for a specific section of the beach. We've pegged the sections out on the sand, but each one runs into the dunes too. Just don't go into any fenced-off parts. But you know that already." Then she looked over his shoulder. "Oh, hi Avery. Glad you could make it."

He turned to see Avery standing behind him, Ace sitting at her feet like butter wouldn't melt in his mouth. Seeing Logan, the dog wagged his tail so hard his rear end went from side to side as well, but he didn't move. Logan decided not to encourage him this time.

"You showed up," Avery said.

"I said I would." He always followed through on his promises. Maybe she'd forgotten that, in the years they'd been apart.

"Hmm." Without further comment, she turned to the others. "Hi, Daniel. Freya, this all looks amazing."

Freya smiled, a little pink spot appearing in each cheek. "Thanks! It took more organizing than I thought, but everything's all set now. I hope. Anyway, let's see who you're teamed up with." She ran her finger down a list of names. "Hmmm...here you are." Her finger stopped at the bottom of the page.

Avery craned over the table, trying to see. "Who is it?"

"Your teammate is Logan."

Something sparked in Logan's chest when he heard that, but Avery was thin-lipped.

"Freya," she said flatly. "Really?"

"You were the last two to register," Freya replied innocently as she handed Avery a pair of gloves, but Logan thought he saw a hint of mischief in her eyes, along with determination.

Maybe sensing that arguing would be a waste of time, Avery sighed. "Alright then. Where are we going?"

"Oh, everyone is drawing their location out of a hat." Freya picked up a battered cowboy hat full of folded pieces of paper. "Which one of you would like to pick?"

Logan spoke up. "Avery, it's all yours." If she was already annoyed about being teamed up with him, he didn't want to get the blame for randomly selecting an unsatisfactory location.

"No, you go ahead," she said impatiently.

"No, no," he said. "You do the honors."

"Fine." She reached into the hat and pulled out a piece of paper, then unfolded it. "Section twenty-seven. Where's that?"

Freya pushed a map across the table. "It's...oh, it's here. At the end of the beach."

Avery let out a loud sigh, and Logan leaned in to look. Their area was the farthest away, right alongside the cliffs. Even if Avery avoided him during the cleanup time, it would mean a long walk there and back together. He checked the fitness tracker on his smartwatch. If nothing else, this would help him hit his target for the day.

"It'll be good exercise for Ace," Freya suggested.

Avery considered this glass-half-full perspective. "I guess." Then she turned to Daniel. "Who are you with today?"

"He's with me," Claudia said from behind them. She tucked her arm through Avery's. "Daniel and I drew section twenty-four, so you'll have the pleasure of our company for the walk along the beach."

Daniel laughed. "Are you sure that counts as a pleasure?"

"Of course," Claudia said. "In my case, anyway."

Freya came around to the front of the table. "Come on,

you guys. I have to get on the microphone and give everyone their final instructions." She clutched her clipboard. "I'm nervous."

"Will you do a number while you're up there?" Daniel asked. "Your singing voice is legendary, after all."

"Enough, sibling," Freya admonished him. "You know yours is just as bad."

At that, Daniel burst into song. "Who says you can't go home?" he warbled.

The women laughed, shushing him, but he continued his tuneless murder of the Bon Jovi tune, drawing sideways looks from the people around them but succeeding in distracting Freya from her nerves.

"Mom loves that song," she told her brother. "Don't kill it."

Following after them, listening to the ongoing banter, Logan felt like a teenager again. Who says you can't go home, indeed. It was almost like everything was just as it had been before. He looked at Avery, laughing now as she walked arm in arm with Claudia, her golden hair glossy in the sun, a spring in her step as Ace trotted alongside…and a vision of what might have been slammed into him. In some parallel universe, he and Avery had both stayed in Austen, and this was his reality—weekends at the beach with the old gang, laughing and joking, secure in their shared history. Or maybe the two of them had left town for brighter lights, but stayed together, coming back as a couple for happy weekend visits to family and friends.

But his reality was something different, for better or worse.

He had left. And then she had left. But now they were back—older, if not wiser. And Avery was suddenly single. For the first time in a long time, he wondered if there might be a way for that parallel universe to somehow intersect with the reality they'd found themselves in.

Chapter 12

As they set off along the beach, Freya's instructions were still ringing in Avery's ears—be back no later than midday, no walking on the protected areas of the dunes, and no dogs off leash. She had clipped an extra long leash onto Ace's collar, and the four of them walked on the hard sand near the water so he could roam without getting tangled up with anyone. He was making the most of it, ranging as far as he could and splashing in the cold water before coming back to check in with her. Each time, he also made sure to nose against Logan for attention. She still hadn't figured out that little love affair, but she wondered if he'd latched onto Logan as a kind of replacement for the missing man in his life. Her dad would want Ace to be happy...but *she* would have been happier if the dog had picked someone else.

Daniel had grabbed Logan and now the two men walked a little ahead, apparently engrossed in conversation. Avery and Claudia followed behind at a leisurely pace, enjoying the chance to catch up some more, and pausing every now and then to wait for Ace. At first there had been a mass of people, but the numbers gradually dropped off as they passed each section marker.

About halfway along, Avery noticed a figure walking

higher up the beach, surrounded by a gaggle of kids. "Is that Hunter Kinnaird?"

Claudia whipped her head around. "Oh! It is." Pink spots appeared on her cheeks and she smoothed her hair, but the wind immediately blew the lengths out of place again. "I guess he's visiting his cousins this weekend. They already have a ton of kids between them."

Avery raised an eyebrow. "Hunter, huh? Tell me more."

"What?" Claudia flapped her hand at Avery, shooing the unspoken suggestion away. "There's nothing to tell. He hardly ever comes to visit, so I'm just surprised to see him."

"If surprised means flustered and blushing."

"Stop it," Claudia said. "That's not what it means at all."

"I don't blame you," Avery said, watching as Hunter raised his arms like a cartoon wrestler, a giggling kid dangling from each bicep. "I never would have picked that he'd grow up so fine." Hunter had gone to Austen Elementary with them, but left town after that with his mom when his parents split up.

"Okay, okay. I'm only human," Claudia conceded. "Sometimes a guy catches my eye. So sue me."

She looked back up the beach again. Hunter had noticed them, and lifted one kid-laden arm in a long-distance greeting. Claudia's cheeks went even pinker, and she gave a half-wave in response before Hunter was swept away toward the dunes by a gaggle of children.

Avery laughed. "I knew it."

"Well, while we're on the topic, I notice that someone has caught *your* eye," Claudia said, neatly diverting as they continued walking. "Someone from your past."

"Nice try, but no."

"There's no point in denying it. I've seen you checking him out."

"I'm not at all. I'm just looking to make sure we don't fall too far behind."

"Yes, his behind is definitely something worth looking at."

Avery groaned. "You are the worst, you know that, right?"

Claudia grinned, and then Ace ran up to them again, scattering salty water droplets everywhere. Avery was glad of the distraction, but she couldn't help glancing in Logan's direction one more time. She was only human too, which meant she had her weaknesses along with everyone else. And, to be fair, the longstanding weaknesses were probably the hardest to shake. Anyway, he'd be gone soon, and she'd have to go back to Portland and decide what to do with her life, at which point she could put him out of her mind again.

A minute later she and Claudia caught up with the men, who had stopped and waited for them.

"This is just like old times," Claudia said cheerily. "Like a reunion, right?" She winked at Avery. "We just need Emma here now."

"Last time we talked, I got the impression that she'd rather be here than in Nebraska," Avery said.

Daniel looked away toward the ocean, saying nothing. Too late, she remembered that he and Emma had been an item in high school. She didn't know exactly what had happened to break them up during their college years— Emma had never given her all the details. In the old days, she and Claudia would have known every last development in their relationship. But time passed, and people drifted away, and it wasn't the old days anymore.

At that moment they came to a peg in the sand marked with the number twenty-four. "This is us," Claudia said, getting out her gloves and snapping them on. "Come on Daniel, let's go clean up this joint."

He grinned at her, seemingly back to his usual lighthearted self. "You know there's something naughty about you snapping those gloves like that, right?"

She adopted a Scarlett O'Hara voice. "Why, Mister Blackwood, I don't know *what* you're talking about."

Despite Claudia's teasing tone, Avery noticed that there was no hint of the attraction she hadn't been able to hide when looking at Hunter. Amid laughter, Claudia and

Daniel set off to do their cleanup, leaving Avery with Logan.

In contrast to their friends' hilarity, the silence between them felt obvious, and Avery was glad to have Ace there. She bent down to adjust his collar, fiddling with the loop where the leash clipped on. When she stood up, Logan was watching her.

"Not far now," she said, indicating toward the cliffs.

"Not far," he agreed. "Shall we go? I have a garbage bag to fill, and something to prove."

Oh, he went there. The last remnant of Claudia and Daniel's frivolity blew away on the wind, and Avery squared her shoulders.

"Let's do it then."

Chapter 13

In their allocated area under the cliffs, the breeze was almost nonexistent, and the air warmer. They pulled on their gloves—Logan couldn't help but notice that Avery didn't indulge in any playful glove-snapping—and got started. With only one garbage bag between them, they were forced to stick close together, but it soon became obvious that there wasn't really anything to pick up.

He looked around. "Do you think there's going to be any trash down here at all?"

Avery brushed the back of her hand against her forehead, trying to shift a stray strand of hair. "Doesn't seem like it."

"Hmm," he said. "Well, this is a problem. How am I going to prove I care, if not with a stinking bag of trash?"

"You'll think of something," she said, and he could have sworn there was a hint of humor in her tone. "Anyway, we can't go back yet. Everyone will think we're lazy."

"I guess we'll just have to wait a while then."

She frowned. "I guess so."

With no other option, they sat on the warm sand, and Avery let Ace's leash out to its fullest length. He collected pats from each of them before going off to forage around, his tail cheerfully swinging.

The silence stretched between them, but Logan wasn't going to make it easy for her. He picked up a shell and tossed it casually from one hand to the other as she determinedly looked out to the breakers. He knew she'd eventually give in and try to start a conversation, if only for the sake of good manners, and then he'd have the advantage. What was the saying? All's fair in love and war? Love and war and trash collection.

And he was right.

"So," she eventually said, somewhat reluctantly, "Daniel said you're doing well in business?"

He shrugged. "I'm doing okay."

"What are you doing okay at?" she asked. "I mean, what business are you in?"

He decided to keep it vague but relatable. "Contracting, mostly. Some residential, some commercial."

"Construction, you mean?"

That would do. "Yeah."

She thought for a moment, running her free hand through the sand. "That makes sense. Your dad was always working on some project or other."

At the mention of his father, he tensed. It was especially disconcerting coming from Avery. "Yeah. He taught me how to do a lot of things." After a moment he added, "He taught me a lot about what *not* to do, too."

Her eyes remained focused on the sand, and he watched the grains sparkle in the sun as she lifted them, then let them fall, over and again. After a while she said, "I guess I could say the same about my mom."

That was an unexpected turn in the conversation. He decided to venture a little deeper.

"You must miss—"

Before he could finish the sentence, Avery's arm was jerked forward and the leash flew from her hand. With a shout, she instantly leaped up and ran after it, calling Ace back. Logan got up to follow, and as he ran he saw the dog was making a beeline for a rocky area at the base of the cliffs, where they met the sea. Near the water, there was something else. He squinted in the bright sunlight, trying to see better. It was a giant, dark mass of something...

Oh, no. An elephant seal.

They both sped after Ace, a repeat of the great boot escapade but with significantly higher stakes than half a pair of hand-stitched leather footwear.

As he caught up to Avery, he could see that Ace was almost upon the seal. It rose up, looming and defensive, its Jello-like body undulating.

"Ace!" Avery bellowed, panic in her tone. "Come! Come here!"

But Ace seemed delighted to make the acquaintance of a fellow fur-covered non-human. He raced up to the elephant seal and play bowed to one side then the other, eager to get a game started. The seal put its nose in the air, arched its back, and let out a series of barking grunts, its proboscis flopping around. In return, Ace barked loudly, then dashed around the side of the animal, the leash trailing behind him.

Avery yelled to him again, but he ignored her. They were close now—too close. The seal was huge. Logan tried to reach out and stop Avery, but she kept rushing onward.

"Avery, don't go near it," he yelled.

As the words left his mouth, the elephant seal lurched forward and around, trying to reach Ace. It lunged over the leash, trapping it between blubber and sand, and Ace yelped loudly as he was brought to an abrupt halt. The seal turned, still pinning the leash to the ground, then rose up again and came down with a powerful downward force.

Logan felt his stomach turn over as Ace cried out again, then suddenly went silent.

"No!" Avery shouted.

Before he could stop her, she dashed forward. In desperation, he darted in front of the seal, trying to distract it. The seal turned toward him and he leaped around, hoping to encourage it away. It raised its head, then opened its mouth and barked at him, clearly feeling aggressive rather than frightened. Out of the corner of his eye, he could see Avery go to Ace and unclip the leash from his collar, then gather him up from the sand. The seal looked back toward her, its attention divided, and Logan let out a couple of whoops to get its attention back.

"Go!" he yelled to Avery as the seal came at him with surprising speed. After one worried glance in his direction, she went, her face white as she clutched Ace close.

With his heart beating out of his chest, Logan dodged backward as the creature surged at him, barking loudly. Then, when Avery and Ace were well clear, he turned and ran too.

They headed down the beach back toward the cleanup HQ, Logan carrying Ace. The dog was subdued after his encounter, but he seemed okay apart from favoring one leg. Avery had called the local veterinarian and discovered that he was taking part in the cleanup too, so they'd arranged to meet him at the registration table.

As they walked, she put both their pairs of gloves in the garbage bag. "I'm still shaking," she said.

He wasn't going to admit it, but adrenaline was still roaring through his veins, making his heart pound. And Ace was no lightweight. "I know," he said, shifting the dog slightly in his arms. "It was like being an extra in Jurassic Park, with Jabba the Hutt playing the dinosaur."

A laugh escaped her at his exaggeration, but it was edged with distress. "Why did Ace think he could be friends with an elephant seal, of all things? He could have been killed. If bad luck comes in threes, I've already had mine for the year. I can't lose Ace too."

Logan had his work cut out for him speed-walking down the beach carrying the increasingly heavy dog, but something in her words caught his attention. "Three bad things?" He knew about her dad, and the baby revelation, but that was only two.

She shook her head, dismissing his query. "At least the seal was okay. I mean, he wasn't injured or anything."

"No, he seemed in good shape. I guess we might have

given him a scare, but he had no trouble sticking up for himself."

"We should go back and check to make sure he didn't get tangled in the leash," Avery said, looking over her shoulder. "I can't see him anymore."

"I'll take care of it," Logan told her. "Let's get Ace to the vet first." At the sound of Logan saying his name, Ace twisted around in his arms and licked his chin. "Yeah, okay, buddy," he said, trying to keep up his pace. "I appreciate the sentiment, but it would be better if you kept still."

Avery was watching them. She bit her lip, then said, "Thank you. For helping us."

He nodded. "That's okay. You were the one who ran straight into the arms of danger. The *flippers* of danger."

She laughed. "He seemed gigantic at the time. I guess he wasn't *that* big though."

"Actually, he was, for a seal. He was a real heavyweight. But not Jurassic Park big."

"True," she said, and her lingering smile gave him more satisfaction than the last business deal he'd closed.

When they arrived at the registration table, Freya and the veterinarian were there to meet them.

"Poor Ace!" Freya said. "Wyatt told me what happened. Is he okay?"

Logan lowered him to the ground, and the vet kneeled down to check him over. Avery sat on the sand next to them, stroking Ace and murmuring to him. Logan stepped away to give them room.

"I think so," he said to Freya as they watched the examination take place. He didn't recognize the vet—he must have moved to Austen after Logan left. "The closer we got to here, the more he squirmed. I would have let him walk, but we wanted to get him checked as fast as possible."

Freya sent him a smile. "That was sweet of you. Ace isn't exactly a purse dog."

"He sure isn't." Logan leaned back, rolling his shoulders to loosen his muscles.

Then the vet got to his feet. "There's nothing immediately

obvious," he said, "but it might be a good idea to X-ray that leg, just to be sure. I can take you both back to the clinic in my truck now, if you like?"

Avery stood up too. "That would be so great. Thanks, Wyatt."

"No problem." He scooped Ace up with the ease of someone who handled animals every day. "If you're ready?"

Looking at Avery's grateful face, Logan worked to squash the feeling that the tall, handsome vet was stealing his thunder.

Avery passed him the garbage bag they hadn't filled. "See you later, Logan. Thanks again."

Before he could reply, she had walked away with Wyatt. He looked down at the bag. He was pretty sure he'd proved something today...so why did it feel like he'd just been handed a consolation prize?

Chapter 14

One of the many things Avery liked about Austen was the central riverside park. The small commercial center of town was set back from the Austen River, separated from the water by a stretch of tree-studded grass. It was a community space that had always been well used for concerts, family get-togethers, and wedding photos. There were bench seats under the trees, a small playground off to one side, and even a traditional round gazebo painted in crisp white.

Today was the Sunday farmers market, and under the blue sky, with people walking around wearing shorts and caps, it felt like summer had really arrived. Even though Wyatt had said Ace was fine, she'd left him at home having an enforced rest so that she could browse the stands in peace.

As a local band played in the gazebo, she wandered around, soaking up the sights and smells of the market: fresh loaves of bread and sweet pastries, lusciously bright vegetables, rounds of cheese, golden-topped jars of pickles and olives, and divinely fragrant coffee. She bought a bag of Italian roast coffee, then stopped at the cheese stall for a wedge of salty pecorino romano. It would be perfect for the dinner she was making for Claudia tonight.

It was a bittersweet way to spend an afternoon; when she was a kid, the farmers market had been a regular family outing before her mother left. Logan's father would sometimes have a stand there, selling wooden trays, cutting boards, planter boxes, and other things he made in his workshop. A love of woodworking was the main thing he'd had in common with Avery's dad...until her mom became what they had in common. She wondered if Jeff and her mom had exchanged glances across the market, something less wholesome than heirloom apples and organic honey on their minds.

She shoved the thought aside as she came to Claudia's flower stand, which was already looking sparse.

Claudia finished serving a customer, then turned to her. "Hi, Avery."

"Hi," she replied. "Looks like you've sold a lot already."

"It's been busy." Claudia adjusted a floral arrangement on the table in front of her. "I guess the weather has brought everyone out. How's Ace today?"

"He's fine, thank goodness."

"I'm so glad he's okay."

"Me too." Avery frowned. "I'm still worried about the seal though. I hope he wasn't on the beach because he was injured or something."

"He wasn't."

At the sound of the male voice, she turned to see Logan standing behind her. He held out Ace's leash. "He's fine. I checked on him after you and Ace went with the vet. This was still lying on the sand."

"Thank you." As she took the leash, their fingers brushed ever so slightly, and she jerked her hand away. Logan raised an eyebrow, but she looked back to Claudia, avoiding his eye. "Are you still okay for dinner tonight?" she asked her friend. "I'm making us my special carbonara. Fancy cheese and everything." She held up the pecorino.

"I'm so sorry," Claudia said. "I can't tonight after all. Briar just asked me to babysit so she and Devin can go to a show in Portland. They're staying overnight, and apparently the girls want me to take care of them."

"Oh...well, another time I guess. Aunt duty is more important."

She had been looking forward to dinner with Claudia, though—a chance to sit down together over a bottle of wine and a simple but delicious meal. Talk and laugh, and maybe figure out what she should do next. She was feeling the need to talk through everything that had happened lately, and Claudia was the only person in town she wanted to do that with. The aunts were great, but they were carrying their own grief.

Claudia's brows knitted. "I really am sorry, Avery. Any other night would be fine." She paused. "Oh, except tomorrow night, because we're going out for dinner for Gramma's birthday. And Tuesday I'm running a night class at the store."

"That's okay," Avery said. "I know how busy you are."

She must have failed miserably at keeping the disappointment out of her voice, because Claudia looked even more guilty. Then she brightened. "If you already have a dinner planned, Logan should eat with you."

Avery took a step back, away from her sneakily meddling friend. "No, no. That's okay. It'll keep. And I'm sure Logan is too busy, anyway."

"Logan is right here," he said. "And he isn't too busy. And carbonara sounds great. I'm guessing that's pecorino?"

She held the cheese to her chest, along with the coffee and the leash. "Yes, but—"

"I heard Logan was great yesterday at the cleanup," Claudia said, leaning forward on the table next to a tall arrangement of lilies and delphiniums. "Taking the heat from that enormous elephant seal so you and Ace could get away, and carrying him to Wyatt. Then he went all the way back down the beach to check on the seal and get Ace's leash. I think the least you can do is give him a nice dinner."

"I don't think—"

Logan nodded. "I would love a nice dinner. I'm

terrible at cooking, apart from basic stuff like bacon and eggs, so I never do it."

"It's not my problem if you survive on takeout food," she said. The three of them stood there for a moment, her abrupt words hanging in the air. Then she sighed. "Okay, fine. Come at seven."

"I never had a more gracious invitation," he said dryly. "It will be my pleasure."

She bit the inside of her lip to stop herself shooting back a snippy retort. "Bye, Claudia. Good luck babysitting."

"Thanks," she replied. "See you soon."

Avery started to walk away, then turned back. "Bring wine," she told Logan.

She was going to need it.

Chapter 15

For the first time in ten years, Logan stood on the Robinsons' doorstep. The last time he'd been on this spot, things hadn't gone so well. He didn't really know why he was here now—Avery was clearly never going to consider rekindling their teenage romance, and despite being hijacked by his own feelings for her, he knew it wasn't a good idea. But maybe they could clear the air, get a little closer to reconciliation. Maybe even friendship, if not closure.

He checked his watch—six fifty-eight—and ran a hand through his hair, then rapped on the door using the heavy round knocker.

He heard doggy nails clacking on the hardwood floors, then Ace snuffling at the door. He resisted saying anything to the dog, but it seemed like Ace had it figured out, because he let out some low woofs of welcome.

After a minute Avery pulled the door open, and as Ace shot out onto the porch, Logan was pulled back to the past yet again. She was clad in jeans and a simple white T-shirt, her hair fell in loose waves around her shoulders, and she didn't seem to be wearing any makeup on her blue eyes. He didn't know if that was her usual style these days, or if she had purposefully not gone to any trouble for the night, just to make a point. Either way, it took him a moment to gather his thoughts. She barely looked any different from that night so long ago, when he'd come for one last try, and she'd given him one last no.

"Are you coming in?" she asked impatiently.

He rapidly refocused. Actually, he did know why he was here. Because Owen had died, and her fiancé had cheated on her. He still didn't know what her third piece of bad luck was, but he knew she needed a friend right now. Claudia's suggestion had been mischievous, but there was method in her madness.

"Yes," he said. "Thanks." As he went through the door along with Ace he gave Avery the bottle of wine he'd brought, then waited for her to lead the way farther into the house.

She looked at the label and raised one eyebrow. "Nice."

He squatted down to accept Ace's enthusiastic welcome. "Needed something good to equal this famous carbonara."

"Don't build it up too much," she told him, heading down the hallway. "It's just spaghetti and cheese."

"That's not what I heard," he said, standing back up.

She made no reply, just continued into the kitchen.

He followed her in, with Ace tagging along. The soft evening air was flowing in through the open back door and there were flowers on the counter and the table, some of them starting to wilt. He realized they must have been sent by well-wishers when Owen passed.

"We could go ahead and open that bottle now," he suggested.

"Good idea." She gave it back to him, then fished in a drawer and passed him a corkscrew. "Unless it has a screw cap?"

"Not this one," he said. He'd heard the argument that screw caps were perfectly fine, but somehow it still felt better buying a high-end wine with a real cork.

Avery took two wine glasses from a vintage hutch cabinet by the window and handed them to him, then went back to the counter and stirred something in a bowl. He opened the bottle, enjoying the sound the cork made as it exited, and poured them a generous glassful each. Then he brought one to where she was cooking and offered it to her.

"Can I help with anything?" he asked as she took the glass.

She shook her head. "No. I don't need your help with anything."

Ouch. Somehow she managed to imbue the word "anything" with all their shared history. Maybe the friend she needed wouldn't ever be him after all.

"Okay," he said, his tone light. Then he gestured to the table. "Do you mind?"

"Knock yourself out," she said.

He took a seat and Ace plopped down at his feet. For a while neither of them said anything as she worked, and instead of conversation, an amazing bacon-y smell filled the kitchen. He took the chance to watch her, trying to be as covert as he could. She was the picture of concentration as she diced, fried, and grated, and every now and then she would bite her bottom lip as she focused on dealing with a sharp knife or a hot pan.

"I hope you're hungry," she eventually said, draining the spaghetti into the sink.

"I am now." And his growing hunger was related to more than the dinner that was coming his way.

Shaking off the thought, he made himself get up and go to the back door. Beyond the porch and the backyard, the river wandered on its path to the sea. From here, it didn't have far to go. On the other side of the water the hills sloped up in the lingering sunshine, and he thought he could pinpoint the spot where he and Patrick had sat on Friday. A lot of the land visible from town was his father's. He took a sip of his wine, narrowing his eyes as he tried to calculate where it started and ended. It was definitely time to get a surveying team in.

"I love this view," Avery said.

He turned to see her standing beside him. As she looked out at the scenery, a hint of the old dreaminess was in her eyes. He hadn't seen that since he came back to town.

"It's pretty great," he said.

"Sometimes you can take things for granted," she said, still looking out the door. "And then it takes something seismic to remind you of what matters."

Her sudden reflectiveness took him by surprise. But before he could reply, she turned around and started back to the table. "Dinner's ready."

They sat opposite each other, with Ace nearby looking hopeful. The carbonara was piled on a big white platter, topped with shaved cheese, and alongside was a fresh, leafy green salad. "This looks amazing," he said.

She shrugged. "I wanted to do something special for Claudia."

It was a not-so-subtle reminder that he was her second-choice guest for the evening. Probably much lower on the list than second, if he was honest. As they helped themselves to the food, he realized that the dinner plates were the same as when he used to come visit—a traditional blue floral pattern. He had vivid memories of eating Avery's mom's ranch chicken off these plates, and apple pie too. And green bean casserole, which he hadn't enjoyed so much.

Now he shook his head as he ate, and made an appreciative sound. "This doesn't just look amazing—it *is* amazing."

For a moment, she let herself look pleased. "It's supposed to be made with guanciale—pig's cheek. But that's not exactly the easiest thing to find, so I use pancetta instead."

"And the salad?"

"Just arugula with radish and an anchovy dressing."

"Wow. I'm impressed."

She snorted. "Don't be. I don't really like cooking. I have a very limited repertoire of dishes. After three dates, I'm done."

"Ah. Well, I hope I make it to the other two."

At that, she seemed to realize what she'd said. "This

isn't a date," she said quickly. "I meant…hypothetically."

He rolled more spaghetti onto his fork before replying, just to let her squirm a little. It was bad, but he couldn't help it. "I meant the other two dishes."

"Oh. Yes, I knew that." Her cheeks were flushed, and he knew it was from more than just the wine. She hurriedly rolled spaghetti onto her own fork and took a mouthful, looking out the window.

He let her be then, and they both concentrated on the food, which really was good. After a while he asked about her life in Portland, and as their conversation picked up he told her about his favorite places in San Francisco. With Ace keeping them company, even the occasional silences weren't completely awkward. In fact, it almost felt companionable. When they finished eating he helped her to clear the table, then he started to rinse the dishes.

"Leave them," she said, waving him away. "I'll do it later."

Most likely she just wanted to get him out of the house, but he wasn't ready to go.

"We didn't get through much of that wine," he said. "Would you like a little more?" She hesitated, and he pressed home the advantage. "It was expensive. I'd hate for it to go to waste."

He saw the exact moment she relented, and went to get her glass. He refilled it, then his own, and passed hers over.

"It is nice wine," she said, as though defending the decision to herself.

Just then there was a series of sharp knocks on the door, and Ace jumped to his feet, barking loudly. Avery shushed him. "It's not anything to get excited about. People come to visit all the time. Just relax."

As she went to answer the door, Logan leaned in the doorway with his glass and watched her go. It was getting to be a habit, but he didn't feel inclined to break it. Her jeans accentuated her curves, and she walked with a little swing in her hips that was hard to ignore. He noticed with satisfaction that she'd taken her wine with her too. He'd chosen well.

He didn't want to seem like he was eavesdropping, so he wandered into the living room and over to the bookcase. As he stood looking at the books and family pictures, he heard Avery's surprised exclamation, then a man's voice in reply. He couldn't make out what they were saying, but the tone of their exchange threw up a warning flag in his brain.

"Everything okay, Avery?" he called.

When no reply came he put down his glass and started for the door. But before he'd taken two steps a tall blond man came striding into the living room, followed by Avery and Ace.

The man looked Logan up and down, then turned to Avery. "Who the hell is this?"

Logan instinctively raised himself up a little straighter and shot back, "Who the hell are *you*?"

"I'm her fiancé," he said. "Carter Cox. And I'm taking her home."

Chapter 16

After his silence over the last few days, Avery hadn't expected to open the door and find Carter on her doorstep. Now his words to Logan—an echo of his inane catchphrase, no less—reignited the pain of his betrayal.

"I *am* home, you idiot," she said.

Carter turned to her. "Baby, just listen, okay? I can explain everything."

"I know enough," she said, putting her wine glass down next to Logan's. "There's nothing you could say now that I want to hear, so let's not waste our time."

She went into the kitchen and collected her engagement ring from a drawer in the cabinet as quickly as she could. It didn't seem like a good idea to leave the two men alone. When she came back in, Ace was standing next to Logan.

"You can have this." She held the ring out to Carter.

"I'm not taking it," he said, holding up his hands. "The only place I want that is back on your finger."

She stared at him. "Have you forgotten something? Karen Frazier? Your baby?"

"You and I can still make it work," he told her. "We were good together."

She exhaled an incredulous *pfft*. Was he reading from a

list of cheater's clichés? "If we were so good, why did you decide you liked her better? So much better that you had to 'network' with her horizontally," she said, making pointed quote marks.

Carter jabbed a finger at Logan. "Who's this then? You're no better than me if you've hooked up with someone already."

The hypocrisy would have left her speechless if she hadn't been so angry. "So what if I do? You were hooking up with Karen behind my back for months."

Carter took a step toward her, his face dark, and fear darted through her as he spoke. "That doesn't give you the right to—"

In an instant, Logan was standing between them. "I think it's time for you to go," he said, a subdued menace in his voice that she'd never heard before. Ace lined up next to him, a low growl sounding in his chest. Avery reached down and took hold of his collar, just in case. He'd never hurt anyone before, but he'd been unpredictable lately.

"Listen, *buddy*," Carter said to Logan, injecting venom into the word. "I don't know what you two have been playing at, but you need to stay out of this. I was here first."

Logan stood his ground. "We haven't been playing at anything. I'm her friend. Or at least I was, once."

At his words, a pang of something bittersweet gripped Avery's heart. They *had* been friends, for so many years. As far back as she could remember, in fact.

Carter tilted his head, his eyes narrowing at Logan. "There's something familiar about you. Do I know you from someplace?"

Logan shook his head. "No, you don't. And we're never going to know each other, because this is the part where you leave."

Avery held her breath as Carter looked at Logan, then at her, then at Logan again, as though trying to decide what to do. Then Logan took the smallest of steps toward him, and he backed down.

"Fine," he said. "I hope you're very happy together."

Logan started to say something, but Avery put her

hand on his arm. "Logan, don't. It's not worth it."

"You'll be sorry, Avery," Carter said. "You'll never get anywhere in radio without me."

"That's fine with me," she said, "because I don't want to be anywhere you are."

"Don't watch any TV then, because that's where I'll be next."

"Back to Karen already?" She laughed at the quick reversal to his original plan. "You'd better hope she doesn't get sick of you."

With a huff, he turned to go, but after a couple of steps he spun back around with his hand out. She dropped the ring into his palm. As he closed his hand around the diamond, Ace let out a loud bark, and her now ex-fiancé made a hasty, undignified retreat.

Logan watched as Avery paced the living room floor. "I can't believe he did the whole 'you'll never work in this town again' thing," she said, waving her wine glass around. "One cliché after another. And 'I was here first.' What kind of Neanderthal attitude is that?"

Now probably wasn't the moment to ask why she'd ever gotten involved with him in the first place. "You can't go back to work with him." At this point, Logan was ready to physically stand in the door of the radio station and prevent her from entering.

She sighed. "I can't anyway, even if I wanted to."

"Why not?"

"They fired me." She raised her glass to him, then took a mouthful of wine.

He sat forward in his chair. "Wait. He cheated, but you're fired?"

"Yes. But he's fired too."

"As he should be." Then he shook his head. "So that was the third piece of bad luck you wouldn't tell me."

"Are you counting for me?" Her raised eyebrow was a scolding in itself. "Because I don't need you to."

"Yeah, I know. You don't need my help with

85

anything." He echoed her words from the kitchen earlier. "Except getting rid of persistent fiancés."

She looked at him, her face unreadable, and for a moment he thought he'd gone too far. But then she cracked a smile and sat down on the sofa. "You did pretty well there. Carter doesn't back down easily."

"I got that impression," he said.

"It comes with the ego. The more famous and successful he got, the more self-important he became."

"I'm sorry," Logan said. "But maybe it's for the best. Better to see his true colors now."

"I think you might be right. He must have known what was coming when Karen called in, but he didn't even try to stop it." She took another sip of wine. "One thing's for sure—no more ego-driven men for me. No more big names or big ambitions or big deals. I just want a regular guy. A nice, regular hometown kind of guy. Like my dad." She laughed. "Speaking of clichés, that's the biggest one ever, right?"

The whole incident with Carter seemed to have broken the ice between them, and she was talking like they really were friends again. Which was good, but also not good. Because he knew that once a woman started confiding in you about other men, you were firmly in the friend camp. In short, you had lost any chance of being the one confided *about* instead of *to*.

"No, it doesn't sound like a cliché to me," he said, as his heart was sinking. "It sounds like exactly what you deserve."

And it sounded nothing like him.

"I guess it's all about perspective, right?" she said. "I mean, at first I was devastated about Carter. But losing him doesn't compare to losing my dad. I've realized now that he isn't half the man Dad was."

"Your dad was definitely one of a kind."

"I miss him." She hesitated for a moment. "Do you ever see your father?"

He shook his head, turning his glass in his hands. "No."

"So…you haven't seen my mom either."

"I haven't seen either of them since the day they left. I'm sorry."

"I was kind of hoping you might have. I mean, I don't really want to see her, I don't think, but…" She leaned back on the sofa, deflated. "I don't know. The whole thing is a stinking mess."

"Yeah." There was one question he'd thought about often over the years. "Why do you think they disappeared so completely? Cut themselves off from us like that?"

She shook her head. "I've wondered the same thing. Was that necessary? Maybe they thought it was. This is a small town, and they hurt a lot of people."

"I guess staying would have meant facing up to a lot of things. Not everyone is strong enough to do that."

They sat in silence for a while, each sipping their wine, lost in their own thoughts. Then Avery sat forward.

"There's something else." She pressed her fingers to her forehead. "I thought Mom might come to the funeral at least, but she didn't. How do we even know…can we even be sure they're…"

He knew what she was getting at. "Still alive?"

She winced at the sound of the words. "I can't help thinking about that. Especially now, with Dad gone."

"I get that. Have you looked for her?"

"I've been too worried about what I'd find out. Or maybe I'd find her, and she wouldn't want to see me." She looked him in the eye. "I mean, she already chose your dad over me."

A hot, heavy guilt weighed on his chest, familiar and unwelcome. "I'm sorry."

She shrugged, but it didn't lighten the impact of her words. Then she drained the last of her wine and stood up. "I'm tired. We'll see you out."

"Oh…sure." He got up too, and they went to the front door.

"Thanks for the fiancé intervention," she said.

"It was nothing," he replied as he stepped outside. "Thanks for the spaghetti and cheese."

She graced his weak joke with a laugh. "You're welcome."

Her brief laughter was a flare of light in the dark, and he was struck with the longing to make her laugh again. To make her happy. They'd been happy long ago, full of possibility, their future stretching ahead. He couldn't honestly say it was an innocent love on his part—full of hormones, aching with desire for the most beautiful girl he knew, he'd wanted more than kisses and handholding and sweet, tentative touches. But even the teenage him had understood that everything would happen when it was supposed to, when she was ready. They were meant to be. They had time.

Except their time had come to an abrupt end. And now their evening was over too, and reality was calling each of them back.

"Goodnight then," he said. More than anything, he wanted to lean in and kiss her, but she was already edging the door closed.

"Goodnight." She shut the door with a decisive click.

He stood on the porch for a minute to wrangle his thoughts. He'd come to terms with his father's absence long ago, but he didn't realize that Avery's mom had cut herself completely out of her daughter's life. Tracking down Jeff Wagner had already been on his to-do list, but only because he wanted to make the river development happen. Now he had one more reason.

Chapter 17

"There must be a way. I—just a minute."

Logan stepped off the treadmill and took a swig from his water bottle. Then he checked his watch. Not as many steps as he wanted, but his heart rate was definitely up. That probably had something to do with the frustration brought on by this conversation. He picked up his phone and switched off speaker mode.

"If he can't be found via the usual channels, we'll have to bring in a professional to help," he said to Lisa as he walked from the vacation rental's small gym along to the kitchen. "At least we know the land is still in his name."

"I'll take care of it," she replied. "It's not the first time we've had to get a bit creative to make something happen."

He laughed. "True."

Lisa had been with him since the early days, when he first took over the contracting company he'd been working for. The business had been on the verge of collapse, and the owner had decided it was easier to walk away than put in the work required to turn it around. It was the first risk Logan had taken, but not the last, or the biggest. So far, most of those risks had paid off.

Keep moving. Do the next thing. Don't look back.

And now here he was, not just looking back, but

literally back in the place he'd left behind. He went out the sliding doors onto the deck. Clouds had settled in over the hills, and there was a dampness in the air—classic Pacific Northwest weather. There was something comforting in its familiar cool closeness.

"There's one other thing," he said.

"No problem," Lisa said. "What is it?"

"I need to know if he's with a woman called Cathleen Robinson. Cathleen with a C. She's from Austen too."

"Got it."

She didn't ask for any more details, knowing that he would only tell her as much as he needed or wanted to. They'd come to understand each other well over the years.

"Thanks," he said. "I'll check in tomorrow, but you know how to reach me if anything comes up."

"I do." There was a pause, then she added, "I'm glad you're having a break. In all the years I've been working for you, I've never known you to have a holiday."

"There was that time in Switzerland," he pointed out.

"That was a trading and investment conference, and you only had an extra day because your flight was delayed. Doesn't count."

He laughed. "Lurking around in my hometown doesn't count either."

"Well," she said, "I can't remember there ever being a Monday morning when you weren't in the office before me. There's obviously something keeping you there, so maybe you should *make* it count."

"I'll be back soon," he said, even though he'd told Barbara that morning that he'd be staying on for several more days. There was no one else booked to stay at the rental, so she'd been only too happy to extend his time.

"Okay," Lisa said, leaving well enough alone. "Talk to you tomorrow."

As they ended the call, he shook his head. Maybe his assistant understood him even better than he'd thought.

A new week, and it was time to take some kind of action.

Even though she didn't really want to. In the backyard, Avery stood aside for the real estate agent to take a photo of the house from a slightly different angle. After an overcast morning, the afternoon sun had started to break through the clouds.

"And that gate opens to the river?"

"Yes, but there's a childproof latch on it, for safety. And for dog-proofing."

She'd never forget the day Ace had figured out how to open the regular latch, and escaped to the river. She and her dad had spent ages trying to coax him out of the cold water, while he swam round and round, happy as a clam. He'd always been a water baby. He was in his favorite spot on the back porch now, looking out over the yard and the view, master of all he surveyed.

"Very good." The agent nodded and jotted something on her form. "A great selling point."

With every new note the agent made, Avery felt sicker about the whole thing. "I haven't decided whether to sell or not," she reminded the woman. "I'd like a rental appraisal first." Selling would mean cutting ties she wasn't ready to let go of. But if she was going to find another job in Portland—or elsewhere—she didn't want to leave the house sitting empty.

"Of course," the agent replied. "But you know this house would be snapped up, right? With the limited number of waterfront properties in town, this would go for a very good price."

"I'm not worried about the money," Avery said. "That's literally the last thing I care about right now."

The settlement from KXIP wasn't huge, but it would be enough to pay off her credit card and see her through a few months of rent on her Portland apartment if necessary. By then she would have found another job...she hoped.

The agent shrugged. "Okay. But knowledge is power. I'm just letting you know."

"I appreciate that."

After one last photo of the river view, the agent put her phone and the paperwork back in her bag. "Alright, I'm done. I'll be in touch in the next couple of days. Call me if you have any questions."

They shook hands and Avery saw her back to the front door. Then she and Ace went upstairs to her dad's bedroom, where Cece and Birdie were going through his things. At least she'd thought they were. When she went in, her dad's closet was open, and some of his clothes were draped on the chair in the corner, but her aunts were both sitting on his bed, propped up with pillows. They were reading what looked like old books.

When they noticed her in the doorway, Birdie lowered her book. "Oh, Avery," she said. "Are you finished with the agent?"

"Yes. She's going to get back to me soon." She came in and perched on the edge of the bed. "What are you two doing?"

Cece held up her book. "We found your dad's notebooks from when he was a kid. He loved to write stories, and make up funny languages. Look, his artwork is wonderful too."

She passed the book to Avery, and she flicked through the pages. Seeing the evidence of her father's lively imagination, she felt a wave of loss roll through her, and tears welled up. She rested the notebook in her lap and pressed the back of her hand against her eyes.

"Oh, honey," Cece said, coming over and putting her arm around Avery's shoulders. "I know. We miss him too."

"I'm okay," Avery said, her voice cracking a little. "I'm just sad I didn't inherit his artistic talent." Safe in the cocoon of her dad's bedroom, surrounded by his things, and his sisters, she let the tears fall.

Her aunts laughed. "Oh, you lovely girl," Birdie said. "You've been so strong. We don't know how you've done it, with everything coming at you at once. Carter, and your job…" She shook her head.

Avery took the tissue Cece handed her. "There has been a lot." She blew her nose. "And I thought…I thought Mom might have come back for the funeral."

Birdie and Cece looked at each other.

"I know you don't like to mention her in front of me," Avery said.

Birdie put the notebook she'd been reading on the nightstand, and swung her legs off the bed. "We thought she might come too. So we tried to get in touch with her, to let her know Owen had passed."

"You did?"

Birdie nodded. "But we couldn't find her."

"She would have been here, if she'd known. Don't you think?"

Cece's arm tightened around Avery's shoulders. "I'm sure she would have."

But Avery caught the look that passed between her aunts. It clearly showed that they weren't sure at all.

"Well, I'm grateful that *you're* both here," she said with a lightness she didn't feel. She didn't want to make them feel any worse than they already did. "Let's get to work."

A couple of hours later, her dad's clothes were neatly bagged, ready to be donated to charity, and his personal items were boxed up or discarded. The linen was stripped from his bed, ready to be laundered. Avery had decided to keep his robe. It was a comforting reminder of him, for both her and Ace.

Now she looked around the room. "We did well."

"We did," Birdie agreed.

They had each had wobbly moments, when emotion crept up on them, but having two others there to empathize and offer hugs had eased them through the lowest points. It had felt like a rite of passage, in a way, and Avery was glad to have shared it with her aunts.

Cece handed her the notebooks. "You'll want these."

"Definitely. I'll put them on the bookcase in the living room." She followed Cece and Birdie out and started to shut the door, but stopped. It didn't feel right to close the door on him. As the aunts went downstairs, giving her a moment alone, she lingered in the doorway. Evening was drawing in, and a pale light was coming through the windows that looked out on the river and the hills. Ace nudged her with his wet nose, and she laid her hand on his side.

"I can't sell this house," she whispered to him, and to herself. "This is our place. All our history is here, good and bad. And maybe we'll make more history here. I think Dad would like that, don't you?"

At that moment there was a knock on the door, and Ace turned and hurtled downstairs. "How do you do that so fast, at your age?" she said to his retreating form. Then her stomach turned over as something occurred to her—it might be Carter back again.

"I'll get it!" she yelled to her aunts, and followed in Ace's footsteps down the stairs, equally fast. She wasn't thrilled at the thought of dealing with Carter again, but Birdie and Cece didn't need to be faced with that either. She'd just have to get rid of him.

Joining Ace at the front door, she jerked it open, ready for battle.

"Hi," Logan said.

"Oh!" she said, her fight replaced with caution. "What are you doing here?"

She couldn't stop her gaze from sweeping the length of him. He was wearing jeans, a blue linen shirt, and a dark jacket, and an expression of confidence edged with uncertainty that did something weird to her heart.

Despite her less-than-enthusiastic welcome, he smiled. "Someone mentioned that you don't like cooking, so I'm here to take you to dinner."

Chapter 18

B efore Avery had a chance to reply, she heard footsteps in the hallway. She turned to see her aunts flanking her, both wearing positively shark-like smiles as they took in the man on the doorstep.

"Hello, Logan," Cece said from behind her.

"Hi, Cece," he said. "Hello, Birdie."

They both brushed past her and received kisses on their cheeks, then hovered around, obviously waiting to see what would unfold. Avery sighed. She could stick a heart-eyes emoji on each of their faces and there'd be no discernable difference. She looked at Ace, whose expression was the doggy equivalent. Seriously, it was Logan, not Prince Charming, or Prince Harry, or whichever prince was the flavor of the month.

He turned his attention to her. "So, what do you say?"

"I can't go out, sorry." She feigned regret. "There's too much to do here before I go back to Portland."

Birdie shook her head. "We just finished for the day. We're going to meet with Freya and the book club to do more planning for the Austen festival. You can go out and enjoy yourself for a while too."

"But tonight I was going to start clearing out the—"

"Avery!" Cece admonished her. "Of course you must

go. Look at him. You can't let that go to waste."

Logan laughed, and Avery wished she could bundle her aunts back inside. She was specifically trying to *not* look at him, because her eyes were threatening to wander and give her away.

"Just dinner at the Clover," he said. "No big deal."

She frowned. "It's not a date."

"Of course not," he said. "It's Monday. No one ever goes on a date on a Monday."

"That's not the reason I—"

"Good," he said. "Then I'll wait while you get ready."

"Perfect!" Cece trilled in a voice Avery didn't even recognize. "She'll be with you shortly."

She steered Avery inside and up the stairs, while Birdie and Ace accompanied Logan into the living room.

"What are you *doing*?" Avery hissed to Cece as they went into her room. "I don't want to go out with him."

"Well, we all have to do things we don't want to on occasion," Cece replied merrily. She directed Avery to the closet. "Choose something nice to wear and put some mascara on."

"Why are you—"

But she was speaking to her bedroom door, as it closed behind her aunt.

She stood in front of the closet, not quite sure what had just happened. Actually, she knew what had happened—her aunts had taken over her life. They seemed to be as enamored of Logan as Ace was. Honestly, a little tall, dark, and handsome and they lost all perspective. They'd clearly been reading too much Jane Austen.

The Clover was surprisingly busy for a Monday night. Logan was glad he'd called ahead and asked Patrick to reserve them a table in a quiet corner.

"You can't go wrong with a pub dinner," he said as Patrick showed them to their seats underneath an old-timey wagon wheel. "Although it's no spaghetti and cheese," he added under his breath to Avery.

This time, she didn't laugh at his feeble humor. They sat down, and she picked up a menu from the table and considered it.

"No, no," Patrick told her. "I have something special for you tonight, an excellent Dublin coddle. It's such a classic, I make it often, but I think I've outdone myself this time. You have to try it."

Avery's brow furrowed, but then she shrugged. "I have no idea what Dublin coddle is, but I'll give it a try."

Patrick took the menu from her, smiling. "Excellent." He turned to Logan. "You'll have the same."

"Uh, okay," he said as Patrick whisked his menu off the table.

They placed drink orders, then Patrick bustled away. Avery's eyes wandered around the pub, and Logan scratched around for something to say to warm things up.

"So...how's everything going? Are you getting organized at the house?"

"I guess," she replied. "The amount of work kind of depends on whether I rent the house or sell it."

Her words sent a jolt through him. "You're thinking about selling?"

"I was. I had a real estate agent come and look around today." The server arrived with their drinks, and she took her glass of wine. "Thank you." She looked back to Logan. "I'll have to go wherever I can find work, so I could end up on the other side of the country."

Logan accepted his beer with a distracted nod and waited while the server lit the candle on their table. "You'd leave Austen for good?"

She laughed. "Don't sound so shocked. You did."

She had a point. But all the time he'd been away, there had been a thread connecting him back: the Robinsons, in their house on the river. Even if Avery wasn't speaking to him, or was away pursuing her career, he knew Austen would always be her place—their place. But now Owen was gone. And if Avery sold up, that would feel like the end of something...the end of what they'd had.

"What about Ace?" he asked.

"Ace would have to come with me. I was going to try to rehome him, but I just can't do it. He's family."

"I get that." Logan nodded. "He's such a great guy."

A smile crept onto her face, and she shook her head in amusement. "He's so into you."

"I'll take that as a compliment."

"You should. Dog approval is like dog years—it counts for way more than the equivalent human measure."

He laughed. "Well then, I'm honored."

"I guess it's not so bad that you're around. He needs a man in his life."

"Not so bad, huh? I'll take that as a compliment too."

She played with her wine glass, her hair falling across her face. "If you like."

He was way out of practice with dating, but he didn't miss the uptick in tension between them. Good tension, not the confrontational kind that had rumbled between them up till now. As he watched her finger run up and down the stem of her glass, the heat of possibility sparked up inside him.

She tucked her hair behind her ear, and he fought the urge to reach out and put his hand on the smooth skin of her cheek, brush his thumb gently across her lips. He knew that after what their parents had done, getting involved with him again would be against her better instincts. And now she'd had three strikes of bad luck in a row, but she was still standing, beautiful and resilient. He couldn't mess with her. If he was going to convince her to try again, he had to be sure. He had to make it count.

Chapter 19

S tanding in front of the ladies' room mirror, Avery ran her hands through her hair and put on more lip gloss. Then she dropped her hands by her side and flung her head back in despair. "What am I *doing*?"

Claudia leaned against the wall by the hand dryer, a knowing smile on her face. Gramma's birthday dinner had happened to be at the Clover, and apparently Claudia couldn't resist the chance to follow Avery into the bathroom and find out what was going on. "Well, my friend, I think you're on a date."

"It's not a date," Avery said, shoving the lip gloss back in her purse. "It's dinner on a Monday."

Claudia pushed off the wall and came over to the mirror. She leaned in and considered her reflection, then smoothed one of her eyebrows. "It's dinner on a Monday with a stinkin' hot guy, you mean."

Heat rushed to Avery's cheeks. In their cozy corner of the pub, in the flicker of candlelight, she had found herself starting to succumb to his undeniable charms. But it was probably just the memories. She'd been under a lot of stress lately—it was only natural that her mind should want to latch onto something from a sweeter time. And their teenage connection had been sweet, infused with a growing, trusting passion. He had never pushed her to go further than she wanted, but there had been times when she was on a knife edge of desire, so close to throwing caution to the wind. She wouldn't admit it to Claudia, but seeing him now, she almost regretted that he hadn't been the one to show her where love could lead. Almost.

"You can't deny he's stinkin' hot," Claudia persisted. "Purely from an objective viewpoint."

"Fine. He's stinkin' hot."

"Ha!" Claudia poked a finger at her. "I knew you thought so. He was always cute, but now...wow."

Avery rolled her eyes. "Listen, just because he looks so good doesn't mean I have to go there. I only just broke up with my fiancé, remember? Anyway, it's not like he's pursuing anything."

Claudia gave her a "duh" look. "Shall we recap? He practically broke his neck on that bichon frise trying to cut the feed during your radio show. Then he came to the beach cleanup and rescued you from a crazed elephant seal, and carried your hefty dog all the way back down the beach."

"It wasn't crazed, it was just defending itself."

"Shhh! I'm not finished. Radio show, elephant seal, hefty dog." She ticked them off on her fingers. "Then he went to dinner at your house and saved you from your rampaging ex."

Why had she told Claudia about that? "I didn't need saving."

Claudia ignored her. "And now he's asked you to dinner. Radio show, elephant seal, hefty dog, rampaging ex, Monday night dinner." She held all five fingers up in the air. "Oh, and he came to your dad's funeral." Up went the pointer finger of her other hand. "And he's *still* here," she added triumphantly. "Why do you think that is?"

Avery shrugged, doing her best to seem disinterested. "I have no idea."

"Well, you can go back out there and ask him now." Claudia took hold of her and turned her toward the door, but Avery spun out of her grip.

"It's not a good idea." There was desperation in her tone, and she wished Claudia would back her up, tell her that too much water had gone under the bridge, that her dad would never approve, that there was no going back.

But Claudia put her hands on her hips. "Because of his dad and your mom? Well, guess what, anyone in this pub can tell that you two still have a connection. You can throw that away, or you can take a second chance at happiness. Which is it going to be?"

The minutes ticked by, and after a while Logan pulled out his phone to check his email. He winced when he saw how many there were—he'd never let things slide to this extent before. Then he looked up to see Ellen the piano teacher approaching, her lips pursed and her shirt buttoned up tight under her neck. He put his phone back in his pocket and braced himself.

She stopped by the table. "Are you *still* here?"

He held his hands out to the side. "Yes, as you can see, I am."

"May I ask why?"

"You may ask, but that doesn't mean I'm going to tell you." His tone was mannerly, his smile cordial, but he knew full well she wouldn't buy it.

She looked at Avery's half-empty wine glass and crinkled her nose, making her rimless glasses rise and fall. "Up to no good, I'm sure. Just like your father."

His faux smile faded. "I'm not like him."

She laughed, but the bitterness in it set his teeth on edge. "Are you sure? Too clever to ever be satisfied. Too handsome for his own good." She leaned toward him. "Just because you *can* do something, doesn't mean you *should*. Remember that, Logan Wagner."

She turned and walked away, somehow leaving him both riled up and deflated at the same time. He was nothing like his father. He hadn't even seen him since he was eighteen. They might look alike, but that was only surface stuff. He took a mouthful of beer, then automatically stood up when he saw Avery coming back to the table.

"Sorry I took so long," she said as she took her seat. Her cheeks were a charming shade of pink, and she didn't meet his eye.

"That's okay. But I'm glad you're back." He sat back down too. "I've been at the mercy of Austen's most frightening music teacher."

Avery looked in the direction he pointed, to where Ellen was now sitting with another older woman. "You mean Ellen? I think she's even scarier now than when she was teaching me to play."

"I never knew you played piano," he said.

"That's because I don't." She laughed. "I only lasted about three lessons."

"I'm not surprised."

"She's not all bad though. She loved my dad—not in *that* way, but he helped her a lot with her house, and in return she always looked out for him. I think they got pretty close over the years."

"That might explain why she's been so tough on me."

"Probably." She looked harder at him. "You do look kind of chastened. What did she say?"

"Ah, nothing really."

With perfect timing, Patrick arrived to take their empty plates, creating a diversion.

"How were your meals?" he asked with a broad smile, clearly ready to accept compliments.

Logan obliged. "Excellent, thank you."

Patrick looked to Avery, and she nodded. "Really great, thanks."

"Of course they were," Patrick said heartily. "Nothing but the best for Austen's favorite reunited couple."

Avery looked startled, and Logan wished they could go back to talking about Ellen after all. "Patrick, it's not—"

But Patrick was on a roll. "And dessert is on the house!" he proclaimed, sounding extra Irish all of a sudden. "Just stay right there, and someone will bring it to you. With my compliments." He half-bowed toward Avery, as though addressing an aristocrat. "It's grand to have you both back."

"Uh...thank you," she said.

He nodded and strode away toward the kitchen, leaving an awkward silence in his wake.

"Sorry about that," Logan said. "I never said anything to give him the impression that we're...you know."

"That's okay," Avery said quickly, waving his words away. "This town is just starving for gossip, as usual."

Half of him was grateful for her easy dismissal. The other half wished there was truth in Patrick's assumption.

Maybe there would be yet.

Chapter 20

A fter dinner they had a token argument outside the Clover, where Avery insisted that she could walk home alone, and Logan insisted on walking with her. Given that he had to go in her direction anyway, to the vacation rental farther along the river, the disagreement didn't last long.

"I didn't even know where you were staying," she said. "I hear that house is super luxurious."

"Yeah, it's nice," he said noncommittally.

She'd never been in there, but talk around town was that the house was spectacular inside, with every possible convenience and then some.

"Pretty fancy for a hometown boy," she joked, but he just shrugged, which piqued her interest even more. Daniel had said that Logan was doing very well in business. Construction must be treating him well if he was staying in such deluxe accommodation. The thought of the Logan she knew working in that industry made sense to her— something honest, practical, and yet creative, every completed building project proof of your hard work. She liked that.

Leaving the main street, they walked through the residential part of town, the darkness broken by the occasional streetlight or passing car. Being a Monday, the familiar streets were quiet, and she could hear their footsteps on the sidewalk. With their difference in height, they fell in and out of sync as they walked.

Logan checked his watch, and she peered over to the light on his wrist. "That looks space-age."

He pulled the sleeve of his jacket down over it. "It just has a few extras."

"Oh, is it like a smartwatch? What does it do?"

"Well, it tells the time," he teased her. "But it has Bluetooth and GPS...a fitness tracker with an ECG monitor..."

She laughed. "You're kidding."

"No."

It was too dark to tell for sure, but she could swear he was blushing. She regarded him for a moment. "You're a geek."

He took it in good humor, as she'd intended. "Apparently."

"So...how's your heart rate?"

He gestured to himself. "I'm still going."

"Good enough." She pressed a hand to her stomach. "I'm surprised I am. That dessert almost finished me off."

"You were a champ," he said.

After the substantial Dublin coddle, Patrick had brought out a decadent sticky toffee pudding accompanied with ice cream. It was absolutely delicious, and completely over the top.

"I think that was more food than I've ever eaten on a Monday, but I didn't want to let Patrick down. It was amazing though."

They came to a house with a white picket fence, and she let her fingers trail along the pickets, bumping over them like on a railway track. She'd done the same as a kid walking to elementary school, and the action transported her back in time.

Logan also seemed to be reflecting on something as he walked alongside her. Then he said, "I'm sorry about that misunderstanding with Patrick."

"Oh. That's okay." After Claudia's comment that everyone in the pub could see their connection, Patrick's enthusiasm hadn't come as a complete surprise. But it was still embarrassing. Better to stay casual about the whole thing. "At least now I know what a Dublin coddle is—just a fancy name for a sausage stew with potatoes on top." She laughed. "But the name almost sounds like something sexy you might do with an Irishman."

Logan thought for a moment. "Or something violent, like a Glasgow kiss is a headbutt."

"I can't imagine Patrick dispensing headbutts in the Clover," she said, laughing. "Or anywhere else for that matter."

"Yeah, he's always been a nice guy."

They came to her house and Logan walked her up the steps to the front door. She dug in her purse for her keys. "Ace will be glad to see you," she said.

He nodded. "My biggest fan."

"Alright, don't let that head get too big," she told him. But she was smiling too.

She unlocked the door and pushed it open, and Ace bounded out, almost overshooting and ending up down the steps. They both laughed as he corrected course and leaped around them. Avery settled him down, then hesitated in the doorway as Logan stood under the porch light. The moment of truth at the end of the night. She made a snap decision.

"Would...would you like to come in for coffee?"

He raised an eyebrow. "You have room for coffee?"

She laughed. "Actually, I don't really—"

"Forget I asked," he said hurriedly. "I'd like to come in."

She gave him a direct look. "You know coffee isn't code for anything, right?"

"Of course. But you're not having coffee anyway, so we're safe either way." Her puzzlement must have shown on her face, because he grinned. "Some more of your company will be stimulating enough."

"That's enough talking around in dubious circles," she

told him sternly, going inside. He laughed as he followed her in. She dropped her purse and keys on the hall table and they went through to the kitchen.

They sat opposite each other at the big table and Ace flopped down underneath it, between their feet. It was quiet in the house. Logan smiled at her, and she tried not to think about all the long-ago times she'd seen that smile—very often, right before he kissed her.

"Maybe I'll just…" She got up and switched on the radio, then sat back down. A country song came on, something about lost love and second chances. They sat in silence as the song filled the room, an aching retelling of a melancholy tale. She itched to switch it off again, but that would be worse. The last thing she wanted was for Logan to think she was imagining the two of them in the lyrics.

She jumped to her feet again. "You know, I think I will have coffee after all."

"Good idea," Logan said, and she thought she detected relief in his tone.

As she made coffee the song ended, and she breathed a little easier even though she was hyperaware of him behind her watching her work. As quickly as she could, she finished up and brought two full cups over, along with milk and sugar.

Sitting down, she passed him a cup. Eager to avoid any more awkward silence, she jumped right in with the question she—and Claudia—had been wondering about.

"So, I thought you would have gone back to work by now. Why are you still in town?"

He reached out and took a spoonful of sugar, let it trickle into his coffee, and stirred vigorously, avoiding her eye. She waited, watching as the spoon created a miniature whirlpool in the hot liquid. Then he cleared his throat.

"I, uh…it just feels like time to revisit things," he said, still focusing on the coffee maelstrom he was creating. "You know."

"Oh, right," she said. "I know."

But she didn't know. And in the gap between her simple question and his vague answer, a notion had crept into her mind.

She thought back to Claudia's words. *Anyone in this pub can tell that you two still have a connection.* Was he staying on to revisit *her?* Surely not. Or maybe. But probably not. He'd been so eager to apologize for Patrick's comments tonight—twice over. She looked at him again. He finished stirring and tapped the spoon extra carefully on the side of the cup. The need to know what he'd meant drove another question from her lips.

"What kind of things did you want to revisit?"

Finally, he looked up. "The past."

"Oh." Clearly she'd have to be more specific, but she could hardly come right out and ask if he meant her. Or could she?

At that moment Ace sprang up under the table, standing on one of her feet. She jerked her leg upward to extract her foot and cracked her knee on the underside of the table. With a loud dragging noise on the floor, she pushed her chair back and rubbed the knee. "Ace! What are you doing?"

But he was already by the door, looking hopefully back over his shoulder at them.

"Looks like he wants out," Logan said. "Are you okay?"

"I'm fine." She stood up, stretching out her leg then putting her foot tentatively on the floor. "No thanks to *you*," she told Ace, but he just smiled and waited. She went and opened the door, and he trotted out.

"He seems happy to have you here," Logan commented as she sat down again.

She nodded. "He is. Hopefully he'll be okay with me wherever we end up. I haven't started looking for a new job yet."

He frowned. "Are you okay for money? Because if you're not…"

"I'm fine," she said quickly. "I have a settlement from the station. Not a lot, but enough to give me breathing space." And there were any number of people she'd ask for help before Logan Wagner. She blew on her coffee and took a sip.

"Okay," he said. "We covered that last night, anyway. You don't need my help with anything."

"It's nothing personal," she said, even though they both knew it was totally personal. "I can take care of myself, financially and in every other way."

"Of course you can," he said. "I can see that." He smiled, and she could see that it was genuine. "But even if you don't want my help right now, the offer stands."

"Well...thanks."

A volley of barks came from the yard, and they both stood up. "What now?" Avery said as they headed for the door. Going outside, they could see Ace in the corner of the yard, barking at something. A sudden thought struck her. "Oh, no. Not the cat again."

"Rescue time?" Logan asked, and she nodded.

They ran down the stairs to where Ace was on high alert. He turned when he heard them coming, and a tabby blur streaked along and then over the fence as the cat took its chance to escape while he was distracted. He came over, looking monumentally pleased with himself, as though cat harassment was the most noble occupation imaginable.

Avery stood and looked at him, shaking her head. "What am I going to do with you?"

Logan ducked down and ruffled the fur on Ace's chest. "It's a guy thing, right? Gotta prove you're still the man."

"Really?" She had to laugh. "Well, good luck to you both."

Logan rolled his eyes at Ace. "Girls. They don't get it."

She let out a *pfft*. "Boys. Always trying to prove something."

Logan stood upright again, and looked at her. The clouds had cleared enough for the moonlight to wash over them, and she could see him clearly. His dark hair, the firm angle of his jaw, his tempting mouth. A nervous laugh escaped her, and he smiled. She didn't want him to know what she was thinking, and yet she did.

He took a step closer, and butterflies tumbled in her

stomach. "Did I prove anything to you yet?" he said.

She held her ground. "Like what?"

"That I care about this town, and the people in it." He reached for her hand and slipped his fingers through hers. "One person in particular."

Her heart was pounding. This was how it had been all those years ago—the sweetness, the moonlight, Logan with his smile and his gentle touch—but now they were all grown up. Now she knew what a man and a woman could do together. She knew where this could lead. And she knew why they shouldn't go there.

She swallowed. "Why should I care if you care? You'll be gone soon, and so will I. The past will be the past again."

"Will it though, now that we've seen each other again?" His voice was low, wondering. "Since I came back, I've realized that a part of me never really left."

Her hand was warm in his, and she didn't want to let go. "Which part?"

"The part that belongs to you."

At that, her heart jumped in her chest. He leaned toward her, and as his lips met hers all she could do was close her eyes and let it happen. Despite every good reason not to kiss him, there wasn't an ounce of resistance in her body. And surrender was so, so sweet. Maybe one part of him belonged to her, but every part of her belonged to him in that moment. The touch of his mouth sparked memories of summer nights and beach bonfires and whispers in the back row of the movies. Stolen moments by their favorite tree along the river path, or behind the gazebo in the park. He slid his hand into the hair at the nape of her neck and stepped nearer, and she melted toward him.

As their bodies finally touched, Ace let out an emphatic series of barks right beside them, voicing his protest. Avery jumped, and they pulled apart. She pressed her fingers to her lips. Ace was right—they shouldn't be doing that.

But she looked at Logan, tall and steady and sure, and somehow she couldn't regret anything.

Ace stood next to her, pressing against her leg, eyeing Logan warily. "Maybe he's not your biggest fan *just* yet," she said.

"Yet?" He tipped his head, a teasing grin on his face. "Does that mean there'll be more chances?"

"Don't get ahead of yourself," she said, but she couldn't stop the answering smile that crept onto her face. She bent down and gave Ace a quick squeeze. "Okay, you made your point. Everything's fine."

"I agree," Logan said, watching her. "Everything is extremely fine."

As they stood in her backyard in the same small town, under the same wide sky, Avery knew that he had proved something. He'd proved that she still wanted him the same way. But there was one thing she'd learned in the years between the past and now—wanting something didn't mean that it was good for you.

Chapter 21

L ogan looked out the plane window at the hills of San
Francisco spread below. He never tired of this view, or
of knowing that the city was his to conquer if he worked
hard enough. And he'd done pretty well so far, leaving his
mark not just here but with projects in numerous cities
across the country. Even now, it still gave him satisfaction
to be the small-town guy who'd come from nowhere to
match—and better—the city players at their own game.

When the jet touched down, he thanked the crew and
then disembarked, walking across the tarmac with his bag
to a waiting car. Lisa had suggested buying his own plane,
but despite the increasing amount of travel he was doing, it
felt like something that would weigh him down. And he
didn't need an accumulation of executive toys to signal his
success. The pleasure was in the chase—finding and
succeeding at new challenges and opportunities.

All the same, he wouldn't deny himself a few
rewards—including his full-floor apartment on the top story
of a historic San Francisco building. It was too big for just
one person, but he'd acquired it at an excellent price as part
of a larger property deal. And if he ever wanted to sell it,
he'd clear a few million on the way through.

Now he reached the car, and the driver hurried round

to open the door.

"Thank you," Logan said, and the driver nodded.

"Pacific Heights today, sir?"

"That's right. You have the address?"

"I do. Please make yourself comfortable. The traffic isn't bad today, so it should be a quick trip."

"Excellent, thank you." The driver shut the door, and Logan pulled out his phone and called Lisa.

She answered after one ring. "You're here."

"I am," he said as the car pulled away. "Thanks for organizing my ride."

"No problem. Will you be in the office today?"

He hesitated. "I think I'll stay home after I drop off my things. Then I'll go directly to meet the private investigator later this afternoon."

"Sounds good," she said. "Let me know if you need anything."

"Thanks, I will."

They ended the call, and he sat back in the deep leather seat and watched the city go by. After his time in Austen, walking everywhere, it felt strange being in big-city traffic again, passing through built-up streets lined with busy sidewalks. He had several days of catching up ahead of him, including a number of appointments, but he could get some work done in his apartment, with the sweeping city view for company. And later he'd find out what, if anything, the private investigator had discovered about his dad, and Avery's mom.

Yet again, his mind went back to the night before, to the moment in Avery's backyard. *Why should I care if you care?* she'd said, and he'd wanted so badly to show her why. He'd said more than he'd even articulated to himself until the words left his lips. He remembered her expression of surprise in the moonlight, the way she softened into his kiss. The car stopped at an intersection, and he watched crowds of people crossing in all directions. Was it any wonder he'd failed at his relationships, if the deepest part of him was still in Avery's keeping? He'd thought it was dedication to business that had maintained a wall between him and the women he'd dated. Maybe he'd been fooling himself…and them. He shifted uncomfortably in his seat at the thought.

Then he retrieved his phone from his pocket and started typing.

Thanks again for last night. Best Monday night dinner I ever had.

He hesitated then added an *x* before hitting send, glad he'd managed to get her number before he left last night. He suspected the night had been a surprise to her. In truth, it had been to him too. He'd come back to Austen knowing he would see her, but not expecting anything—just the funeral, then a quick look at the riverside land to get a feel for its potential, and out again. But he'd been fooling himself again. Because from the moment he saw her at the funeral, sweet and stoic, his plan had been going steadily off course.

He kept the phone in his hand as the car turned onto his street. There was no answering ding of a message notification. Maybe she hadn't seen the text yet. Or maybe she had no intention of replying.

Avery pulled into the parking lot underneath her building in Portland and breathed out. It had felt like a long drive, her mind turning over the events of last night again and again. Logan standing on her doorstep. At the Clover. Walking home. And finally, in the backyard. Carefully, assuredly bringing her closer and kissing her so perfectly that she went to putty right there on the grass.

It was kind of annoying, actually. Turning up out of the blue and turning her head when she least expected it. Or wanted it.

She got out of the car and retrieved her bag from the back seat, then headed up to her apartment. It felt weird opening the door and going in, like returning to a life that she no longer had. Last time she'd been here, she still had a job and a fiancé…and then she'd gotten the phone call about her dad. She threw her things on the sofa in the living room and opened the windows to let in some fresh air. The ghost of that phone call still lingered in the room. She sighed and went to make coffee.

Armed with a good strong brew, she sat on the sofa with her laptop and checked her emails. Among the million and one messages about the situation with Carter and Karen, there was a message from her landlord. The rent was going up. She stared at the words on the screen for a while, thinking. With a rent hike and no job, should she even stay? There was no guarantee she'd get another job in Portland, especially after the on-air "love triangle wrangle," as the tabloids had called it. Valerie was right that everything would blow over eventually, but if Carter did end up on TV with Karen, that would drag it all out.

And did the developments with Logan complicate things, or not? He'd said a part of him belonged to her, but she didn't know what that meant in the cold light of day. He'd been gone for ten years—you don't just walk back in and pick up where you left off, as though nothing had changed. Especially when *everything* had changed. Back then, deep in her dreamy teenage love affair, she couldn't think of a single reason why she and Logan couldn't be together forever. Not anymore.

When he left last night—escorted out by a watchful Ace—he'd seemed eager to keep in touch. He'd taken her phone number, saying he had to get back to work but he'd see her soon. He hadn't said when or where though, and for all she knew, she might not see him for another ten years. Even if a little part of her was tempted, she couldn't start making decisions with him in mind.

Now, sitting in her small, dogless apartment, her only view the building across the street, she closed her eyes and leaned her head back against the sofa. In her mind's eye she was back home by the river, breathing the fresh, soft air and watching tiny hummingbirds flit in the backyard while Ace snuffled around the fence in search of eau de cat. It was a scene so familiar, and yet so rare in her life these days.

She opened her eyes and sat up. She should check on Ace. Claudia had taken him for a few days so that she could come back and deal with things here—including signing the settlement agreement with the KXIP lawyers. She was sure Ace would be okay, but with everything that had happened, she wanted to make sure.

She put her laptop aside and reached for her purse. When she pulled out her phone, there were several new messages. Claudia had already texted to say that Ace was fine, hanging out with her at the store and being petted by all the customers. Avery smiled imagining it, and texted back her thanks. She hadn't mentioned anything about the kiss to Claudia when she dropped Ace off—she'd still been processing it herself. The aunts had been at Persuasions, so she hadn't had to give them a report on the Monday night dinner either, but she knew that time of reckoning would come eventually. She laughed to herself remembering their breathless enthusiasm for the man who'd turned up at the door.

Then she scrolled down and found a text from the man himself, sent a couple of hours before.

Thanks again for last night. Best Monday night dinner I ever had. x

He must have sent it from San Francisco. She sat on the edge of the sofa and read it again, soaking up his words. And that x. One little x. She tapped her thumb against her finger, thinking about what to reply.

Thanks, she started. No, he'd already thanked her. She deleted it. Tension built in her chest as she considered and discarded various options. Then she shook her head and stood up. What was she, fourteen? All she had to do was send a polite reply and be done with it.

It was lovely, thanks. Have a great week.

Her thumb hovered over the x key. Should she reciprocate? Maybe a smiley face would do. On the other hand, the lack of an x might seem very pointed. Finally she took the plunge, added an *x*, and sent the message.

What the heck, right? She was pretty sure that now he was back in San Francisco he'd get immersed in his real life again, and their backyard kiss would be nothing but a memory to add to those from years before. And she would move on to something else herself, somewhere or other. And that would be for the best.

The past would be the past again, just as it ought to be.

Chapter 22

One of the advantages of running your own business was the ability to work from anywhere, and Logan liked to make the most of it. Now he waited for the private investigator at a booth in his favorite coffee shop, just around the corner from his apartment. With his laptop open in front of him and an espresso at hand as he worked, he kept one eye out for the private investigator, Rick Miller.

A couple of minutes before their appointment time, the man walked in. He quickly spotted Logan and came over.

Logan stood up and held out his hand. "Logan Wagner. Thanks for coming."

Rick gave him a short nod and a firm handshake. "No problem."

"Coffee?" Logan asked as they sat opposite each other in the booth.

He shook his head and set a folder on the table. "No thanks."

Logan recognized the gruff, no-nonsense demeanor of a man who'd seen plenty, and said little. "Let's get to it then."

Rick opened the folder. "Well, I found them both." He looked at his papers. "Jeff Wagner is in Pahrump, Nevada."

"Nevada? What's he doing there?"

"Best I can tell, he's managing one of the smaller local casinos. He lives in an apartment out back."

He turned the papers from the top of the folder around and pushed them over to Logan. There was a candid snapshot of his father standing by a slot machine, a little older but otherwise unchanged. He looked well enough. It was a strange feeling to see him after so long. Logan had wondered if he might be emotional at this moment, but instead he felt numb.

"So he's in Nevada. What about Cathleen—is she with him?"

"I had to look a little harder to find her. She's on the housekeeping staff of one of the cruise lines that runs down the coast from LA to Cabo. Looks like she shares accommodation with some of the other staff when they're on shore."

That was unexpected. "Do you know if they're still in contact? Still a couple?"

"Doesn't seem that way. Wagner moved to Pahrump three years ago. Before that he was in Boise, and before that, Seattle. He was involved with a woman in Seattle, but he seems to be single now. Cathleen's been employed by the cruise line for nine years."

Logan nodded, but his head was spinning. Nine years. That meant they'd stayed together for a year at most after leaving Austen. That huge betrayal, so much pain and heartache, for one measly year. Somehow it was way worse than if he'd discovered they were still living happily ever after in their new lives. Presumably the woman in Seattle had been the end of things.

He sat in silence for a while, rereading the information in Rick's documentation while the man waited. Then he looked up. "There's something else."

"Sure."

"Please tell Cathleen that Owen Robinson has passed. But don't say it came from me."

"Will do. I'll let you know when it's done."

"Thanks for your help with this."

Rick nodded. "Any time."

When he left, Logan stayed on in the booth, his coffee going cold beside him as he processed the details that Rick had uncovered. Now he knew where to find his father, he could approach him about the riverside land in Austen. But instead of being pleased about making progress, he felt sick thinking about how the news would affect Avery. She'd been in the dark all this time. For a moment he wondered if he should even tell her—maybe some things were better left alone. But he knew that the information would eat away at him, and not telling her would be a betrayal in itself. He slapped the folder shut. This wasn't something he should tell her over the phone, or via email. He should do it in person. He owed her that.

At that moment his phone sounded with a message notification. He picked it up and saw that it was from Avery herself.

It was lovely, thanks. Have a great week. x

That was...perfunctory. Not exactly the words of a woman who was still starry-eyed after a kiss in the moonlight. At least she'd added the *x*. Judging by this reply, it seemed likely that she wouldn't be bursting with enthusiasm about seeing him again. Probably even less so once she found out what else his dad had done.

Coming to a decision, he stood up and gathered his things. He'd let Rick contact Cathleen, get through the essential tasks and appointments for the week here in the city, and reach out to his father—although he had no idea how he'd be received. It wasn't like Jeff Wagner had made any effort to contact him over the last decade. Regardless of how that turned out, he'd go back to Austen for the weekend and talk to Avery...whether she was pleased to see him or not.

Chapter 23

The sound of rain on the window woke Avery on Saturday morning. She snuggled deeper under the bedcovers, enjoying the coziness of knowing she didn't have to get up any time soon. She was home. And not just home for the weekend—home for the foreseeable future. She'd taken the plunge and left Portland.

Ace had been ecstatic to see her when she picked him up from Claudia's house the night before, and it felt like confirmation that she'd made the right call. And Claudia's reaction when she found out had cemented it.

"You're *staying?*" she'd said, her voice rising half an octave in those two words.

Avery laughed. "For now. I had to give thirty days' notice on the apartment, so I'll lose that money, but once I made the decision I just wanted to get out of there."

"I can't believe it!" Unable to suppress her excitement, Claudia gave Avery a hug right there on the front porch, swaying her from side to side. "It'll be *so* nice having you here. Even if it's only for a while."

"Aw, thanks," Avery said, squeezing her friend right back. "I'm excited to have some hometown time."

"It's the best medicine." Claudia let her go and looked over her shoulder toward her car. "What about all your stuff though?"

"It's all in there," she said. "I'm traveling light these days."

It had taken a few days to go through her things and decide what to bring home and what to ditch or donate. Her apartment came furnished, so there was nothing big to deal with. In the end, everything fit in her car. With all her belongings on wheels, she'd hit the road back to Austen with an exhilarating sense of lightness.

"You free bird," Claudia said. "I'm actually kind of jealous."

"You have a gorgeous house though, and your own successful business. Everyone in town thinks you're amazing, with what you've achieved all on your own. Don't shake your head, it's true! You shouldn't be jealous of *me*."

"I am pretty blessed in that way, I guess," Claudia admitted. "But it would be nice to have someone to share it all with. I haven't done very well at that side of things."

Avery threw her hands up. "You and me both. But it'll happen," she said, wagging a finger at Claudia. "Just you wait and see."

"My mom is doing all the waiting for me," Claudia replied with a wry smile. "You know how traditional she is. The house and the business are great and all, but marriage and family are her real yardstick." She sighed. "The pressure's on for more grandkids, and I'm not delivering."

"She *should* be proud of you," Avery said indignantly. "Not just for what you do, or the babies you produce, but for the person you are."

"Aw. Thank you." Claudia blushed pink and reached down to stroke Ace's head. "Anyway, it's nice to have your fur baby visit. I'm happy to have him whenever I can."

Now Avery rolled over to see Ace asleep on the bed next to her, and smiled. That was obviously going to be a thing. After some hesitation last night, she'd decided to sleep in her dad's room. If she was going to stay for a while, it would be nicer to have a big bed, and she didn't think he would mind, if he knew. In fact, she suspected he'd kind of like it. And judging by the way Ace looked so comfy, this might have been their usual routine anyway. Her aunts had made the bed again, so it had been all too easy to fall in and sink into sleep, dog or no dog.

Thinking about her aunts reminded her—the Jane Austen festival was today. She sat up and looked out the window. Oh, no. Rain was not ideal, especially with long dresses and carefully arranged Regency hairdos. Hopefully they could put up some marquee tents, or maybe relocate to the community hall. If Freya was involved they'd have some fallback plan, she was sure—she seemed to be doing a great job in her new role.

Now that she was upright, Avery suddenly felt extra awake. She threw back the covers and got up, leaving Ace in his cozy spot. Job-hunting and other adult decisions lay ahead, but for now, she was giving herself a weekend to relax.

After breakfast the rain eased and then stopped, and Ace started agitating for a walk. Avery took his leash from the hook by the back door, laughing as he danced around in anticipation.

"Come on then," she said. "I could do with some fresh air too."

Just then the landline rang, giving her a start. No one called on that number anymore—even her aunts had switched to mobile—but her dad had insisted on keeping it in case of some apocalyptic digital collapse.

"Hold that thought," she told Ace, putting the leash on the kitchen table. Then she went into the hall and answered the phone. "Hello?"

"Avery?"

That voice. A sprinkle of goosebumps went up the back of her neck. "Yes."

"It's me. Mom."

She stood in silence, holding the phone against her ear. Everything she'd imagined saying to her mother over those long, silent years flew out of her head.

"Are you still there?" her mom said.

She blinked, and sat down on the three-legged stool by the hall table. "I'm here. Where are you?" What she really meant was, *Where have you been? Why did you leave us? How could you do that to us?* But suddenly she wasn't sure she wanted to know the answer to any of it.

"I'm in California. I've been trying to call this week. I heard about Owen...your dad. I'm so sorry, honey."

The endearment grated, and Avery could only manage a diffident sound in response.

"I want to come and see you," her mom said.

Oh, no. Too much, too fast. "I don't know if that's a good idea right now. Can you just...can I just let you know? Call you back sometime?"

"Oh...sure. Of course."

Avery thought she sounded disappointed, but what did she expect, calling out of the blue after all this time? She read out her phone number, and Avery wrote it on the pad by the phone. Then she put down the pen. "Okay, well...I'd better go."

"Alright. Talk soon?"

"Sure. Bye."

With the call over, she sat for a moment with her elbows on her knees, looking at the phone. Ace milled about, sensing something was up. Her weekend to relax was suddenly feeling not very relaxing at all.

Chapter 24

A ll Avery's fondest memories from her childhood and teenage years were set against the backdrop of the river or the beach. Kayaking with her dad, encased in the safety of a stiff life jacket as rain tickled her nose. Building sandcastles in the sunshine with her mom, the ocean breeze whipping her hair across her face. Sneaking over the narrow footbridge with Claudia early on a weekend morning, laughing as they answered the call of freedom. Hanging out with friends on the beach over the slow weeks of summer.

Now she found herself heading for one other special place, just off the river path along from her house—the wishing tree. It was set on a slight rise, with a view over to the hills on the other side of the river. At some point the tree must have been damaged, but it had kept growing with two trunks in a wide V. Now she stepped into the V and lay back against one trunk, just like she used to when anything was troubling her. Just like she and Logan used to when they wanted to escape from the world and be together. As Ace panted on the ground alongside, she closed her eyes, trying to banish her mom from her mind. A few lingering droplets of rain drifted onto her cheeks and eyelids, but she let them be. You didn't grow up in this part of the country without understanding the comfort of a little rain.

After a while the sun peeked through, and she felt the warmth on her face. Then she heard footsteps, and Ace leaped to his feet with an eager woof, followed by excited whining. She opened her eyes and turned to see Logan coming through the trees from the direction of the path.

She sat up. "Are you stalking me, or...?"

"No." He frowned, apparently taking her seriously. "But I was coming to see you, and I thought I'd walk this way. I heard Ace bark. Are you alright?"

She schooled her features, trying to wipe away any trace of her internal conflict about her mom, as well as the sweet, hot rush that was the memory of their kiss. "I'm fine."

"This was where you always used to come when—"

"I know, but I'm fine."

He held up a hand. "Okay, just checking." Then he eyed the other trunk. "I guess I'll just..." In one quick movement he was inside the V, leaning back opposite her, his feet on either side of hers and his hands behind his head. "This takes me back."

"Yeah, me too." Despite the effect he was having on her, something about being here with him again was taking the edge off her tension. She breathed deeply. "Everything smells so good. It always does after a rainstorm."

"There's a word for that," he said as Ace lay back down and rested his head by their feet.

"For what?"

He gestured to the scenery around them and the wild country over the river. "That special smell that only comes after it rains."

"I bet it's German," she said. "They have a word for everything, the more obscure the better. Schadenfreude and all that."

He laughed. "Actually I think it's Greek. Petrichor, it's called. Strictly speaking, I think the term only applies when it rains after a long dry period, but long dry periods aren't exactly a feature of the climate around here."

She folded her arms, considering him. "You really *are* a geek."

"Apparently," he said, echoing their conversation from the previous weekend. "But didn't you hear? Girls like geeks. It's a whole thing now."

She shrugged and reached down to pet Ace's head. "No one told me." With his strong physique, dark hair, and teasing, tempting expression, he was far from geeky. And that kiss had been ample proof that—geek or not—part of her did still like him. But she wasn't going to tell him that.

"So what's up?" he said, looking at her.

How was it that ten years had gone by, but he could still read her so well? "My mom called."

His gaze stayed level. "What did she say?"

"She wants to come and see me."

"Huh. What do *you* want?"

She passed a hand across her forehead. "I don't know. When she first left, I never wanted to see her again. Then after a while I felt like I wanted to see her—to thrash things out, you know? But then I got kind of numb. I got used to her not being in my life. And now..."

"Now?"

"I guess hearing her voice on the phone stirred everything up again."

"I get that," he said, and she was suddenly reminded that this had something to do with him too.

"I didn't even think to ask about your dad," she said.

"That doesn't matter." He waved a hand, but his expression told her that his words weren't the full story.

"It does matter though. I'm sorry." She stepped out from between his feet and gathered up Ace's leash. "Do you want to come back for coffee?"

He stood up too, mischief back on his face. "That's not code for anything, right?"

"No." She sent him a squashing look. "Not on a Monday night, not on a Saturday morning, not ever."

"Gotcha," he said, laughing. "A man can hope."

She started heading back to the path, Ace in tow. "Are you with me?" she threw over her shoulder.

"I'm with you," he said emphatically.

And in that moment, she had the feeling he really was.

All the way back to the house, Logan wrestled with the knowledge he had about Cathleen and his father breaking up so long ago. He'd come back to Austen just to talk to Avery about it, and now was the ideal moment. But if Cathleen had made contact, and wanted to see her, it seemed like she should be the one to tell Avery what had happened. Of course, that all depended on whether Avery would maintain their contact. He understood her ambivalence—he hadn't reached out to his father yet. The week had gone by, busy with work projects and meetings, and the task had remained on his to-do list. Walking along with Avery now, he realized that he'd been focusing on the business aspect of it—the land and the potential development. But once Rick handed over Jeff's contact details, it became something more personal. Suddenly he was someone's son again. Someone who'd walked away without looking back.

They came to the gate at the bottom of Avery's backyard, and he unlatched it then held it open for her and Ace to go in. They went up the slight slope of the yard and inside through the back door, and Avery hung Ace's leash on a hook.

"Coffee, then," she said.

"Looks like it," he replied in a faux-sad tone, and she rolled her eyes. But she was smiling. And that made him happy.

Just then there was a knock at the door. Avery hesitated, then said, "Could you start the coffee while I go see who that is?"

"Sure." He came over to the counter. "You don't think it's Carter, do you?" It would be just like her to try to keep the two of them apart.

But she shook her head. "I don't think so. He'll be too busy with his new TV career now to give me another thought."

He hoped that was true. Because he didn't want her ex-fiancé anywhere near her.

She went along to the front door, and he tried to listen as he started making the coffee. Instead of a man's voice, he heard a woman—two women—and he relaxed. Then there was a clattering of footsteps in the kitchen doorway, and he turned around.

"There he is!" Cece said.

"We've been looking for you," Birdie told him. "Barbara said you were back in town."

"What's going on?" he said, leaning against the counter. It was difficult to imagine what they could want him for, but with the aunts, you never knew.

"Well," Birdie said. "We have a problem with our Jane Austen festival."

Avery nodded. "Yes, the weather isn't—"

"It's not that," Cece said. "It's worse."

"Oh, no," Avery said. "What is it?"

"Our Mr. Darcy has *let us down*," she said in a doom-laden tone. "That's why we're here. We need Logan's help."

He frowned. "Who's Mr. Darcy?"

All three of them turned to him, their brows furrowed in apparent amazement.

"Please don't tell me you don't know who Mr. Darcy is," Avery said.

"Should I?" He looked between them, searching for a clue. He was obviously missing something. Maybe this Mr. Darcy was supposed to help with the setup today.

Birdie stepped in. "Mr. Darcy is the hero in Jane Austen's timeless masterpiece Pride and Prejudice. He is without doubt the most beloved hero in fiction."

"He's mesmerizing," Cece said dreamily. "And very rich."

"He's grumpy but extremely hot," Avery added helpfully.

They all had a slightly glazed look about them as they thought about this imaginary person. "So...he's a character in a book."

"No," Cece said, fixing him with a stern glare. "He's so much more than that. He is an *archetypal romantic hero*."

"Ah. Okay then." Clearly it would be safer to say nothing more about the wondrous Mr. Darcy. "And how would you like me to help, now that this fictional person has managed to let you down in some way?"

"It's not Mr. Darcy who's let us down," Birdie said. "It's Daniel."

This was getting more confusing. "Daniel Blackwood?"

"Yes," Cece said. "He was supposed to appear in period attire as Mr. Darcy tonight, but something came up at the last minute and he can't get back to town. So we need a replacement."

All at once it dawned on him. "You want me to be Mr. Darcy."

"Yes. You'll be perfect." She turned to Avery. "I think he's a much better choice than Daniel anyway, don't you? His hair is darker. More Colin Firth."

Avery nodded. "I agree."

Logan wasn't sure which fictional character Colin Firth was, or why it was an advantage to have hair like his. But he did know one thing. He wasn't dressing up in a costume and pretending to be anyone, no matter how beloved.

"No. I don't think so."

He turned back to his coffee making, hoping they'd give up. But Cece came and touched him on the arm.

"Please? We need you."

He turned back around, his resolve weakening, and looked at Avery.

"You would make a lot of women very happy," she said, a small smile playing on her lips. "Including me."

At that, he knew they'd won. But he wasn't going to go down without a little more fight. "So, just to clarify—you're saying this Darcy guy is a beloved hero."

Birdie nodded. "Absolutely."

"Mesmerizing."

"Completely," Cece said innocently.

He looked directly at Avery. "And extremely hot."

"Don't push it," she said. But he noted a satisfying

tinge of pink in her cheeks as she looked away.

"Alright, ladies," he said. "You have your new Mr. Darcy."

Chapter 25

B y the time Avery set out for the Austen festival late that afternoon, the clouds had cleared and there wasn't a whisper of wind. When she arrived, she found the riverside park transformed. Lots of people were there already, milling around chatting and laughing, and she was surprised and impressed to see how many were dressed in full period costume. There was a big screen set up right in the middle of the park, with rows of low folding chairs for the audience. Closest to the screen was a collection of oversized beanbags, which had been claimed by teenagers, two or three in each. Fairy lights were strung in the trees, ready for sundown, and a string quartet played suitably elegant music in the gazebo. Alongside, a demonstration of Regency dancing was underway. At one side of the park, there were stands with all kinds of Jane Austen books and period memorabilia, and trucks selling food and drinks.

She was glad the rain had cleared so everyone could enjoy themselves. She waved hello to Emma's Aunt Maeve, who was wearing what looked like a riding habit, with a little top hat. Even though Avery didn't have a costume herself, she was feeling thoroughly historical after spending a few hours reading an old copy of Pride and Prejudice she'd found on the bookcase in the living room. It had been a surprisingly effective way to take her mind off her mom's phone call.

Logan had gone to meet the aunts earlier, to get fitted for his Regency clothing. She was curious to see how he'd look. She suspected it would suit him very well. He'd texted to say they were in a tent off to the side of the screen, so she made her way over there.

Going in, she squeezed past a table where a couple of the book club members were teaching visitors some kind of card game, and found Logan behind a screen at the back of the tent. He was being fussed over by Cece and Birdie, who were both clad in their empire-style dresses. He looked up and sent her a half-defeated grin as Cece straightened the upright collar of his shirt. "I'm at their mercy."

She stood back to get a better look at him. The white shirt was tucked into cream-colored, high-waisted trousers, and topped with a dark waistcoat. At his neck, a length of white linen was tied in an elaborate arrangement. His long boots were dark leather, with a turned-down top of a lighter color. The whole effect was very striking.

"You look very dashing," she said—and she meant it.

He adjusted one shirt cuff. "I believe the term you're looking for is 'extremely hot.'"

She shrugged. "Okay, that too."

He caught her eye and sent her a smile, and she couldn't help but return it.

"Right," said Birdie as she stepped back, finally satisfied with his appearance. "So after the movie, all you have to do is take off the waistcoat and neck cloth, and your boots, dive into the river, and then walk back out of the water and stride over to where everyone is waiting."

His jaw dropped. "I'm sorry, what?"

Avery pressed a hand to her mouth, trying to stifle her laughter.

"It's the most famous scene," Cece told him. "With Mr. Darcy's wet shirt."

He raised an eyebrow. "Is this story classic literature or something more racy?"

Cece and Birdie glanced at each other. "Okay, it's true,

that scene wasn't actually in the book," Cece conceded. "But it was in the BBC version, and it's everyone's favorite."

"I thought the rule was that the book is always better," he said obstructively.

"There's a place for both," Birdie said firmly. "And our Mr. Darcy gets wet. We just have to use the river, because we don't have a lake."

He looked out of the tent toward the water. "It'll be cold."

"Daniel had agreed to do it," Avery said in a casual tone.

"Just making an observation," he said, visibly straightening. "I'll do it."

That was too easy. She nodded, keeping a straight face. "Good for you."

Birdie was looking up something on her phone. "Here," she said, holding it out to Logan. "This is the scene with Colin Firth."

They crowded around to watch as Colin took off his outer garments, dived into the lake, then strode back toward his stately home.

"My hair doesn't look anything like that," Logan said, running his hands through it.

Birdie put her phone away. "Nevertheless, you'll do a fine job. You absolutely look the part." She handed him a long tailored coat. "You can wear this too."

He obediently put it on. "What do I do when I've finished my striding around?"

Cece stepped forward. "I'll be there to meet you. I'm playing Elizabeth Bennet."

"My love interest?" he asked doubtfully.

"Yes." She patted the ringlets above her ears.

"Oh...okay."

Avery thought he looked like he was about to say something more, but he wisely decided against it. If Elizabeth Bennet was a woman of a certain age in this live-action replay, it would only make it all the more relatable for many of the ladies in attendance.

As she looked at him in his costume, a whisper of possessiveness crept in. But she pushed it away. Backyard kisses and flirty teasing were all very well, but the repercussions of their complicated past still lingered. And unlike the Bennet women, she was not in need of a man. Not even one who was arrestingly handsome in his Regency best.

After some final tweaks to Logan's apparel, Cece and Birdie went off to check that the projectionist was all ready, and Logan and Avery went to find somewhere to sit in the audience. Birdie was going to come and get him just as the movie ended. He'd noted a general sense of regret among the book club members that the screening was the movie version, rather than the BBC series with Colin Firth—which he now knew was acknowledged as the very best adaptation, and the only one with Mr. Darcy dripping wet in a lake. But Birdie said that even the book club enthusiasts had accepted that a series almost six hours long was too much to expect people to sit through.

Out by the seating area, they scanned the crowd and spotted Claudia waving from the third row, where she'd saved them two seats.

"Wow, you look quite the gentleman," Claudia said when they reached her, taking in his attire.

He bowed slightly. Dressed as he was, it felt weirdly natural. "Thank you, ma'am."

She laughed and turned to Avery. "Where's Ace tonight?"

"Safely at home," Avery said as they took their seats. "I thought that would be better."

Claudia nodded. "He's seemed much more settled lately though." She passed over a blanket, and Avery spread it across her own knees and Logan's.

"He has," she said. "It's a relief—I was worried about him."

"I'm glad you won't have to give him away," Claudia said.

"Me too." Avery lowered her voice, but Logan could still hear her next words. "It would have been a bad deal if I'd kept Carter but lost Ace."

Claudia reached out and squeezed her hand. "Truth."

A very ungentlemanly sense of victory came over him. Ungentlemanly, and unwarranted. Carter may have lost her, through his own messed-up actions, but Logan hadn't won anything himself. He wasn't even sure he should be trying.

Then the screen flickered to life, and a round of applause rippled through the audience as the movie started. Next to him, he felt Avery lean back in her chair and relax as they were transported to England. But despite the bucolic scenes of English meadows, elegant ballrooms, and grand stately homes, he couldn't relax. She was too close—her shoulder against his, her knee tantalizingly near under the blanket, the smell of her hair, the sweetness of her profile as she concentrated on the movie. He forced himself to focus on the screen, and the imminent prospect of his freezing river swim—apparently the Regency equivalent of a cold shower. It seemed that he and Mr. Darcy had more than just dark hair in common, but his own happily ever after might turn out to be complete fiction too.

Chapter 26

A ll too soon, Birdie crept alongside Logan's seat and whispered, "You're on!"

Reluctantly, he slipped the blanket off his knees and folded it back over Avery, so she had a double layer.

"Good luck," she whispered.

He nodded, then followed Birdie to a point halfway between the seats and the river.

"Wait here," she told him. "And look dashing." With a stern look, she turned and went back toward the big screen.

He waited at the exact spot she'd left him, wondering again how he'd ended up in this situation. He was a businessman, a man of decisive, efficient action. He didn't dress up and draw attention to himself. He didn't—

"Ladies and gentlemen," Birdie said over the speaker system. "Thank you again for coming to our first ever Austen in Austen Festival! Although our town is fortunate to share a name with this most beloved author, the path to this particular day began when Lila Marshall started our Jane Austen book club. I talked to Lila last night, and she and her husband Theo would have loved to be here...if they weren't busy in Vermont with their newborn."

The crowd cooed in unison at the baby news. Then,

with a quick glance in Logan's direction, Birdie spun her finger in a circle, implying that he should get moving.

"As Lila always used to say," she continued, "Jane Austen is…"

He stopped following her speech as he pulled off his coat and deposited it on the grass, then bent down to remove his boots. When he looked up again, all eyes were on him. Ellen the piano teacher was in a seat near the back, sending him a look that threatened to freeze the blood in his veins. He pulled himself together and unbuttoned the waistcoat, purposefully trying to do it in a matter-of-fact, non-sexy kind of way. But as he took it off, someone wolf whistled. He dropped it with the coat then turned abruptly and headed for the water, wrestling to undo the fabric cloth tied at his neck. If this was what Mr. Darcy had to wear every day, it was no wonder he was grumpy.

Finally he tore the cloth from his throat, letting it fall to the ground as he reached the river. With a shallow dive, he hit the water. The chill smacked into him, just as cold as he'd imagined. He stayed under long enough to turn around and head back to the bank, then burst out of the water with a deep gasp of air. He ran his hands through his hair, wiped the water from his face, then looked up. At that moment, the crowd burst into applause. Dying inside, but remembering Birdie's strict instructions, he reprised his bow from earlier. Then he waded out of the river and picked his way up the bank, hoping he looked dashing rather than ungainly as water sluiced from him.

Right on cue, he slipped on a muddy patch and went down on one knee, to the sound of laughter from the crowd. Great.

He stood back up and made it to the grass, then strode toward the seats, the cold fabric of his shirt clinging to him. He could feel the tension in his own brow, and knew he must have a face like thunder. He vaguely remembered that Colin Firth had looked more relaxed after his swim than before, but he didn't think Colin was frozen to the core. This reenactment wasn't exactly true to the original. None of it was true to the *real* original anyway, so he wouldn't be interested in hearing any complaints.

As he reached the audience, Cece stepped forward. She patted her ringlets again, and sent him what he guessed was meant to be a flirtatious smile.

"Oh, Mr. Darcy!" she said loudly, in a passable English accent. "Imagine seeing you here."

He hesitated, and she raised an eyebrow and nodded, encouraging him. He cleared his throat.

"Miss Bennet. How delightful to see you."

She held out her hand, her eyelashes fluttering, and he took her cue. Taking her hand, he bent over and bestowed a cold kiss upon it.

At that moment Birdie came over with the microphone.

"Ladies and gentlemen," she said as Cece turned to the crowd and held his hand in the air. "I give you Mr. Fitzwilliam Darcy!"

The assembled guests stood up, whooping and cheering, and when he saw Avery's smiling face, he couldn't help but grin. *You would make a lot of women very happy,* she'd said. *Including me.* And she did look happy. He nodded and waved to the crowd, ignoring the clammy shirt stuck to his body and the death grip Cece still had on his hand. Maybe there was something to be said for a little fiction after all.

Avery fought her way through the gaggle of women surrounding Logan and her aunts. For genteel Regency ladies, they were remarkably unbending as she tried to get closer. She blamed the Logan effect. A sort of viral swoon had gone through the audience as he emerged from the water and came across the grass. Going down on one knee had only added to the drama of his performance.

"Excuse me." As the band played from the gazebo, she elbowed her way between two women wearing blue dresses topped with cropped jackets. "Pardon me."

They reluctantly parted to let her through, and she found herself standing in front of Logan Fitzwilliam Darcy.

"You seem quite popular," she said.

He shrugged. "I'm an archetypal romantic hero. Comes with the territory."

Up close, the effect of his wet shirt was even more striking. She tried not to stare at his strong torso, emphasized by the clingy fabric. "Uh…well, you did great. Claudia and I are going over to the food trucks to get steamed buns. Will we see you after you get changed?"

"Sure," he said. "I need something hot after that swim."

"Okay," she said, trying not to dwell on how the words *steamed buns* and *something hot* seemed to take on new, inappropriate nuance. "Well, we'll catch you there." She made her escape, leaving him with his fans.

When she reached the food area, she found Claudia with Freya and a few other Austen locals. Freya was in full historical gear, including long gloves and a bonnet.

"You look great," Avery told her.

"Thanks," she said. "I'm so happy with how it's going. Your Logan did a spectacular job filling in for Daniel as Mr. Darcy."

"He's not my—" Avery started, but Claudia spoke up.

"We need to get him back here every year. An Austen festival tradition."

Freya laughed. "I think he'd be a big drawcard."

Avery held her tongue, but she suspected they were right.

They joined the line for steamed pork buns. When she reached the counter, Avery bought one carton for herself and one for Logan. Then they went over to the beanbags, which had been vacated by the teenagers, and plunked down into one each.

"I'm going to have serious trouble getting out of this seat when we're done," Freya said, gesturing to her long dress.

Then Logan arrived, dry again and in his regular clothes. "You all look comfortable," he said, looking around at them.

Avery held up the takeout carton with his steamed

buns. "Here. You earned it."

"Thanks," he said, taking it from her. Then he made a waving gesture. "Move over."

"What?"

But he was already lowering himself onto her beanbag. She shuffled over as quickly as she could, but found herself tilting against him as he touched down. She considered struggling out of the beanbag and sitting somewhere else, but he was warm next to her, and there were no other empty ones anyway. And then he turned and smiled at her, and heat flooded not just her cheeks but the rest of her too, and she lost all will to move away. He grinned at her, obviously knowing exactly the effect his closeness had, but she concentrated on eating a bun.

"Hey, Mr. Darcy," Claudia said. "You did great."

"I think Daniel blew it," Freya added. "He won't be getting another chance after your performance."

"Another chance?" Logan said. "You're going to do this again?"

"Sure. It's been such a huge success, we're definitely planning to make it an annual thing. Even bigger and better. This is going to be the biggest Austen festival in the country." She pinned him with a determined look. "You're in, right?"

Avery tried not to laugh at his slightly panicked expression. "I don't know," he said hurriedly. "I mean, I might not always be available. Because...work commitments. I travel a lot."

"I'm sure we'll be able to make it happen," Freya said.

He made an indecipherable noise and took a bite from one of his buns.

Claudia leaned forward in her beanbag. "What kind of work do you do?"

He took his time over his mouthful, then shrugged. "Construction...property. This and that."

"Huh." Claudia nodded thoughtfully. "Keeps you busy then."

"It does." He bit into the bun again.

Avery thought Claudia looked like she was about to

say something else, but then Patrick arrived.

"Hello, kids," he said cheerily. "Great night!"

"Really good," Avery said, scrunching up her napkin and putting it in the now-empty takeout carton. "Did you enjoy the movie?"

He rubbed the back of his neck. "Not my style exactly, but I'm not against broadening my horizons. Can be worthwhile." Then he looked at Logan with a grin. "Seems like you feel the same."

"I don't know about that," Logan said. "But apparently it takes a stronger man than me to resist the persuasive powers of the Robinson women."

"They're a force of nature alright," Patrick said fondly. "Especially Cece."

Avery gave Logan a shove. "Come on, you enjoyed it."

"I think *you* enjoyed it more," he said, a wicked glint in his eye.

She rolled her eyes. "And I think some of Mr. Darcy's pride has rubbed off on you."

Amid good-natured laughter, she turned away to ask Freya about the plans for next year's festival. There was no way she'd admit Logan was right.

Chapter 27

E vening turned into night, and as the darkness crept in the fairy lights sparkled even more brightly in the trees. There were lights around the gazebo too, and soon couples were dancing on the grass, making a charming scene.

Logan levered himself up from the beanbag and held his hand out to Avery.

"I'm not a romantic hero anymore, but will you honor the regular me with a dance?"

"You know I'm only interested in regular hometown guys now anyway," she said jokingly as she let him pull her up, reminding him of their conversation after Carter's appearance. *No more ego-driven men for me,* she'd said. *No more big names or big ambitions or big deals.* He pushed aside the suspicion that she would put him in that category and gestured for her to go ahead.

"We'll have a regular hometown dance then," he said.

They made their way over to the grass in front of the gazebo and joined the other couples. He held out his arms and she stepped into them, one hand on his shoulder, the other in his grasp. Hyperaware of all the places they were touching, he let his hand rest lightly on her waist. Then, despite their proper dance pose, they proceeded to shuffle slowly around like everyone else.

"That was fun," she said as they circled. "You made a pretty good Mr. Darcy. Critically acclaimed, even."

He nodded. "I hope after that I might be mostly forgiven by the town. Apart from Ellen, of course."

She looked up at him. "You were never in need of forgiveness. You weren't to blame for what your father did."

"Really? That's not the impression I got from you."

The words had come out before he could stop them, and he saw her flinch as they hit home. But she didn't let go of him.

"I guess you're right. I did give you that impression." She sighed. "I didn't *blame* you, not really, but I didn't see how we could ever be the same again. My dad was devastated. *I* was devastated. It was a lot to process."

She looked down, and he took his hand from her waist and gently lifted her chin. "I'm sorry. I wish I could undo the pain that you both went through. That you still feel."

Her eyes glistened, reflecting the fairy lights and what he hoped was a new connection between them. "Thanks," she said. "I was doing fine, really, but with Dad passing, then seeing you again, and the thing with Carter, and now Mom making contact..." She shook her head.

His heart ached for her, guilt and regret and lingering anger all blurring into a desire to make things better. "I know you might not feel like I'm the right person to help, but I'll do whatever I can."

"You're not the right person," she told him, meeting his eyes. "But...I think you're the person I want."

At her words, something in him lifted and lightened, the weight of years receding. He wanted to take her sweet face in his hands and kiss her, erase all the lost weeks and months and seasons, take them back to that hopeful, happy place they used to inhabit. But they were surrounded by people, and he didn't want to give the town anything more to talk about. So he put his arm around her and pulled her closer, holding her hand tight as they moved to the music.

"And you're the person I want," he murmured into her hair. "It's always been you."

She pressed closer, sliding her other hand around his neck and nestling in against him. As the band played and the wild stars shone overhead, he realized he might be getting the second chance he'd never believed would come. He just hoped he wouldn't mess it up.

When the band stopped playing and the food trucks closed up and drove away, Avery and Logan helped Freya, Maeve, and the book club members fold the chairs and tidy things up. The hire company was coming in the morning to dismantle the screen and the tents and take them away. With the work done, everyone drifted away to home, or to the Clover for a celebration drink. Avery found herself lingering near Logan, waiting to see what he would do.

Birdie and Cece came over. "Thank you for everything," Birdie said to them both.

"And especially to you, Logan," Cece added, "for braving the cold water for the sake of authenticity."

He accepted a kiss on the cheek from each of them. "I would say it was my pleasure, but I'm not sure that's true."

"Ah, we know we'll see you as Mr. Darcy next year," Birdie told him. "Right, Avery?"

She nodded. "After tonight's show, no one else could fill your boots."

He laughed. "We'll see."

The aunts left for the Clover then, promising to see Avery tomorrow.

She and Logan looked at each other, the last people left in the park, and she held her breath. Since their dance, a fragile connection had been running between them, something tender and new. She didn't want to break it, but she didn't want to assume anything either. "Well, I guess I'd better..." She waved vaguely in the direction of home.

"Would you like to sit a while first?" He gestured to the gazebo, which was still lit with fairy lights.

"Okay," she said.

They made their way over and sat down next to each other inside, facing the river and the hills. The clouds had stayed away, and moonlight draped the tops of the trees. The heat from his body warmed her side from shoulder to knee, and she let herself relax sideways, leaning against him just a little more.

He looked down at her. "That was a good night. Apart from the swim."

"You definitely did that outfit justice," she said. "But the swim was what took it to the next level." The image of him in that clinging-wet shirt and pants was burned into her memory.

"You liked that?" he asked, his voice teasing.

She nudged him. "Stop fishing for compliments. I think you already know my opinion."

"I do," he said. "Extremely hot."

She laughed. "If that will make you happy."

They sat in silence for a while then, looking out at the landscape that had defined their youth, that made their town what it was. She was surprised how easy the silence was, how little she felt the need to fill it with words. Close against Logan, she could feel his arm rise and fall slightly with his breathing. She took a peek at his profile, so familiar but now with stronger adult lines. What had he been doing all these years, that had made him who he was now? Because she liked the man he'd turned into—not just because he was tall, dark, and yes, extremely hot, but because he seemed honest and funny and substantial. Someone her father would have liked too. And yet, he'd walked away from her—from them—all those years ago, and never looked back. Was it safe to want someone who was capable of that?

Finally he spoke. "So…what do you think? Do we have a shot at something here?"

"I have to be able to trust you," she said. "Maybe you felt like you had to leave back then. But you went without a word to me…to anyone."

He frowned. "My father created one of the biggest scandals Austen had ever seen, and then left me alone in a rented house with only enough money for a few months. I was supposed to go to college, but that dream was over.

Everyone in town was talking about us, looking at me...I felt like I couldn't go anywhere." He pressed his fingers to his forehead.

She swiveled to face him, tucking one leg under herself. "No one wanted to drive you away. You shouldn't have worried what they were thinking about you."

"Maybe it was pride," he said. "But like I said, I had nothing to stay for. No mom, a father who'd shamed my family and destroyed yours, and no prospects. What would I have done once school finished—worked behind the bar at the Clover for the rest of my days? And even if I thought you might speak to me again one day, you were leaving for college, while I had no way to go. You would have been leaving *me* in more ways than one."

How could she have been so self-absorbed, so caught up in her own grief that she couldn't see his? "If you'd given me some time..."

"You said it was better if we didn't see each other at all. And you stuck to that. It seemed pretty clear that we were done."

"I understand that now." She sighed. "I'm sorry. I should have seen what you were going through too."

He looked out across the river. "We were just kids."

"I guess I just...I thought you'd always be there."

He turned back to her and took her hand. "I'm here now. If you can take that chance."

She hesitated. Was there really any reason why not, or were her doubts tied up in the past, and in Carter's betrayal too? When she didn't reply, he reached up and put his warm hand gently on her cheek.

"Avery. You said I wasn't in need of forgiveness. But can you forgive me for leaving?"

His touch and his words jolted her out of her doubt. This was Logan. Logan, who had been there all along, her whole life, until something huge and unexpected had blindsided both of them. She put her hand over his. "Can you forgive me for shutting you out?"

They looked into each other's eyes, searching for something unspoken, something true. Then in the same moment they moved just a breath closer, instinctively drawn together. He put his other hand on her cheek, cupping her face, and she let her hand stray to the back of his neck. Anticipation made her heart race, all the more because now she knew what his lips felt like on hers. How a grown-up kiss from him could make her feel. That he was going to make her feel that way again, but this time, there could be more.

When he leaned in, and his lips finally touched hers, she couldn't help the small moan of relief and desire that escaped her. The sound seemed to ignite them both, and he deepened the kiss, a sudden urgency gripping them. She was ready, wanting more, welcoming his hunger for her. She buried her fingers in his hair and he put his arms around her, pulling her closer in the dark. In that moment she was seventeen again, not sure where things were going, but knowing that Logan was there, loving her, taking care of her, and that she wanted him. Wanted *them*.

When they parted, he was smiling. "Seems like we can call it even," he suggested.

She couldn't keep the matching smile off her own face. "Seems like we can call it a second chance."

Chapter 28

They walked home under a moonlit sky, an unspoken knowing between them. Logan held tight to her hand, half in disbelief that this was actually happening. She shot him a glance every now and then, a smile playing on her lips, and he wondered if she felt the same.

Ace was waiting for them when they walked in the door. After a quick round of welcome pats, and a pit stop in the backyard, Avery took him into the living room and put him in his crate.

"I'll come get you soon," she told him as she secured the door. "Don't worry."

"Not *that* soon," Logan told her. "Sorry, Ace."

The dog snuggled down with his blanket and his toys, but there was a definite frown on his face, and Logan felt the force of his reproach.

"I don't think he feels the same about me anymore," he said to Avery.

She laughed as he grabbed her hand and pulled her out of the living room into the hallway, away from the dog's watchful eyes. But when he took her into his arms her laughter faded, replaced with an expression of trepidation, and she bit her lip.

"*I* feel the same about you," she said.

He brushed a thumb across her lip, knowing there would be time to explore all the sweetest parts of her. "Me too."

They stood for a moment at the bottom of the stairs, looking at each other. Years ago, this was the moment he'd hoped they'd have before they each left for college. When he would finally get to show her how he felt, in the most tender, intimate way possible.

But that hadn't happened. And ten years had gone by—ten years of trying not to think about her, of building something through his own efforts, of becoming successful and self-sufficient. Standing in Avery's house, with her finally in his arms, it seemed to have taken forever to get back here. So many years lost.

On the plus side, he knew what he was doing now. There would be no teenage fumbles, no awkward first-time surprises. Now, he planned to take her to bed and make up for every one of those missed years. More than once.

He didn't want to think about the fact that he wouldn't be her first. They had each gone out and lived, and finding their way back to each other was all the sweeter.

She reached up and pushed his jacket back off his shoulders, and he shrugged out of it. She took it and draped it over the stair rail, then eased out of her own coat and laid it over his.

He glanced up the stairs, and she took his cue. Turning out of his embrace, she clasped his hand and wordlessly led him up, slowly climbing each step. He followed behind, watching the sway of her hips, the contours of her curves, feeling his pulse pick up. There was something else too— not nerves, but a kind of anticipation he'd never felt before. This had been a long time coming.

Standing by the bed, with moonlight flooding in the window, crickets in the garden, her childhood sweetheart before her, Avery knew they were at a turning point. Before and after. Finally fulfilling the promises they'd made to each other so many years before.

"You're sure about this?" Logan said carefully. Maybe he was feeling the same.

She smiled. Without saying anything, she reached for the hem of his T-shirt and lifted it up, just a little. He didn't need any more encouragement. He dragged the shirt over his head and tossed it away. She pulled her own T-shirt off and reached for his belt buckle, needing to see more of him, to be closer, skin on skin, heart to heart. He took off his shoes and jeans and then helped her out of hers, his hands warm where they brushed against her skin. Then he paused for a moment, looking at her. It wasn't cold in the room, but a scattering of goosebumps tickled her skin as she stood in her bra and panties under his tender, hungry gaze.

He took her face in his hands, his eyes full of a conflict she thought she understood. "Why did I let you go?" he said, but it didn't sound like a question. It was a rebuke to himself, full of regret.

"Don't think about that," she told him. She knew she could ask the same question in reverse. "Don't think about anything except how we are right now."

He smoothed her hair away from her face, his eyes fixed on hers. "And how are you right now?"

She looked up at him, at his serious, handsome face, his sculpted shoulders, his broad, strong torso. Of its own accord, her hand reached out and traced a line from the side of his neck, over his chest, down to his flat stomach. Grownup Logan had turned into a spectacular man.

"I'm in a pretty good place," she said, half laughing. "But...this is uncharted territory. Like we're going back, but going forward."

His eyes were dark, intense under his brows. "You can trust me."

At his words, her last hesitations melted away. Complications, history, all the reasons to not be here, doing this...she refused to let any of it in. Outside this room, outside this house, the past was waiting to catch up with them. But in here, it was just the two of them. Nothing could reach them.

They were Logan and Avery, meant to be, and there

was nothing commonplace about that.

When Avery stepped away, Logan had a sudden stab of doubt. Maybe she didn't trust him enough to take this step after all. But then she took his hand, a promise in her eyes, and he went eagerly, following her onto the bed. He gathered her close, then reached around and unfastened her bra, only fumbling a little. She helped him slip it down her arms and away, then he reached for her panties, made of the same pale blue lace. She lifted her hips from the bed as he slowly, slowly eased them off. Then, when she was free of every covering, he sat back and looked at her.

He shook his head, almost overwhelmed by the moment. This was Avery, the girl he'd loved, now a beautiful, accomplished, complicated woman. Vulnerable and exposed, trusting him at last. Trusting him with all of herself. Her skin had a pale glow in the moon's soft illumination, like she was some otherworldly creature sent to captivate him. Which was exactly what she'd done.

Under his gaze, she suddenly seemed to be struck with shyness, crossing her arms in front of herself. He took both her hands and raised them over her head, gently pinning her to the mattress underneath him. "I want to see you."

Her eyes met his, and her expression was a tantalizing mix of demure and daring. He grinned. Oh, he accepted that dare.

Starting at the most tender spot under her ear, he planted one kiss after another, down her neck, across the delicate skin of her throat, and between her breasts. Then he ran his tongue across the peak of one nipple, gently at first, then harder as she squirmed underneath him, small appreciative noises slipping from her lips. He repeated it with her other breast, feeling his own arousal insistent against her thigh.

She fought free of his hold and flung her arms around him, pressing her fingers into his back. "Kiss me," she said, a yearning hunger in her voice. "Kiss me."

So he did. As his mouth met hers, her lips parted and

their seeking tongues found each other. A flare of desire overtook him and he crushed her to him, the kiss intensifying, two starving people finally finding sustenance in each other's arms. She wrapped her legs around his hips, pressing upward, and he slipped his hand under her bottom to hold her close against him.

In his mind he'd had all kinds of ideas for the moves he'd make, but now there was nothing but wanting, need, a blur of heat and the desperate urge to get closer to her. As close as two people could get. And it seemed like she felt just the same.

She broke the kiss, letting out a frustrated growl. "Logan...come on." She released him and reached down for his boxer briefs, trying to shove them down and out of the way.

He rolled over and dragged them off, then returned to her. She immediately reached down, taking him firmly in her hand between her legs. He glanced down, and the sight and sensation of her hand wrapped around him quickened his already intense arousal.

"God, Avery," he said. "You're—"

But her grip strengthened, and whatever he was about to say was lost as his breath caught in his chest. Their mouths crashed together again, and she writhed until he was pressing against the sweet place between her legs, and they were so close, so close to being one.

Then, with a crushing disappointment, he realized something, and pulled away. "Oh, shit. I don't have any—"

"Over there," she said breathlessly, pointing to a toiletry bag sitting on a dressing table by the window.

Like a cartoon superhero, he was up and back within seconds. After so long, he didn't want to waste a minute of their time together. He tore open the foil packet and covered himself at lightning speed.

"Where were we?" he said, taking her into his arms again, and she gave a low laugh.

"I think you were about to show me how good a second chance can feel."

He smiled. "That's exactly what I plan on doing."

"Come on then," she said, a teasing impatience in her voice as she pulled him on top of her. "I think we've waited long enough. I'm ready."

Now that the moment was here, he didn't want to rush anything. There would only be one first time with Avery, and he wanted to make it memorable for her. He kissed her again, drawing on all his restraint as her hands ran over his body, leaving a tingling warmth every place they touched. But she wriggled closer, insistent, angling her hips until they were perfectly, teasingly aligned. So, with his eyes fixed on hers, he slowly, carefully slid inside her, a little at a time, loving the way her expression went from determined to hazy. When he was finally deep inside her, she drew in a breath and let it out in a ragged sigh.

"I missed you," she said, her voice barely more than a whisper.

With his thumb, he gently brushed away a tear that had escaped onto her cheek. "You don't have to miss me anymore."

They started to move together, neither of them breaking eye contact, like a silent promise strengthening between them. But it didn't take long before their rhythm picked up, an irresistible pulse building. She let out a small, husky exclamation, her head tipping back on the pillow as she grasped his shoulders, and he dropped his mouth to lavish nips and kisses on the pale curve of her exposed throat. Supporting himself on one elbow, his hand under her neck, he explored her soft, luscious curves with his other hand, wanting to feel, taste, love every part of her. As her hands roamed over his heated skin in return, her breathy sounds of pleasure and encouragement filled the room. All too soon he felt a relentless rising heat, and saw the answering urgency in her eyes, and knew that despite his best intentions, all his restraint would probably be for nothing this very first time. When she suddenly cried out, lifting her hips and clinging onto him as her climax rushed upon her, he knew he was lost too. He gave in, driving harder, letting the rush overwhelm him, his face buried in Avery's sweet-smelling hair, her gasps in his ears, her body and her heart the home he'd been missing all this time. They had all night ahead of them for him to make up for the years they'd been apart, and all weekend. And maybe the rest of their lives, if she'd let him.

Chapter 29

A very had a definite spring in her step as she set out from home with Ace the next morning. The sun was shining, jewel-like hummingbirds were darting in the pink honeysuckle cascading in her neighbor's yard, and she was about to embark on a very unexpected second chance.

Ace picked up on her good mood, trotting alongside with his tail held high. They were on their way to meet Claudia for breakfast at the Riverbend Café in town. She knew her friend would pepper her with questions about Logan, but she wasn't sure how much she wanted to share yet. Their fledgling reconnection felt so delicate that she wanted to shelter it a while longer, let it grow safely and secretly.

It had been a night to remember—as tender and passionate and, yes, delightfully dirty as she could have imagined. There was no doubting that Logan was a grownup now. A man who knew what he wanted, and who seemed to know what *she* wanted before she even knew herself. A warm thrill went through her as she recalled his big hands roaming her body, his breath against her skin, that moment when he was finally inside her and she clung to him, years of waiting culminating in sensations so intense she could barely think straight. And they'd gone back for more, and more, until they were so deliciously spent that she could barely move.

When they'd finally had their fill of each other, Logan went downstairs and let Ace out of his crate. Then they lay tangled in bed talking, the dog snoozing at their feet. She'd told Logan about college, and her slow but steady rise in radio; he'd told her funny stories about some of the people he worked with when he first moved to Oakland. She was impressed that he'd managed to find a job and a place to live, building a new independent life along with the houses and commercial properties he worked on. In contrast, her time at college in Portland had been safe and predictable, even though she'd worked hard too.

Before he said goodbye that morning he had taken her in his arms at the front door, and given her a kiss so full of promise and tenderness that she'd almost thrown her breakfast plans to the wind and pulled him back inside. But then he let her go, gave Ace a hearty pat, and walked away down the steps and out the gate. She'd watched him go, her heart full, knowing that this time he'd be back.

Now she came to the Riverbend and went in, calling out good morning to Ilona, who had owned it for as long as she could remember. Then she and Ace made their way to the back courtyard, where dogs were allowed to accompany their owners as long as they behaved well. Claudia was already there, and she stood up when she saw them coming.

"Good morning," she said, giving Avery a hug. "You're looking very cheerful. I wonder why that is."

"Alright, alright," Avery said as they sat down. "Get it all out now, then we can get on with breakfast."

"I *knew* you still had a connection," Claudia said. "Did you..." She raised her eyebrows. "You know."

Avery felt herself blushing. "Getting right to the point, huh?"

"You said to get it all out now," Claudia reminded her.

"Okay, fair point." She picked up her menu, pretending to be engrossed in the breakfast options, but she knew her smile gave her away. "We did."

"Oh, Avery. After all this time."

Something in Claudia's voice made her look up. Her friend's expression was a mixture of nostalgia and fondness, but there was something else Avery couldn't identify. Before she could ask Claudia what was up, the server came to their table. She put a bowl of fresh water on the ground for Ace, then asked, "Are you ready to order?"

"Oh, yes," Avery said. "I'll have the eggs Benedict with bacon, please. And coffee. Oh, and orange juice."

The server nodded and wrote down the order, then turned to Claudia. "And for you?"

"Blueberry peach pancakes please. And coffee."

With their orders noted down, the server took their menus and went back inside.

"Still an eggs Benedict fiend, huh?" Claudia said.

"I know. It might seem boring, but you can't beat a classic."

"True." Claudia fell silent, fiddling with her cutlery.

"Okay, what's wrong?" Avery asked her. "I thought you'd be all over this news about me and Logan."

She sighed. "Well...I don't want to be a gossip, but I found out something you might want to know."

A sharp flare of warning leaped in Avery's chest. "What is it?"

"It's about Logan."

A dozen scenarios flashed through her head. He was a convicted felon. He had a terminal illness. He was married. "Oh, God. Just tell me."

"Okay. Did you know he's a millionaire?"

Avery stared at Claudia, the words not computing after her dire imaginings. "A what?"

"A millionaire. As in someone who's made a million dollars. Or more than one million, I guess, but less than a billion. It's kind of a plural noun in itself, so it could mean—"

Avery held up her hand. "I know what a millionaire is."

"Sorry."

"Are you sure? How did you find out?"

"After we talked about his work last night, I got curious. He was so vague about it, you know?" She passed over her phone. "I googled him."

Avery took the phone. The Finance Today website was on the screen, with an article titled *Self-Made Mavericks: Ten Young Millionaires to Watch*. She scrolled down and found a picture of Logan. Underneath was a timeline of his work history and achievements. His start as a contractor's assistant in Oakland, then turning the ailing company around. Expanding operations statewide, then dabbling in property development. Funding and managing major national projects, then investing his money in the futures and options market. The article attributed his success to his fearless approach to business, and his ability to move decisively when an opportunity arose—something that could have been his downfall if he'd lost his nerve at a crucial moment or picked the wrong risk to take. And it predicted that he would be among the first of the ten profiled entrepreneurs to hit the billion mark.

She looked at Claudia. "Wow."

"So you didn't know anything about this?"

She shook her head. "I had no idea."

"He didn't mention it to you?"

"No. He was vague with me too. He just said he was in contracting...construction..." She put down the phone and pressed her fingers to her temples. He hadn't given her any hint of the extent of his business dealings. "I can't get my head around it. He doesn't *look* like a millionaire. I mean, he doesn't dress like one."

"No, he doesn't," Claudia agreed. "He seems more casual, like a jeans-and-T-shirt kind of guy. Like he really could be a contractor."

At that moment the server came back with their order, and Avery sat back to let her put everything on the table, thinking. Those expensive hiking boots—half eaten by Ace—made more sense now.

When the server had gone, Claudia reached for her coffee. "It's not a *bad* thing, is it? I mean...a millionaire. A *multi*-millionaire. That's a lot of money."

"I don't care about the money," Avery said abruptly, her conflicting emotions threatening to spill over.

"I'm not implying that you'd want him for his money," Claudia said calmly as she dropped a spoonful of sugar into her coffee and stirred. "I'm just saying it's not necessarily a negative thing."

"I know, I'm sorry. I just thought he'd been honest with me about everything. I thought he was still my Logan...a regular hometown guy. That's what he seemed like. That's all I want."

Claudia nodded. "You'll have to talk to him about it."

The thought made Avery's stomach knot up.

"Eat your eggs," Claudia told her, nudging her plate closer. "You don't want to be heading into this on an empty stomach."

She picked up her knife and fork, but her appetite had gone, even for her favorite breakfast. She'd started the day on the high of a second chance. How could she take that chance with someone who'd purposefully hide something so huge from her?

Logan walked into town from the vacation rental, enjoying the fresh morning air and the optimistic feeling buoying his steps. Last night with Avery had been a breakthrough that he'd sorely needed—and not just because they'd finally made love. He'd been carrying so much baggage around the events of the past, it had been cathartic to talk it through with her, to smash through the barriers and connect with her in such a real way. And yes, the sex had been everything he'd imagined and hoped for. *She* was everything he'd imagined and hoped for.

She and Claudia had arranged to meet at the Riverbend at nine this morning, so he'd left her place earlier and gone back to the vacation rental to get changed and go for a run. He didn't want to crash their breakfast—that would be leaping straight into very unattractive needy-boyfriend territory—but he'd decided it would be okay to catch her afterward. So at ten, freshly showered and full of anticipation, he turned the corner onto Main Street and slowly started along the sidewalk, keeping an eye on the café's entrance.

Okay, maybe this *was* needy-boyfriend territory. But he'd think of it as being ready to take a risk for the sake of a priceless reward.

As he got closer, he saw Avery and Claudia come out of the café with Ace. They spotted him, and he gave a casual wave. He saw them glance at each other, then Claudia gave Avery a hug and walked away in the opposite direction. That was weird—he'd thought she would stay and say hi. Maybe she had somewhere to be.

Avery stepped away from the café door, then waited for him to arrive. She wasn't smiling, and he wondered if she was tired after last night, or maybe Claudia had needed to talk through a problem. Ace was doing his usual waggy welcome though, straining at the leash in delight and anticipation as Logan came closer. He was grateful for the dog's enthusiasm—it had done him a big favor when he and Avery first met again. As he reached the two of them, Ace's propeller tail looked like it might lift him off the ground.

"Ace, sit," Avery said, steel in her voice. The dog sat at her feet, uncharacteristically obedient.

"Hi," Logan said. He knew he was grinning like a Cheshire cat, that all his casual cool had gone out the window, but he didn't care. After last night, after all these years, he just wanted to keep rolling with their second chance.

"Finance Today," Avery said sharply. "Ten Young Millionaires to Watch."

Instantly, the grin fell off his face. That explained the look from Claudia. "Oh. I didn't know that had been published already." He guessed the reporter hadn't spared any details about his career—the same details he'd skipped over when talking to Avery about his work.

"I thought you said you were in construction."

Her expression was level, unreadable, but he knew he was in trouble here. "I am."

161

"That's not exactly the whole story though, is it?"

"Construction, and...other things."

Her hands were gripping the leash so tight her knuckles were white. "How could you lie to me about something so big?"

"I didn't lie. I just...left out some details."

She snorted. "What are you, twelve? The truth is the truth."

He waited as someone walked by, then said, "I'm sorry I didn't give you the whole picture. But I would have sooner rather than later."

"It's already too late," she said.

"I don't get why you're so angry about this. You don't hold Mr. Darcy's money against him," he pointed out. "Doesn't the book say he's a single man in possession of a good fortune, like his friend Mr. Bingley?"

She stared at him. "I thought you hadn't read Pride and Prejudice."

"I looked at the first few chapters yesterday afternoon, before the festival. For research purposes."

"Oh. Well, anyway, I'm not holding your money against you," she countered. "However good your fortune might be, the point is that you didn't tell me."

He felt like they were getting nowhere. "There was a reason for that. Money complicates things. Once I got back here, I just wanted to be myself for a while—the same regular guy I always was."

"You're not that guy though, are you?"

He blew out a frustrated breath. That was the guy she wanted—a regular hometown guy, no fancy deals, no ego...no risk of ending up with another Carter. And although he was still the old Logan in some ways, he knew he hadn't achieved so much by being a "regular" guy. He'd pushed the limits, found a deeper well of self-belief that allowed him to deal with the big players of industry and finance. If that equaled ego, so be it.

"You said I could trust you," she said.

"You can," he insisted. "I would never intentionally do anything to hurt you."

"You don't get it." She laughed, but it was a weary sound. "I'm going home. I need to think." She clucked to Ace and he stood up.

"Let me come with you," Logan said. "We can talk about this."

She shook her head. "No." Then she turned to go.

That no was something he'd heard from her before. He'd give her space while she was in this frame of mind, but this time he didn't intend to give up so easily. He stood and watched her walk away, in case she had a change of heart. But only Ace looked back.

Chapter 30

The *devil is in the details*. Never had a saying seemed so apt. Avery strode home at a brisk pace, charged by irritation. Ace trotted by her side, probably thinking fond doggy thoughts about Logan, untroubled by his double-crossing tendencies.

Money complicates things, Logan had said. Did he think she was the kind of person who'd act based on greed? Because that wasn't her. Unlike him, she hadn't changed.

Or maybe she had. After Carter, her heart had quietly put up an extra layer of protection. Sure, she was better off without him, but that knowledge came with a deepening cynicism and caution. Logan had broken through that all too easily, because of who he was—her small-town childhood sweetheart. Despite everything, that history counted for something.

Except that wasn't who he was…not anymore.

Although he'd seemed the same, on the surface. Well, apart from the fancy boots maybe.

Ugh. She shook her head as she walked along. She didn't know what to think, other than he'd had plenty of time to tell her the truth. She'd had enough lies to last her a lifetime—she didn't need them from Logan too.

They reached the house and went up the steps, Ace

panting slightly after their speed-walking. She pulled her keys out of her purse and went to open the door...but it was already unlocked. Then there was a dull thud from inside the house. Instantly, her whole body went on high alert. Someone was in there.

Beside her, Ace tensed too, which only set her nerves even more on edge. Heart pounding, she slowly, silently turned the handle, holding Ace's collar firmly so he wouldn't rush in.

The door swung open.

A woman was standing in the hallway holding a dusting cloth.

"Oh, Avery, you're home," her mom said, as though she'd never been away.

Avery stood in the doorway as the years telescoped in on themselves, not wanting to go in, unable to go back.

Her mom waved her forward. "Come in, honey." Her gaze fell to Ace. "Oh, and who's this?"

"How did you get in?" Avery asked, still holding tight to Ace. She could tell by the way he was quivering at full attention that he knew something was wrong.

"Well, I used my key of course. I wanted to surprise you. I know you said you'd call, but you sounded down, so..." She held out her hands. "Ta-da."

"You still have the key? After all this time...after what you did?"

Her mom had the grace to look a little guilty. "Sure. I guess...just in case."

"In case of what?" Avery heard her own voice rise, saw her mom flinch, but didn't care. "In case you wanted to stroll back in like nothing ever happened?"

She sighed. "Can we start again? Because this isn't going how I planned."

Finally Avery stepped inside with Ace and closed the door behind them. She unclipped his leash but he stayed close by, standing guard next to her.

"How did you imagine this would go, Mom? We'd fall into each other's arms, like in some Hallmark movie?" She walked past her mother into the kitchen and hung Ace's leash on the hook, then went to turn the coffee machine on, Ace trailing after her. But there was already a pot of hot coffee ready to go. She turned back around. "This isn't your house anymore. You don't get to come in and make yourself at home and do dusting and make coffee."

Her mom dropped the cloth on the kitchen table. "I'm sorry, honey, but that's where you're wrong."

"What?"

"This *is* my house. I talked to the lawyer. Your dad never changed his will." Her voice took on a more gentle tone. "You must know that by now."

Confusion and anger sparred in Avery's heart as she looked at her mother. That couldn't be right. She cursed herself for putting off the paperwork around her dad's death. She'd assumed it would all be straightforward—she was the only child, so everything would come to her. But apparently her mom was first in line.

"Anyway, you'll be going back to Portland, won't you? Last I heard you were working at a radio station there."

"Not anymore," Avery said. "I'm living here at the moment." She definitely wasn't going to tell her mother about her on-air embarrassment and subsequent firing.

"Oh, well then," she replied lightly. "You're welcome to stay with me until you find something else."

Avery's rage at her mother's blithe invitation was a physical force expanding in her chest. "I'm welcome to..." She threw up her hands. It wasn't worth it. "Never mind."

She had to get out. She went into the hallway and grabbed up her purse. She didn't need it where she was going, but she didn't trust her mom. Didn't even recognize her anymore. Then she went back into the kitchen and collected Ace's leash from the hook, and clipped it to his collar. "I was obviously stupid to think you might say you're sorry. Acknowledge what you did...what you put us through."

"I am sorry," her mom said indignantly.

Avery rolled her eyes. "Right. Sorry enough that you waited until Dad was dead, then came rushing back here to reclaim the house." She opened the back door. "I'm going out."

"We'll talk when you get back," her mom said in a lecturing tone, like Avery was seventeen still.

Without a word she went out the door with Ace, down the back steps, and across the yard. Usually she'd stop to smile at the whirring hummingbirds ducking their heads in and out of the foxgloves her dad had planted for them along the back fence, but now she unlatched the gate and went right on through.

She had gotten used to her mother not being around, but she always knew there was a possibility they'd see each other again somewhere, sometime. Of all the ways she'd imagined that happening, this wasn't one of them.

Logan pushed through the greenery along the side of the river path and made his way to the wishing tree. Just as he'd suspected, Avery was there, wedged into the V. Her eyes were closed, and Ace was lying patiently on the ground next to her. When he saw Logan he lifted his head and thumped his tail on the ground, but he didn't leave his mistress. Logan knew that was a sign things were serious.

"Thought I might find you here," he said. Avery ignored him, so he added, "I went to the house."

"You saw her then," she said, her voice dull.

"Yeah. I'm guessing it didn't go well."

"She's come back for the house. Dad never changed his will."

He sucked air through his teeth. "That's not good."

She sat up, and her eyes were dark with emotion. "I can't go back there right now. I'm too angry, and she's too..." She made a sound that was somewhere between frustration and anger, and slumped back against the tree trunk.

"She did seem very casual about the whole thing when she answered the door."

Avery's eyes widened. "I didn't ask her about your dad. If he's not with her, maybe she's just planning to sell and go back to wherever they are."

Logan shook his head. "I doubt that." Now probably

wasn't the time to admit that he knew exactly where Jeff Wagner was—and had done for almost a week.

"Or maybe he's going to move in too," she suggested.

Then again, he owed her the truth about what had happened after Jeff and Cathleen left Austen. Especially after skimping on the details about his own situation. He took his place opposite her in the tree, and braced himself for the fallout.

"I found out something you should know."

She groaned and leaned her head back against the trunk. "I've already had one conversation start that way today. I'm guessing this isn't going to be good either."

"Uh...not really."

"Okay, what is it?"

He tried to think of the best way to put it, but there wasn't one. So he got straight to it. "Jeff and your mom split up about a year after leaving here."

Her mouth dropped open. "What?"

"Yeah. They went their separate ways."

Her eyes narrowed. "Why?"

"From what I understand..." He cleared his throat. "From what I understand, there was another woman."

"Well, isn't that just lovely," she said. "And did Jeff tell you this himself?"

"No, I haven't spoken to him." That much was true, at least so far. "I hired a private investigator to find them."

"So that's how Mom found out about Dad's death?"

"Yes."

"So it's thanks to *you* that she's back here."

He could have kicked himself for not thinking this through better. But he'd never expected that Owen would have left his will unchanged.

"How long have you known all this?" Avery asked.

He looked away to the wild hills over the river, then met her eyes again. "Since Tuesday."

"Are you kidding me?"

"No. Sorry."

She shook her head. "I can't believe she never came back or got in touch after they broke up. I guess it shows where her priorities lay. I don't want to go home and deal with her right now. If it's even my home anymore."

He watched as emotions ran across her face, wishing he could undo the events of the past. He had determinedly put his father out of his mind, gone on to create something Jeff could never take away. But Avery had clearly missed her mom, and now Cathleen was back, she could potentially take away something on top of the lost years— Avery's home.

She looked at him. "Well, I came here to think. Now I have even more to figure out, thanks to your sleuthing. You can leave me to it."

But he had no intention of being dismissed. He tried a small smile. "You always used to say things made better sense when we talked them through."

She huffed. "*Used to* being the operative words."

"They don't have to be." He hesitated, an idea solidifying in his mind. "If you don't want to go home, come back to San Francisco with me. Do your thinking there."

"Why would I want to do that? Did you not hear anything I said outside the café?"

He nodded. "I did. You said it was already too late for me to tell you the truth. Why is it too late?"

"For the same reason I can't go away with you now."

"And that is?"

She glared at him. "Because I already fell for you again."

Chapter 31

A very stepped out of the small terminal building at the municipal airport, and stopped in her tracks. A sleek white jet stood on the tarmac, its steps lowered ready for boarding. It looked completely out of place, and absolutely gorgeous.

She turned to Logan. "Is this what we're going in?"

"This is us," he said. "Would you rather fly commercial?"

She could see the twinkle in his eye, but she was too distracted to think of a smart comeback.

"This is fine." Did her voice sound a little breathless? "Is it yours?"

He shook his head. "No, it's a charter. My assistant thinks I should get one, but I've been putting it off. What do you think?"

"I, uh…maybe?" She was starting to realize that Logan must be heading well upward on Claudia's scale of millionaire to billionaire.

He smiled. "Let's go."

Following him across the tarmac, she resisted the urge to pinch herself—or him, to make sure he was real, not some imposter pretending to be Logan Wagner from Austen, Oregon.

She had been a hundred percent sure she wasn't going anywhere with him. But when he walked her back home from their tree, she stood in the backyard and looked up at the house, and couldn't make herself go inside. In that moment, everything had come crashing down on her—her mom's departure, her dad's passing, Carter's very public betrayal, the loss of her job, even Claudia's revelation that morning. Not to mention her blurted confession to Logan that she'd fallen for him, which she'd wanted to swallow back down the moment it was out. She'd seen surprise and hope cross his face, but he'd just nodded and stepped back, and gestured for her to go first toward the path. She was grateful for that. Outside the house, she'd put her hand on Ace's warm head to draw from his steady presence, but her legs wouldn't take her any farther.

Logan had rested his hand lightly on the small of her back. "You can do this."

But she'd realized something. She didn't want to. And she didn't have to. She didn't owe her mom anything.

She turned to him. "Does your offer still stand?"

His face had lit up. "To come with me? Of course. I said I'd help any time you need me."

"Just as friends though," she told him firmly, trying to push aside the lingering memory of the night before.

He hesitated, then nodded. "As friends."

So they'd gone inside, and Logan had kept her mom talking in the kitchen while Avery went upstairs, tore the sheets off the bed, and packed her things. Cathleen hadn't been pleased to hear they were leaving, but Avery kept her equilibrium, and said she'd be back in a few days. Then they collected Logan's bag from the vacation rental, dropped Ace with a very surprised Claudia—Avery had to promise under her breath that she'd message her with an explanation as soon as she could—and headed for the nearest airport.

Now she followed Logan up the plane steps, where a smiling flight attendant was waiting to greet them. Avery turned the corner and took in the interior: understated pale décor with cream leather seats, a small but well-appointed galley kitchen, TV screens on swivel arms, and even vases of flowers.

The flight attendant showed them to their seats and ran through a quick safety briefing. Then she served them drinks and retreated discreetly behind the cockpit door.

"How did you organize this so quickly?" Avery asked Logan.

"My assistant Lisa. She's used to me throwing her travel challenges."

"Well, she did good," Avery said, sipping the champagne the flight attendant had given her.

They passed the short flight in a quiet bubble of luxury, making small talk. Avery was thankful that Logan kept the conversation light. At the airport in San Francisco they were met by a driver with a big black car, and driven to Logan's apartment building in the city. Looking out at the passing streets, she felt some of her tension lift. A new city, away from everything, would give her breathing space. Here she was nobody, could be anybody.

"This is us," Logan said, and the driver slowed in front of an elegant 1920s apartment building. Avery craned to take it in—nine or ten floors, maybe—but then they turned the corner and entered a basement parking garage.

The driver parked the car and got out to open the door for her. Then he and Logan unloaded the trunk and put everything in the elevator. Logan thanked him and said goodbye, then ushered Avery into the elevator too.

"Going up," he said, putting a key into the elevator panel and pushing a button.

She couldn't help smiling. "How far up?"

"All the way."

"That's not code for anything, right?" she joked. Well, half-joked.

"No," he said, giving her a wry grin. "Not on a Monday night, not on a Saturday morning, and not on a Sunday evening. Not if we're just friends."

"You got it," she said, trying not to think about how it had felt in his arms last night—the moonlight slanting through the window, his warm, intoxicating kisses, his murmured endearments as he made love to her in the house beside the river.

But they weren't going back to that place. He'd promised she could trust him, but he hadn't told her about her mom and Jeff...hadn't even been willing to tell her the truth about his life, thinking money would complicate things between them. How could he have so little faith in her? And keep so many secrets?

With a tasteful ding that snapped her back to attention, the elevator opened into a small vestibule with an inner door. They stepped out with their bags, then Logan pressed his finger to a keypad and the door unlocked with a click. He pushed it open and gestured for her to go first.

When she went in, her breath caught in her chest. They were in an expansive living room with sleek hardwood floors, long, low sofas, and white walls decorated with tasteful abstract artworks. But her eyes didn't linger on the inside—she was immediately captivated by the incredible views from the wide windows. She went over to look more closely. Dusk was just beginning to settle over the bay, and lights were coming on along the streets and in the buildings that clad the city's hills. The harbor reflected the cerulean-blue evening sky, and Alcatraz was in clear view.

"This is incredible." She shook her head, trying to process the surreal feeling of going so quickly from their simple little hometown to the pinnacle of urban luxury. "Where are we exactly?"

"Pacific Heights," he said, standing back to let her take it all in.

"That's the Golden Gate Bridge." Lit up as it was now, it did look golden instead of red.

He smiled. "Correct."

She pointed toward another bridge. "And that one?"

"That's the Bay Bridge."

"Oh, right." She nodded, drinking in the unbelievable vista, then turned to him. "Logan. Seriously. This is *crazy*."

He looked at her steadily for a moment, then his smooth veneer cracked and he laughed out loud. "I've never shown this to anyone from home."

In that moment it felt like they were two awestruck kids who'd stumbled into someone else's apartment, and couldn't believe their eyes.

"I don't think anyone would believe it," she said. "I can't believe it, and I'm right here." She held out her arms, turning to encompass the luxurious room and the stunning view.

"Well, you'd better believe it," he said. "Because I want you to make yourself at home. Relax. Are you hungry?"

She thought for a moment. "Actually, I really am."

"I'll order in," he said. "What would you like? Anything at all. Most of the really good restaurants near here will take an order."

"Oh," she said, remembering something. "When we were at the market, and you said you never cook, and I assumed you lived on takeout...I wasn't exactly right."

He laughed. "You were only half wrong. Do you like Thai food?"

"I do. I mean, I like anything I don't have to cook myself. You already know about my culinary deficiencies."

"I think you do better than me on that score," he said, and pulled out his phone.

Once the order was made, he showed her around. They went from the main living area to the other side of a double-sided fireplace, where there was a kitchen, breakfast area, and comfortable family room. Farther around, there was a formal dining room, an office, a library with shelves up to the ceiling, and several bedrooms and bathrooms. Every room boasted a different view of the city, and she wanted to linger and soak in each unique perspective. But she followed him, knowing she'd have time to look at them again. Then he took her into a large bedroom with a huge bed and a built-in fireplace.

"Here you go," he said, putting her bag on the bed.

She hesitated. "But this looks like the master suite. I didn't come here to—"

He shook his head. "I know. I sleep in one of the smaller rooms. I tried this one to start with, but it felt all wrong being alone in here."

"You must have had company sometimes, at least." She had to say it, even though she didn't want to let her mind go down that path—or his. She knew there would have been women in his life, who'd come after her and shared things with him she never had. It was ridiculous to feel jealous or resentful about that, especially now they were back to just friends, so she wouldn't. She definitely wouldn't.

He shrugged, his eyes fixed on the bed. "Not for a long time now."

It was the best answer she could have hoped for.

Then he turned and grinned at her. "Come on, let's have a drink to celebrate your escape."

"Sounds good," she said.

With one last look over her shoulder, she went ahead out of the room, and he followed. So she would have that enormous, inviting bed all to herself. In that moment, she wasn't sure whether she was relieved or disappointed.

Chapter 32

Logan woke up in his apartment on Monday morning with the sense that something was different. It took him a moment to remember what, and when he did, it still didn't seem real. Avery had been unbelieving of the apartment; he was equally unbelieving that she was here in it, currently sleeping in the room down the hall.

He checked his watch: five thirty. Despite the upheaval of the last week or so—and despite lying awake last night doing battle with the desire to burst into her room and repeat the events of the night before—his body clock was still running exactly to schedule. He got up quietly and showered in his bathroom, then dressed and went down the hall, only hesitating for the briefest moment by her bedroom door. All was quiet. Good. She needed the rest—physically and emotionally.

He left a note for her on the table in the breakfast area, then slipped out. She'd be fine to come and go as she pleased—last night he'd told her all the practical things she needed to know about the apartment, and as well as giving her a key for the elevator he'd programmed the control panel in the vestibule to accept her fingerprint.

But that was all they'd talked about—that and light, easy topics like their best and worst TV shows, bands they'd seen, movies they loved. They didn't talk about their parents, or their work, or their sweet, hot, long-awaited connection the night before. They were just two people enjoying a meal, having a drink, and watching the city lights from a perfect San Francisco vantage point.

The only wrong note had come when he tried to give her a credit card, and she had been aghast.

"This isn't Pretty Woman," she told him. "I don't need your money. I don't want it. I told you that. Money doesn't complicate things unless you make it that way, and that's what you're doing."

"Okay," he said, trying to find a way back out of the hole he'd dug himself. "I just want you to feel free to do whatever you like in the time you're here. It's an expensive city."

"I don't need to do anything expensive," she said firmly. "But if I do, I'll use my own money. Thank you anyway."

He'd considered himself told.

Now he walked the few blocks to his building and went up to his sixth-floor office space. Lisa usually arrived at seven thirty, and his few other staff at eight thirty, so he had the place to himself for a while. The fresh hours just after dawn were when he did his best work. He liked the uncluttered feeling of that time of day.

He had a lot to do, but there was one glaring task that had been waiting on his list—a call to Pahrump, Nevada. It was too early yet—especially to call someone who worked in a casino and was surely not an early riser—but it had to be done today. He needed to talk to his father about what had happened with Cathleen. And there was still the question of the development, which was what had started him on this whole journey.

Last week he had quietly sent a small team of surveyors and engineers onto the Wagner family land along the Austen River, and now he found the report waiting in his email inbox. He opened the file and read through it. Their assessment was that the land was suitable for multistory development, and it would be possible to create a landing area to ferry machinery, equipment, and supplies across the river. He just needed a suitable access point on the opposite shore.

The report went on to outline approximate costs for stabilizing and preparing the land. He read through the details, then crunched some numbers on a scrap of paper. At first reckoning, it seemed like there would be enough land to make the project worthwhile. And he'd remembered Barbara's comments about the need for more accommodation in town, and the positive effect of tourism. Even if it was borderline in terms of profit for him personally, it would be good to provide a further boost to the local economy. Assuming he could get it off the ground—and that all hung on Jeff Wagner.

He went through to the small kitchen and made coffee. He wasn't hungry for breakfast yet—Lisa usually brought something in for both of them. As he added milk, he wondered whether Avery was awake yet. Even though he'd stuck to small talk last night, he hadn't forgotten her confession. *I already fell for you again.* There had been nothing romantic about it—she'd snapped it out in frustration, under pressure. But didn't the things people say in unguarded moments hold the most truth? Hearing her words, his heart had jumped in his chest. And when she immediately clapped her hand over her mouth, dismayed at herself, he knew she'd revealed something true.

But he also knew she needed time to think, to process everything, and she'd been pretty clear about her expectations for this visit. He wouldn't deny he was disappointed, but he could play the long game—he'd done it before in business, and he could do it now, with something a million times more important. So he planned to deliberately give her plenty of space. He'd stick to his usual early-morning routine, leaving before she woke up, and let her spend her days exploring the city before coming home to meet her in the evening. Just like in business, there was a time for action, and a time to be patient. If she missed his presence, started to want more of his company, that could only be a good thing.

For now, he immersed himself in work. After a while, he heard Lisa arrive. She came in and gave him a breakfast burrito and a fresh coffee, but left him to it. She knew he'd emerge later in the morning as usual, ready for conversation.

When he judged it late enough, he pulled out the folder from Rick and found his father's number. Without hesitation, he dialed the number.

After several rings, his father answered. "Wagner."

"Dad, it's Logan," he said.

There was silence for a beat or two, and Logan let it hang in the air, waiting to see how his father would react.

"This is a surprise," he said, stating the obvious.

"Yeah," Logan agreed. "I hear you're in Nevada now."

"I am. Been here a while."

"You okay?"

"Pretty good," he said warily.

"Just you there?"

"Mostly."

Logan could see that the whole conversation would be nothing but bare bones if he didn't take it up a notch. "Listen, I think you're a man who'd prefer to skip the small talk. Let's get to the point."

"Alright," his father said. "What is the point?"

Logan pushed aside his growing disappointment at his father's distance. No "great to hear from you" or "how are you?"—just defensiveness.

"Why did you and Cathleen cut yourselves off from everyone?" he asked. "From your kids?"

"It was better that way."

"Better for who?" Logan asked.

"Did you call to argue, or what?"

"Maybe," he said.

Unexpectedly, his father laughed. "Nice to see a bit of spirit in you. Maybe you do take after me."

That wasn't something Logan would count as a compliment. "I also heard the two of you split up."

His father sighed. "Yeah, a long time ago."

"Did you know she's back in Austen?"

"Damn, really? Huh. I wonder what took her back there after all this time."

"Owen passed," Logan said bluntly. Owen, one of his dad's best friends before he betrayed him.

"Oh." There was a pause, then Logan could hear him blow out a long breath. "Damn shame."

"Yeah. He was a good man."

If his father registered the implication that he didn't live up to the same description, he didn't let on. "Is that why you called? To tell me about Owen?"

"Partly," Logan said. "But I also have a business proposal for you."

"Is that so?" Suddenly his father's tone had changed. "Well, alright. I'm listening."

Chapter 33

C laudia was right. Logan being a millionaire wasn't necessarily a negative thing. In fact, there were some definite positives.

In San Francisco, Avery quickly fell into a routine. Each morning she woke up to find Logan gone, and a simple note on the table wishing her a happy day. She helped herself to breakfast in the beautiful modern white kitchen, and ate looking at the panoramic San Francisco view. She went back to her bedroom with the giant bed and showered in the en suite bathroom, which was like something from a five-star hotel. Then she pulled on her clothes, tucked her phone and wallet into a crossbody bag, and hit the city.

What she'd said to Logan about not doing expensive things was true. She didn't feel the need to pay for touristy activities. She just wanted to walk, and watch, and think. Or not think, really. Just let the events of the last couple of weeks settle. The aunts had called to check on her, having seen her mom in town, and Avery assured them she was doing okay. She could only imagine how it must have gone when her mom came face to face with Owen's fiercely devoted sisters again.

As she explored the city, she enjoyed seeing how many

people had dogs with them as they went about their days, even though it made her miss Ace. She knew he'd be fine though. She'd gotten a message from Claudia on her first night away, lying in the big bed.

What's the deal? Claudia had typed. *Are you two an item again?*

No, Avery had replied. *He's just letting me hang out here while I freak out about my life, lol.*

Hugs. xxx What's it like there?

Ridiculously luxe. I'll send you pics in the morning.

Okay. Ace sends sloppy licks.

She followed with a dog emoji and a red heart, and Avery sent a trio of hearts in return. The next morning she took some photos and sent them through, and Claudia's reaction made her laugh.

Still think the millionaire thing is bad?

It wasn't about that, of course, but with each day she navigated around San Francisco, hopping on and off trams with the tourists and climbing hills with the locals, she started to forget why she'd been so mad at Logan. And the evenings were an increasing reminder of why she'd fallen for him way back when…and now.

She'd tried to tell him she was happy eating at home, but every night he took her to a different restaurant—Vietnamese, French, Japanese—where they were received by a super-solicitous maître d' and ushered to a private table in the perfect spot.

Every night she tried to pay her share for the spectacular food and the first-rate wine, but he refused.

Every night she told him about her day's adventures, laughed at their shared jokes, and learned something new about his life.

Every night she looked at him across the table—his broad shoulders, his square jaw with just a hint of five o'clock shadow, his warm brown eyes focused attentively on her as she talked about her own life—and felt herself wanting more.

Every night they went home to his apartment, he said goodnight with a kiss on her cheek, and she lay in her extravagant bed fighting the urge to get up, go down the hall, and knock on his door.

Neither of them mentioned that passionate night after their dance under the stars, or her confession that she'd fallen for him. At first, she was grateful. But after a while, as he stuck to a friendly, easygoing demeanor, she wondered if he'd changed his mind about the things he'd said, or regretted what they'd done.

In contrast, she was thinking about it more and more. And she knew what she had to do, before she did something she'd regret.

On Thursday night they walked home from their early dinner at an Italian restaurant just a few blocks from the apartment. It was a perfect evening, clear and still, with just an edge of coolness in the air and no sign of the infamous San Francisco fog. At each intersection the street dropped away to one side, and they could see for miles across the city and into the harbor and the headlands beyond. Logan had his hands in his pockets, seeming perfectly relaxed as they walked along, but Avery had been stewing on something. It felt like now was the moment. She took a breath.

"Logan."

He turned to her. "Mmm?"

"I think it's time for me to go home."

"Really?" He stopped in the middle of the sidewalk. "Why?"

"I love being here, and I really appreciate you giving me this time away, but I should get back to my real life."

"There's no rush," he said. "You're welcome to stay. We could bring Ace here if you're worried about him."

The fact that he'd thought of Ace made her like him even more. "No, it's not that. I have to face up to things eventually—deal with my mom, find a new job. I can't keep putting it off."

"It's only been a few days," he pointed out.

"I know, but..." She didn't want to say what she was really thinking. *But this platonic thing we have going on is driving me crazy.* "It's time."

He rubbed the back of his head. "But has it helped, being here?"

"Definitely." That was true. She knew now that even if her mom had reclaimed the house, a new place could give her breathing space, and maybe a fresh start that could lead to something good. Portland was out, and she wouldn't look for work in San Francisco—that was too close to Logan for comfort—but there was a whole country out there for her and Ace to explore.

"Good," he said. "That was all I wanted."

He smiled at her, but she felt something wither inside. That was all he wanted? That wasn't quite *You're the person I want...it's always been you*. Her anger at him had apparently cured him of that.

"I have some things to work on here," he added, "but I'll ask Lisa to organise a flight for you."

"Oh no, that's okay," she said quickly. "I can take a regular flight."

He looked at her as though trying to gauge whether she meant it or not. "I can't fix everything for you," he said. "But let me do the little things I can."

She opened her mouth to argue, then changed her mind. If chartering a jet for her at short notice was a little thing, she could let him do that. And in truth, she would love to have that experience just one more time.

"That's very kind of you," she said. "Thank you."

He nodded, then pulled his phone out of his pocket and started typing. Watching him, she was gripped with a panicky remorse—*no, I don't want to go*—but she tamped it down. She couldn't linger here. She'd already started to think of him as home again, but the feeling didn't seem to be mutual. She had to find her own way home—wherever that might be.

Logan tucked his phone back in his pocket and looked around. The car wouldn't be long—this was the home of Uber after all. He'd suddenly realized that in trying to give Avery space, he'd played it too cool. He couldn't throw their second chance away without a fight. So now he had a plan for one last special moment with her, one chance to turn things around. What use was money if he couldn't use it to wow his childhood sweetheart?

"There's one other thing I'd like to do tonight," he told her. "Do you mind?"

She shook her head. "I guess not. What is it?"

"No big deal," he said. "We'll just grab an Uber, and you'll see."

"Do millionaires even travel by Uber?" she said, laughing.

He grinned. "In San Francisco they do."

"Goes with the permanently casual attire, I guess." She gestured to his jeans and shirt.

"*Smart* casual," he said, feigning offence, and she laughed again.

The car arrived just then, and he held the door open for her before getting in himself. He had a quick, quiet word to the driver, then sat back with her. "Just a short trip."

"Okay," she said, looking intrigued.

As they drove he sent one more message, and a reply quickly came back. Everything was in place.

They drove down the side of AT&T Park and stopped in the parking lot at South Beach Harbor marina, by the yacht club. Logan got out and opened Avery's door for her. She stepped out of the car and looked around, taking everything in. The sun was setting, the marina was a delicate forest of yacht masts, and the Oakland Bay Bridge was lit up like a finely stringed instrument. Behind them, the city was beginning to sparkle against the dusky sky.

"Oh, this is gorgeous," she said.

"Come on," he said. "There's more."

They made their way to the gates and the after-hours security guard let them in. Then Logan led the way along to where his yacht was moored. At thirty meters it wasn't the biggest in the marina by a long way, but he'd bought it years ago and hadn't felt the need to upgrade. His skipper came out to greet them, and Logan shook his hand.

"Thanks for doing this at short notice."

"Any time," he replied, in his distinct Australian accent. Then he turned to Avery and held out his hand. "Trent Holland. Pleasure to meet you."

"Avery Robinson," she replied, receiving what Logan knew would be Trent's usual firm handshake.

"Are you ready to go, Avery?" Trent asked.

She looked at the yacht, with its classic deep blue hull and several stories of crisp white decks, then at Logan, and he nodded encouragingly.

"Sure," she said. "I would *love* to."

They boarded the yacht and Logan took her up to the sundeck. He grabbed a bottle of champagne from a small refrigerator at the back of the deck, and poured them a glass each. Then she sat on a lounger, and he pulled blankets out of a storage hold and tucked one around her before sitting down himself. "It'll be colder out on the water."

Soon Trent had maneuvered them out of port and into the harbor, the engines quiet but powerful. Logan watched as Avery gazed around, drinking in the new perspective of the bay as she sipped her champagne. There was an ocean breeze out here that played with loose strands of her hair, and he had to stop himself from reaching out and tucking them behind her ear.

"You didn't tell me you had a boat," she said, turning and catching him looking at her. "This is like a super yacht or something."

He shrugged. "Not really. But I like it. And it's easier than dealing with sails."

"Yes, that would be a terrible struggle." She laughed.

"Just drink your champagne," he told her with a grin, and she leaned back in her lounger and obeyed.

He watched her taking in the view of harbor and city and passing boats, the fresh night air bringing a charming pink to her cheeks, and hoped that even if she had to leave, she would remember this moment. These days when they had been friends again. Because if they could be friends, after everything that had happened, anything was possible. Maybe she would even decide that it was safe to have fallen for him after all.

Keep moving, he'd always told himself. Do the next thing. Don't look back.

But for once, he only wanted to stay exactly where he was. And he wanted her to stay too.

Chapter 34

The elevator felt extra small as they rode up to Logan's apartment. Avery still had sea air in her lungs, salt in her hair, and the taste of champagne on her tongue. Close beside her, Logan stood quietly, watching the numbers count upward on the elevator panel. This was the last time she'd take this ride up to the top floor, the last night she'd spend in his apartment. Austen awaited, and her mom, and her jobless real life. She sighed, and Logan looked down at her.

"You okay?"

"Yeah. Just…thinking about tomorrow."

He caught her little finger with his own, a tiny gesture of solidarity. "It's not tomorrow yet."

A whisper of heat went through her at his touch, but then he let her go. She resisted the urge to grab his hand, and checked her watch. "Actually, it is." She held her wrist up to show him that it was ten after midnight.

But he shook his head. "It's not tomorrow until the sun comes up."

She laughed, still feeling the fizz of champagne in her veins, and he smiled. Then the elevator stopped and the doors opened. He gestured for her to go first, and she stepped out into the vestibule. The muted lighting and subtle, dark décor made it feel like a refuge—tiny, hushed neutral ground after the brisk breeze of the moonlit bay, and before the territory of his apartment. Behind them, the elevator doors closed.

She turned to him, suddenly not wanting to step back into the real world. "How many hours until the sun comes up?"

He tilted his chin, thinking. "About six, I guess."

"Okay." She nodded. "Six hours."

"Do you have plans for those hours?"

All at once his voice held a different tone…something she thought she recognized. She'd been battling temptation a little more every day, but the more she was tempted, the less likely it seemed that he would do anything different. Just friends, she'd said, and he had agreed, and like the gentleman he was, he'd stuck to his promise.

Until this moment, when his words seemed to give something away. Something he might be battling too.

Or…maybe she was imagining it. Four nights in a row, they'd come through this vestibule, full of good food and great wine, and parted ways in the hallway. Four nights in a row she'd looked over her shoulder as she closed her bedroom door, only to see his back as he went without hesitation into his own room. Even tonight when they'd been out on the harbor, the downtown lights reflecting in jewel-like strips on the water and the stars determined to shine despite the city glow, he'd seemed immune to any sense of romance.

So now she reminded herself of the reason why she'd insisted on the just friends rule—all the *many* reasons—and shook her head.

"No plans." She glanced toward the apartment door, but didn't take a step, wanting to delay the moment when they would say goodnight and go their own ways for the last time, and be just friends forever. If they ever saw each other again. Their lives were so very far apart. "You?"

He shrugged. "After the harbor trip, I'm all out of plans. But I'm open to ideas."

There was that tone again—deeper, with a touch more

gravel than usual. She was sure of it now. *I'm open to ideas.* And they were standing closer, but she couldn't say if he had moved, or if her body had taken her nearer of its own accord. Either way, she could feel his warmth, smell the night air on his clothes, see the way his eyes went a little bedroomy as she met his gaze. And she remembered the last time she'd seen that look, and all the delicious, intoxicating, lustful things they'd gone on to do. And how very, very well he'd done them.

One more night. When she was gone, and this was over, she didn't want to have any regrets. And she was starting to think there was one thing she would regret not doing. Not doing *again*.

She reached out and tucked her little finger around his.

He looked down at the connection, then back at her, and she knew that he got it. Her heart rate picked up and she felt her own eyelids become heavy with desire as they held each other's gaze, each of them weighing the moment, waiting to see what would happen next. Then he slipped his free hand along the side of her neck, letting his fingers tangle in her hair. He dipped his head and laid a slow, soft kiss on her lips, long enough to show her that he meant business, brief enough to leave her wanting more.

So much more.

When he stepped back, a small, regretful noise fell from her lips. She put her free hand to her mouth, but her secret was out. She wanted him. And now he knew it.

He considered her, anticipation and caution dueling in his eyes. "Are we doing this?"

With the warmth of his hand on her skin, and his eyes on hers, she knew that any thoughts of regret, one way or another, were irrelevant. This was happening.

Without a word, she reached out and pressed a finger to the keypad, and the door to his apartment clicked open. She stepped inside, then turned to look back at him. "We're doing this."

In an instant, he was through the door, scooping her up into his arms. Laughter burst out of her, and he strode into the living room, a wickedly determined look in his eye as he carried her effortlessly toward the sofa. She let her shoes fall to the floor as they went, clattering on the hardwood. When he set her down, her laughter trailed off. The lights were off in the apartment, but the city lights sent a glow into the room through the wide windows behind him. His features were in shadow, and in that moment she wondered what the hell she was doing. But then he came closer, and she could see the truth written on his face. He wanted her as much as she wanted him.

He sat beside her on the sofa, then pulled her to him, and she swung a leg over his lap to sit astride him. His body was warm between her legs, and when he ran his hands up her thighs under her three-quarter length dress, she tugged at the fabric and wriggled until it came free, allowing him better access. The full skirt covered them both from the hips down, hiding what his hands were doing, but she felt every move he made. Every slow, teasing touch of his fingers as they found their way closer, closer to the place she wanted them to be, stroking and caressing her skin. He didn't try to kiss her, didn't say anything, just kept looking right at her in the soft city glow as her heart rate climbed and her breath came faster, caught in his gaze. By the time he finally reached her panties, and slipped his fingers under the lace, she was helpless with lust. With a moan, she pressed herself against his hand, and he slid his fingers into the waiting heat. It was exactly what she'd hungered for, known was coming, but the luscious shock of it sent a cry from her lips. Through the blur of her desire, she saw him smile, just a little. As his fingers expertly played between her legs, the intensity rose up, and she slipped over the edge into a sudden, heady climax.

When the peak passed, she let herself fall against him, her arms around his neck, and he held her close as she tried to catch her breath. She didn't want to look him in the eye. Because if she did, he would see how she must look— flushed and disheveled and vulnerable, her almost instant orgasm proof of how helpless she was in his hands. How her body and her heart had conspired to bring her to him again, needy and open. But when he took hold of her and

191

held her away from him a little, she couldn't look away.

He cupped her cheek, considering her. "You're so beautiful, Avery. Do you even know how beautiful you are?"

Her heart jumped in her chest, but she demurred, not knowing what to say. He just smiled, and kissed her. Then he twisted a little to pull his wallet from his pocket, and took out a small foil square.

"You put that in there for tonight?" she asked, suddenly suspicious.

He shrugged. "No, this has been waiting in there since high school."

She stared at him, disbelieving but unsure. "Really?"

"No."

With a groan, she gave him a shove, but he just laughed. And then she took the condom from him, and he stopped laughing. Good. She'd teach him not to tease her. She toyed with the little packet, as though debating whether to get rid of it. He raised one eyebrow, then slipped his hand under her skirt again, going straight to the exquisitely sensitive spot between her legs. She jolted under his hand, a fresh wave of heat rushing through her body. Okay, so maybe she didn't want to teach him anything. Not when he already knew exactly what to do. She went to tear the little packet open, suddenly desperate to get to the next base, but he put a hand over hers.

"Oh no," he said. "Everything got away on me last time, way too fast. Tonight, we're taking it slow."

"Slow?" she said, hearing the frustration in her own voice. "I don't—"

But he tossed the packet onto the coffee table, then lifted her off him and laid her back on the deep sofa. When he pushed her dress up to reveal her black lace underwear, a shiver wafted over her skin.

"Actually, I think you do," he said conversationally, sliding the lace down over her thighs. "And I'm going to prove it."

As he lowered his head between her legs, his breath hot and his tongue insistent, her own head sank back and her eyes closed in surrender. Whatever he was going to prove, using delectably nefarious means, she had no choice but to let him. And she had the feeling she wouldn't regret it.

Eventually, when Logan was sure he had nothing left to prove, and they were both spent and languid, they made it back to Avery's big bed in the room he had left empty for so long. They climbed in and curled up together in the cool, crisp sheets, sighing in appreciation of the luxurious comfort. He had teased another climax from her before retrieving the condom from the table and making love to her on the sofa. And a few other places. In total, it had been the perfect end to an already great night.

Now he trailed his fingers down the side of her neck and around the curve of her breast. "So you liked the yacht," he said.

She squeaked a little as his hand traced the dip of her waist, passing over a ticklish spot. "Of course I liked it."

"That was the plan."

She snorted. "I bet you say that to all the girls."

"Sure, but not everyone gets my most expensive champagne, you know," he said jokingly.

Her smile faded and she sat up, pulling the sheet with her to cover her body. "I didn't sleep with you because of your yacht. Or your expensive champagne."

"That wasn't what I meant," he said, a flare of alarm jolting him out of his blissfully sated state. "I was making a joke."

But she had latched onto the idea and was running with it. "Is that why you took me out there tonight? One last try to impress me with your fancy lifestyle, so I would fall into bed with you again?"

He opened his mouth to deny it, but hesitated. In truth, that kind of *was* what he'd been thinking, but the way she put it made it sound so...tacky. And there was nothing tacky about his feelings for her. He started to protest, but his hesitation had been his undoing.

"Oh my God," she said, holding up a hand to stop

him. "So this whole visit wasn't about helping a friend. It wasn't about us being friends at all. It was about..." She gestured between them, still holding the sheet firmly with her other hand. "This."

"No," he said. "It's not like that. We are friends, you know that. But you also know there's more between us. There always has been. And...is *this* so bad?" He echoed her gesture, trying not to look at the contour of her sweet, soft curves beneath the white sheet. The curves he had been worshipping only a few minutes before. "Because I thought it was pretty damn good. And you seemed to think so too."

Her brows were a V of disapproval, and she made a disgusted noise. "What were you doing all this week...some kind of reverse psychology? Making me think you didn't want me, so I would want you?"

He grabbed at the straw she'd handed him. "You wanted me?"

"No! I didn't say that." She frowned.

"Oh. You *didn't* want me, but you slept with me again anyway."

"What? No. I mean..."

Seeing she was at a disadvantage, he took the chance to steer them away from the reverse psychology angle. It was uncomfortably close to the truth, but she had the knack of making everything he did sound so seedy. "Don't turn me into the bad guy just because you regret sleeping with me again."

"I told you I just wanted a regular hometown guy, but you still thought you could use your money to get me into bed. Is that what you think of me? That my head can be turned with expensive restaurants and luxury yachts and penthouse apartments?"

"Avery, stop. You're twisting everything around."

She grabbed a pillow and held it in front of herself. Her cheeks had been deliciously flushed after their lovemaking, but he knew the high spots of color on them now were a bad sign. She ran a hand through her tousled hair. "I think you should go."

He stayed where he was, determined to drag them back

from the cliff she was forcing them off. "Okay, it's true. You're right. I'm not a regular guy. Regular hometown guys don't achieve the things I have. But that doesn't make me a bad person."

"It does if you keep it a secret, and make me think you're someone you're not."

He reached for her hand, but she gripped the pillow tighter. "I said I was sorry for misleading you before, and I really am, but my intentions weren't bad. I know you're scared to let me in, but I'm still the person I always was." Something else occurred to him. "And Avery, you knew exactly who I was when you decided to fool around with me this time."

"I can't do this," she said, shaking her head. "This is all wrong."

With a sigh, he got out of bed and stood up, not trying to cover his nakedness. He didn't miss the way her eyes swept the length of him before coming to rest somewhere above the fireplace.

"If it's all wrong, tell me you regret sleeping with me. Tell me you wish you hadn't done it." Her eyes stayed fixed on the same spot near the ceiling, and she said nothing. The tiniest flicker of hope remained lit inside him. "I don't think you can."

"Please," she said. "It's for the best. Let it go."

Her words took them back to that morning on the river path, when he'd clumsily told her the same thing. *Let it go.* He would leave for now, but he had no intention of letting her go. Because what she didn't say—couldn't say—had revealed more than what she did say.

He left the room, closing the door quietly behind him.

She didn't regret it.

Chapter 35

The flight back to Oregon the next day was just as luxurious as the flight to San Francisco, but despite everything, Avery couldn't help feeling that it wasn't so much fun alone. She'd thought Logan might go into work that morning to avoid seeing her before she left—in fact, after the way their night had ended, she'd hoped he would—but he'd stayed home to say goodbye. During breakfast they were scrupulously polite with each other, and she tried not to look into the living room, where they had done inappropriate things on nearly every surface. Then he took her down in the elevator to the parking garage. The same driver was waiting for her in his big black car.

"So," Logan had said as they stood by the car. "Good luck with everything."

She sighed. "Thanks."

He stepped closer, unsmiling, studying her as though there was some secret only he knew. Then he took her face in his hands. She considered pushing him away, but a hot shockwave went through her as he buried his fingers in her hair, his thumbs brushing her neck. He tipped his forehead toward hers, and she fought to prevent her lips parting in expectation. Four days of being without him, four nights of intimate candlelit dinners and chaste goodnights in the hallway, and then she'd given in to one night of abandonment. Well, maybe *given in* wasn't an accurate description, considering her part in proceedings. The strength of her freak-out afterward had matched the intensity of her desire, and her overwhelming need for him. The fact that he had seen right through her only made it worse. But now, in a cold concrete basement parking garage, she was burning up for him again. Her chest rose and fell with her rapid breathing, her heart raced, and even though she'd told him to let it go, all the contrary part of her wanted was for him to start the kiss she knew must surely be coming.

And then he diverted and laid a slow, tender kiss on her cheek.

"Have a safe trip," he murmured in her ear before stepping away, leaving her dizzy with desire and confusion.

Then he opened the car door, and there was nothing for her to do but get in and be driven away, wondering what on earth had just happened.

When they arrived at the airport, the driver escorted her right to the plane, carrying her bag. And although the flight attendant was very nice, and the view from the window was amazing, and she knew she was all kinds of lucky to be traveling in such extreme luxury...it just wasn't the same.

When they reached the municipal airport, she was relieved to find Claudia waiting for her in the terminal. Logan had wanted to arrange for a car to drive her back to Austen, but she hadn't wanted to turn up in something conspicuous. And Claudia was desperate to hear about the trip, so she'd been more than happy to pick Avery up.

"Avery," Claudia breathed now, her eyes wide as she looked through the terminal window at the jet. "Are you freaking kidding me?"

Avery looked back at the plane, glistening white in the sun. "I know. It's nuts."

"How did some kid from Austen end up with his own plane?"

"Oh, it's not his," Avery said, setting her bag on its

wheels. "It's just a charter."

Claudia laughed. "Would you listen to yourself? It's just a charter. How fancy have you gotten already?"

"Claude, stop. I haven't."

But Claudia gave her a gentle push. "I'm just teasing. You can fly charter any time you like."

"Okay, that's enough," Avery said, laughing. "Where's my pup?"

They went out of the terminal and into the parking lot. Straight away Avery could see Claudia's car, with all the windows rolled halfway down and Ace straining out of one of them. When he saw Avery, he boomed out a giant bark of welcome and started wiggling so hard Claudia's little car was rocking.

They both laughed. "He was fine, but I think he's missed you," Claudia said.

"I missed him too."

Claudia opened the car door and he sprang out, doing his best to leap into Avery's arms. She staggered slightly, then ducked down to give him a hug and be anointed with enthusiastic slobbery kisses.

"I know, buddy," she said. "I know. Did Aunt Claudia take good care of you? I think she did. Yes, I do."

After a little more loving, they finally got on the road back to Austen, Ace happily sitting in the back seat. Every now and then he came forward and rested his head on Avery's shoulder, just to show his pleasure at having her back.

"Thanks for coming to get me," Avery said to Claudia. "I know you're busy with the store."

"No problem," Claudia said. "My part-timer Prue came in to cover for me. Anyway, I knew if I had you trapped in my car you'd have to tell me *everything* about your time away with Logan."

"You're even more devious than I realized," Avery told her.

"You have no idea," she said, raising a wicked eyebrow. "The photos were unbelievable, but now I want the gossip directly."

"Okay." Avery pushed her sunglasses higher on her

nose. "So I spent the days looking around San Francisco while he was at work, and then we had dinner at a different fancy restaurant every night. And on the last night he took me out on his boat. Well, not just a boat—more like a super yacht. He had a skipper and everything, and we drank champagne, and sailed under the Oakland Bay Bridge...it was heavenly."

"It sounds blissful. And after the super yacht?"

Avery fiddled with the strap of her purse. "We went home."

"And?"

"And, uh, we...you know."

"I do know!" Claudia said triumphantly. "Although why you waited so long is beyond me. All those nights you could have put to good use."

"Well, we were supposed to be just friends. I made him promise before we went."

"Just friends?" Claudia briefly took her eyes off the road to send a frown Avery's way.

"We kind of agreed on it at the start." She shrugged.

"Okay, let me get this straight." Claudia lifted a finger from the steering wheel, holding it up. "You were staying in a spectacular penthouse apartment in one of the most ritzy neighborhoods in the city, with a tall, dark, and handsome millionaire, being wined and dined every night. On the very last night, you finally let him in again. And it was amazing."

"I never said that," Avery protested.

"You didn't have to—your face gave it away. And now you're back here without him...why?"

"I kind of...I had second thoughts, I guess." She couldn't even begin to explain that supercharged kiss in the parking garage.

"You've seen him, right? You know how hot he is."

"Uggghh," Avery said, throwing her head back against the seat. "I know." Ace took the opportunity to slather her with a kiss of his own, and she pushed him gently away. "But I can't go down that path with him again."

Claudia clucked her tongue in disgust. "I don't even

know what to say to you right now. That would be a tragic waste of a perfectly good millionaire."

Avery laughed out loud. "Well, when you put it that way."

"You know I'm right," Claudia said, grinning. Then she looked over at Avery again. "Seriously though. You two. You obviously still have the old chemistry. I mean, we all saw you dancing at the Jane Austen festival. And I know what you did after that."

Avery felt her cheeks heat. "Yeah, there's chemistry. Or there was last night, anyway. Before that, he totally backed off while I was staying there."

"Could that be because you yourself made him promise to only be friends? And because you were all mad at him again, for being successful and wealthy?"

"You know that's not why I was mad! But...yeah, maybe," she conceded.

"And are you still angry at him, after a night that was so good it scared the hell out of you? Or are you ready to admit that you want him after all?"

Logan's words echoed in her head. *I know you're scared to let me in.* "You're ruthless," she said.

Claudia smiled. "Ruthless, but right. And you know it."

"Argh! Fine. I want him, okay? But it's so damn *complicated*. And anyway, I think I messed it up by pushing him away again."

"It'll work out," Claudia assured her. "Just you wait. He'll be back, and you'll see."

"Okay. We'll see." Avery wasn't sure if she wanted Claudia to be right or not. But from the disaster area of their past, it did seem like there had been the possibility of something truly good.

They drove on for a while, then Avery decided she'd better ask the question that was hanging over her. "Have you seen my mom?"

"Oh. Yes." Claudia looked across at her again, her brows knitted. "She's been walking around town like she never left."

"That's what she was like when I found her in the house," Avery said. "I don't get it. I mean, I don't want people to be mean to her or anything, but it seems so tone deaf."

"Maybe she thinks so much time has gone by that people will have forgotten."

"Maybe." Avery thought for a moment. "And maybe they have. People move on." Like Valerie had said, everything blows over eventually.

"They do," Claudia said. "But it doesn't undo what she and Jeff did to you and Owen and Logan. Even Patrick is still cut up about it."

"I think he found it really hard. The three of them had been so close."

"I wonder why your dad never got a divorce," Claudia mused. "Did he ever say anything to you about it?"

"No. That's why the whole thing with the house was such a shock. I've made an appointment with the lawyer for next week—hopefully I can figure something out."

Claudia thought for a moment. "Your dad was always a loyal kind of person."

Avery nodded. "He was. Maybe he just never stopped loving her, despite everything."

"Oh, God." Claudia put a hand to her chest. "My heart."

"Yeah. Mine too." Avery could hardly bear to think about it.

They were drawing closer to Austen now, and she could feel her own chest getting tighter with every mile. As they crossed the bridge into town, the tension turned into a brick behind her ribs. "Hey, Claude. Can I...can I just hang with you for a while when we get back? At the store?"

"Sure," Claudia said. "But come back to my place and have lunch if you want. Prue can hold the fort for a bit longer."

"Thanks. That would be great."

She'd told Logan that she couldn't keep putting off dealing with things, but now that she was back, she just needed to put it off a *little* longer. Just long enough to catch her breath. Because she'd need all her inner strength for the upcoming conversation with her mom. After all this time, she was going to get the answers she needed.

Chapter 36

After a very nice lunch, which Avery managed to drag out way longer than she should have, Claudia dropped her outside her house. Well, her mom's house. After wishing her luck, Claudia drove away, headed back to Beach & Bloom. Avery felt like running after the car.

Instead, she squared her shoulders and went up the path with Ace. She unlocked the door and lifted her case over the threshold, setting it carefully inside so she didn't scratch the floors with the one slightly wobbly wheel. Ace skittered around, excited that they were both home again.

Then they heard a noise in the kitchen. Her mom was home. Okay, might as well get on with it. They made their way down the hall.

In the doorway, Ace came to a halt, his hackles rising.

Avery gasped, her heart in her throat.

Jeff Wagner was in her kitchen.

Buck. Naked.

"What are you *doing*?" she hissed.

The shock on his face would have been funny in a different situation. Caught off guard, he slapped his hands over his front, trying to cover the relevant bits and pieces.

"Oh, for the love of—" She held up her hand to obscure his bottom half. "Why are you in my kitchen, *naked*?"

He ducked down slightly so that his modesty was protected by the kitchen island. "I thought you were Cathleen."

"It's the middle of the afternoon!" She had no idea why that was the point she'd seized on first. "Why would you be lurking here with no clothes on, waiting for my mom? You broke up years ago. You left her for another woman!"

"I'm not lurking," he said. "I—"

Ace was making his way slowly toward him, his lip curled and a rumbling growl sounding in his throat. Jeff inched farther along behind the island, clutching himself.

"Tell your dog to back off," he said, his voice rising to a thin squeak as Ace gave a low warning bark.

She shook her head. "First you tell me why you're here."

"I'm not waiting for Cathleen," he said hurriedly. "She's upstairs taking a nap." He reached the corner of the island nearest the back door, keeping his eyes fixed on Ace. "I just came down for something to eat."

"Taking a nap?" With that, Avery knew what was going on. "So you're saying this is an afternoon delight scenario."

"If you like."

"Actually, Jeff, I don't like," she said. "I don't like it at all."

He reached for a floral dish towel that was hanging nearby and held it in a rectangle in front of himself. Emboldened by having a little more protection, he stood up straighter and looked her in the eye. The bright, flowery cloth was weirdly at odds with his graying chest hair, but she couldn't help noticing that he was in good shape for his age.

"Cathleen invited me to come over," he said. "So if you'll excuse me..." He nodded toward the door behind her that lead back out of the kitchen.

A hot rage was simmering in her guts at his brazenness. She walked over to the back door and opened it wide. "And now *I'm* inviting you to leave."

"What?" He laughed. "I don't think so."

"You're excused," she said, gesturing to the door. Then she walked back to the kitchen table, giving him room to pass.

"Oh, come on," he said. "I'm not—"

"Ace," she said, clapping her hands. "Go get him!"

Ace obliged, lunging toward Jeff with an enthusiastic bark. Uttering a sharp curse, he turned and made a break for it. Avery averted her eyes as he hotfooted it out the back door, the dish towel fluttering at his groin and Ace in eager pursuit.

"Ace!" she called sternly. "Come!"

Fortunately, he decided to listen and come back to her side. The last thing she needed was a lawsuit brought on by an unfortunate personal injury.

With Jeff out and Ace in, she shut the door and locked it, then went and locked the front door too. Then she put Ace in his bed in the living room and went straight upstairs. Her mom was just coming out of the master bedroom clutching a robe around herself, her hair mussed up.

"Avery! What's going on?"

Avery strode past her without a word. In the bedroom, she gathered up Jeff's clothes, then flung open the window and threw them out into the backyard with as much force as she could muster. It was more than he deserved—she'd seriously considered leaving him out there to fend for himself.

"Avery!" her mom said, grabbing up a black sock that had escaped. "What on earth are you doing?"

"What are *you* doing, Mom? How could you hook up with Jeff Wagner again? How could you bring him here, into our house? This is Dad's room!" She gestured to the bed, a tangle of sheets and blankets evidence of what they'd been doing. "Dad's bed!"

"Please, honey, calm down." Her mom reached for her, but Avery flinched away.

"Mom. We have to talk. About everything." They could hear Jeff yelling something from outside, but Avery closed the window. "Come and meet me in the living room."

She nodded, subdued. "Okay."

Avery went back downstairs, her heart still pounding, and a few minutes later her mom joined her in the living room. She was dressed, and she'd tidied her hair. It still felt jarring to look at her, suddenly so much older—she'd walked away not quite forty and come back almost fifty. Avery wondered if it was equally weird for her mom—she'd left a behind a teenage daughter and come back to a grown woman.

They sat in separate armchairs, looking at each other. There was no sound from outside—Jeff must have given up and gone away. Finally, Avery took a breath.

"I just want to know why, Mom." She hesitated, then started again. "Not why you cheated on Dad. I don't want to know any of that stuff. But why did you just disappear like that? Didn't you ever think about me? Wonder how I was? Worry about me?"

Her mom pressed her fingers against her forehead and dragged in a shuddery breath. "All the time. *All* the time."

"So why didn't you call, or email, or message me? There was nothing. I didn't even know if you were alive or dead."

"I'm sorry," she said. "I didn't know what to say. And the longer I let it drag on, the more impossible it felt."

"You could have come back after you split up."

"Oh, honey." She shook her head. "That only made it so much worse. I broke up our family, and for what? Some grand love affair that turned out to be an illusion. There was no way I could come back and face you after that. Your dad. Everyone."

"So you were too proud to come back," Avery said flatly.

"No," her mom replied. "I was too ashamed."

Despite that sad confession, Avery couldn't feel any sympathy for her mother. "And yet you managed to overcome that shame enough to hurry back and claim the house once Dad was dead."

"I'll be honest," she said. "That was a real shock. And

sure, I'm not doing great financially. But the house isn't the reason I came back. I knew then that I *had* to come and see you."

"Right." Avery rolled her eyes. "And the house was just a nice bonus. Can you imagine what it was like for me, to walk in and find you here acting like nothing had happened?"

"I guess I didn't know how to begin again. I'm sorry, Avery."

"I'm sorry too. I'm sorry I spent all those years missing you, when you couldn't even pick up a phone and call me. And I'm sorry that one of the first things you did when you got back here was hook up with Jeff Wagner."

She shrugged and gave Avery a sad smile. "I guess he's my weakness. We all have them."

Her words hit home. Yes, Avery had a weakness. And he was a Wagner too. But that wasn't the same. Would never be the same.

"Are you going to keep seeing him?"

"Truthfully?" Her mom threw up her hands in a helpless gesture. "I don't know."

Avery didn't know what to say to that. It wasn't like she'd expected her mother to be perfect, but this was a twist she hadn't bargained for. Now that her mom was here, very much alive even if still causing trouble, Avery would just have to figure out what to do with their imperfect, messy reality. She looked at Ace asleep in his bed in the corner, twitching as he dreamed of catching cats, or expensive boots, or naked interlopers. Half of her was glad her dad wasn't here to see this. The other half wished he was, so that she could run into his steady arms for comfort.

"Avery?" her mom said tentatively, leaning forward in her chair. "Can we start again? Somehow?"

Unlike the first time she'd asked, the question seemed to come from somewhere genuine. Somewhere unsure but hopeful.

Avery threw up her hands, a mirror image of her mom's earlier gesture. "I don't know how either. But maybe."

As relief lightened her mom's face, Avery felt herself

relent a little more. She didn't know where they would go from here, but maybe the truth was a start.

Chapter 37

S even o'clock on Friday night, and Logan was sitting alone in his living room. On Friday nights he would usually be at a local bar, a regular get-together with a group of friends from his earliest days in the Bay Area. But he hadn't felt like it tonight.

He turned his glass of whisky slowly in his hands as he looked at the expansive, glittery view Avery had loved so much. It felt all wrong here without her. Especially after what they'd done on this very sofa...and in a number of other places. When he came home from work that day he'd gone down the hall to Avery's room—as he thought of it now—and stood in the doorway wondering what she was doing at that moment back in Austen. She'd still been determined to leave, after their night had gone from unbelievably good to unbelievably bad, and he couldn't stand in her way. Whatever happened between the two of them, he wanted her to figure things out with her mom, find her own way forward. Hopefully he'd be able to convince her that he should be a part of that.

As for him, he was still getting to grips with his father. Jeff had immediately been interested in his proposal for the land. Logan had already gone ahead and instructed his engineers and architects to draw up plans for the project, and his project manager had started talking to the county about permits, but he was still working out the best way to approach it from a legal standpoint. He didn't want to shortchange his own father, but as their discussions had continued that week, it became obvious that Jeff was in precarious financial circumstances and would press for the greatest advantage possible. Logan couldn't fault that—it was only what he would have done himself—but it made him realize that it wouldn't be a feel-good family project. And when Jeff mentioned a lawyer in Pahrump it confirmed that this was business, through and through.

But business was what Logan did best. And it would be worth it. He didn't want to mention it to anyone in Austen until everything was confirmed though.

His phone dinged, and he smiled when he checked the screen. Avery. She'd texted earlier to say thanks for the flight, and that she was having lunch at Claudia's place, but he hadn't heard anything since. He'd been hoping things were going well with her mom.

But when he read the message, his smile faded.

Came home to find Jeff in the kitchen. Naked. Looking for postcoital snack. He and Mom have hooked up again.

He slumped back in his chair, blowing out a breath, and ran a hand through his hair. What was his father playing at now? He hadn't mentioned anything to Logan about going to Austen. And the thought of Avery walking in on that made him sick to his stomach.

I'm so sorry, he wrote back. *I could kill him. I'll come back and sort it out.*

There was a long silence before his phone dinged again.

No, that's okay. Mom and I are talking.

Well, that was something. But their conversation would be all the more difficult with this added complication. He never would have seen that coming.

Is he still there? he texted back.

No. I kicked him out without his clothes. Ace helped me.

At that, Logan laughed out loud in surprise and admiration. What a woman.

So Jeff Wagner is wandering Austen in the buff?

Sadly no. I took pity on him and threw his clothes out the window. Better than leaving him out there with only a dish towel for cover.

He was still laughing as he replied, *Probably for the best.* Then he added, *Are you alright?*

I'm fine.

Okay. Call me if you need to talk. x

She replied with a thumbs-up emoji, but nothing more. It didn't exactly fill him with confidence. It seemed like they were still talking—or texting, at least—but he had a long way to go to win her over.

He drummed his fingers on the arm of the chair for a while, then got up and went along to his room and changed into running gear. He suddenly felt adrift, and there were two sure ways to ground himself—work or exercise. And he didn't feel like working tonight.

He went down to street level and out of the building through the marble-floored foyer. He paused for a moment by one of the ornate columns outside the main doors, holding onto it as he did some quick stretches. Then he put in his ear buds, turned on some music, and set off. Once he reached a pace that was registering as ideal on his smartwatch, he settled in, navigating the familiar streets with ease.

About an hour later, he circled back to his building, feeling like he'd burned off some of his tension. He noticed someone waiting outside the building, hovering between two of the columns. He held himself ready as he approached. Although he was confident in his ability to defend himself, you could never be too careful.

Carter Cox stepped out of the shadows, wearing a baseball cap.

"I've been waiting for you," he intoned.

"This isn't a spy novel, you know," Logan told him as he took his ear buds out. "You could have called me, or emailed."

For the briefest moment Carter looked sheepish, but he regrouped. "I was in town for a TV thing anyway," he said.

"With Karen," Logan said.

"Uh…yeah."

"The mother of your child, who you were going to dump for Avery, after you dumped Avery for her."

Carter's face was satisfyingly red under the cap. "This isn't about them, okay?"

"Alright," Logan said, swiping sweat from his brow. "So what's up?"

"I'm here to let you know that there'll be a story on Statewide Scoop tomorrow night about developers planning projects on pristine land. Including your proposed development on the Austen River."

Logan frowned. "How did you know about that?"

"Good journalism," he said smugly.

"You're not a journalist," Logan pointed out. "You're a talking head."

"I'm a *presenter*," Carter snapped. "I contribute to the stories too."

"Okay, fine. But why me? There are plenty of more significant developments going on."

He shrugged. "To start with, I was just curious about you. I thought I recognized your face from somewhere, and when Avery said your name I had a head start. It didn't take much digging to find you, and look into what your business is doing."

"Nothing I'm doing is illegal."

"Illegal, no. But if you cared about Avery, you wouldn't desecrate the hometown she loves."

"Desecrate? I'm trying to help the town, not harm it."

"Are you sure that's how she'll see it? I was with her long enough to know how she feels about that backwater. Destroying the wild country in her backyard is not the way to her heart."

Logan had the unpleasant feeling that the balance of their conversation had shifted in Carter's favor. "I thought you said this wasn't about Avery."

"Well, maybe it is."

Logan wanted to knock the sly look off his face with a sharp uppercut. "You don't care about her," he said. "Why

212

would you get in the way of her finding happiness with someone else?"

"First off, I do care about her. And second, you're not just someone else. You already left her once. Your father screwed up her family. I might have let her down, but you're not the right person to make her happy either—no matter how much money you have."

Logan's jaw tensed as he heard the echo of Avery's doubts in Carter's words. "How do you know all that?"

"You're not the only one who hires private investigators," Carter said. He started to go, then turned back. "Someone from the show will be in touch to get your comments on the report. You might want to think about what you'll say to them." He smiled. "And what you'll say to Avery after she watches it too."

Then he tipped his hat and walked away, just like the villain in a spy novel.

Chapter 38

Higher hopes, lower expectations. Avery was trying to be realistic as she and her mom began navigating their way through the early stages of getting to know each other again.

They'd had a late breakfast together that morning, sharing some details of their lives. Cathleen had told Avery about her job with the cruise line, and that she'd been able to get a few weeks off by swapping around shifts with her friends. Avery had glossed over her breakup with Carter and the loss of her job—luckily her mom hadn't heard about the fateful broadcast—and focused on possibilities for the future.

Neither of them mentioned the house, but Avery hadn't forgotten. She would be discussing it with the lawyer at their meeting next week. She figured it was better to be fully informed before bringing the subject up again.

After breakfast, she suggested they go outside to pull weeds. Working on something practical together, out in the fresh air, seemed like a good way to ease the lingering tension, and take her mind off Logan. Plus, her dad would hate it if he knew his garden was being neglected. Ace joined them as they retrieved gardening tools from the shed, then nosed around where they were working before wandering off to lie in the sun.

After a while her mom looked at her watch. "Oh, I'd better get moving," she said, standing up. "I have a few things to do in town today."

Avery looked up from her spot by a cotoneaster shrub smothered in white flowers. It was one of the plants her dad had chosen specifically to attract hummingbirds to the garden. "Okay. Do you want me to come with you?"

"No, no, you enjoy the sun here. I won't be too long."

Avery sat back on her heels and watched as her mom went into the house, brushing off her hands. She had a pretty good idea where she was going. They hadn't mentioned Jeff that morning, but yesterday Claudia had texted to say she'd seen him going into the A-OK Motel at the far end of town. With a sigh, she went back to her weeding, and before long she heard her mom's car start up and drive away.

By four thirty, she still hadn't returned. Avery wasn't surprised, but she couldn't help being disappointed. She'd been busy though. She'd spent the first part of the afternoon on her laptop, researching big-city radio networks and browsing employment websites. But she'd soon realized that she wasn't sure she wanted to continue in radio. She'd worked toward that dream for so long, but it had turned out to be better in her imagination than in reality. Still, she'd achieved it, and now she could tick it off her list and move on to the next thing. But what would the next thing be? Most of all, she'd like to do something that was her very own—no more corporate masters—while still using her broadcasting skills.

Podcasting, maybe? She looked down at Ace, who was keeping her company as usual. A dog-related podcast of some kind? A little spark lit up inside her, and she switched over to a new document to make notes. The ideas started to flow as fast as she could type, and the more she thought about it, the more excited she felt.

And alongside that, she found herself itching to share her ideas with someone. Specifically, and inconveniently, that someone was Logan. He'd get it—he'd understand the attraction of building something from nothing, because he'd been there.

But that wasn't the only reason she found herself wanting to talk to him. Leaving him behind in San Francisco had been even more of a wrench than she'd expected, and she couldn't get him out of her mind. Couldn't stop remembering how it felt to be in his arms. Annoyingly, he and Claudia were right—she was scared. Scared to take the risk of letting him in again. Of falling for the man he was now—so different from his younger self, yet just the same in the ways that really counted.

Despite everything in their past, they'd been finding their way to somewhere good. And although the shock of her mom and Jeff hooking up again had totally thrown her, did it need to get in the way of her and Logan? Would she let their parents ruin things all over again?

She stared at her notes on the screen, the tentative beginnings of something that might be her future. A future that she wanted to share with Logan, no matter how much the thought scared her. She could only hope some part of him felt the same, and that she hadn't killed their second chance by pushing him away yet again.

At that moment, her phone rang. With a sudden burst of expectation, she picked it up, thinking it might be him. But it was Carter's name on the screen. For a second or two she toyed with the idea of ignoring the call and dealing with him later—after his visit a couple of weeks ago she didn't feel inclined to speak to him. Then again, putting things off hadn't gone so well for her yesterday. She accepted the call.

"Hello."

"Avery. It's Carter."

"Yeah, I know," she said. "What do you want?"

"How are you?" he said thoughtfully, as though their conversation was between two dear friends who actually liked one another.

"Carter, seriously? Can you just get to the point? If you have one."

"I do," he said, not sounding even slightly discouraged. "So I got a job as a presenter on a current affairs show called Statewide Scoop."

"Yay, congratulations."

He ignored her tone. "We have a report tonight about something happening in Austen that you should probably know about."

Tuning in to watch Carter do his thing on TV was not her idea of a fun Saturday night. "Why don't you just tell me about it now?" she said. "Unless you're so desperate for ratings that you're calling everyone to beg them to watch you."

"No," he said indignantly. "Our ratings have been great so far. For a new show."

"Good for you. So what's happening in town that I should know about?"

"You'll have to watch and see," he insisted.

She'd play his game. "I might have other plans."

"Listen, Avery, I'm telling you this because it's important, okay? You always used to talk about how much you love your hometown. I'm just trying to do the right thing here."

She sighed. "Ugh, fine. I'll watch your show." Trust him to be so dramatic, just to get some attention.

"Good. Tune in at seven." There was a pause, then he asked again, "How are you?"

The overly concerned note in his voice grated on her. It came across like he was feeling sorry for her because he'd already made his leap into TV, while she was still hanging around at home.

"I'm doing great," she said, a level of enthusiasm in her voice that she would have had to force if he'd called her twenty-four hours ago. "I'm loving my freedom, really enjoying having a break here and catching up with friends. And I'm planning something exciting for my next work project."

"Oh, well...good. That's good to hear."

Time to wrap this up before he wanted to get deep and meaningful. "Alright, so thanks for the heads up. I have to go now. Bye."

"Bye," he said, and she quickly ended the call.

Maybe she should have asked how Karen and the baby were, but she just couldn't bring herself to open that can of worms. In any case, she could probably keep up with that situation online. Karen had always been an open book, using social media to her best advantage. Maybe that was why she'd had no compunction about revealing their affair and her pregnancy over the airwaves, knowing it would be all over the internet within minutes. The bigger the splash, the bigger the audience.

Anyway, none of that was her concern now. She had a new start to get on with.

Feeling hungry all of a sudden, she checked the time and realized it was getting close to dinnertime. Looked like it would just be her tonight—so much for her and her mom getting to know each other again. Well, that was fine. She'd just call Patrick and ask if she could order something to go, then she'd be back here in time for Carter's show. And after that she would call Logan, and see if their second chance had withstood her second thoughts.

Chapter 39

A very picked up the remote and switched off the TV, cutting Carter's farewell spiel off midsentence. She understood now why he'd been so insistent about her watching the show, but she wasn't going to listen to him for a moment longer than necessary.

She stood up and paced the living room floor, too antsy to stay still. So Logan had one other secret up his sleeve. A luxury development on the Austen River—right opposite her house. And planning permission was already underway. She closed her eyes, imagining how it would go. Trees gone, land cleared, the roar of machinery...construction and concrete and chaos. And then multistory structures staring them down from the other side of the river, where once there had been wild Oregon forest.

No wonder he'd kept it a secret. He must have known that she'd be against this. That no one in this town—a place where the last parcels of riverside land had been bought by the council for protection and preservation—would want to see it happen. She bit her lip as she paced, trying to think. Surely he didn't need to do this. He had bigger fish to fry. If they talked about it, he'd understand that the project couldn't go ahead.

Wouldn't he?

Or had he kept it secret for good reason?

She grabbed up her phone and called him, but it went to voicemail. She hung up without leaving a message.

"Oh, sure," she said to Ace, who was curled up in his bed. "*Now* he's unavailable." The dog opened one eye at the sound of her voice, then went back to sleep. "Of course *you'd* be on his side," she told him.

Saturday night—Logan was probably out in San Francisco at some fancy function for millionaires under thirty. A self-made mavericks meetup.

Or maybe he was avoiding her.

She went along to the kitchen and made coffee, then took her mug to the table and sat down, thinking. She could talk to Mayor Whittaker, see what he thought. Maybe something could be done. A legal challenge maybe, although that would be costly, and she guessed Logan would have access to the best lawyers.

Not that it would come to that. Logan was a reasonable guy. He'd wanted to prove he cared about the town by joining her at the beach cleanup. And despite his worries, he'd been accepted back by everyone—embraced even, after his arresting performance as Mr. Darcy. Well, everyone except Ellen maybe. Here was the chance for him to prove, once and for all, that he'd put his money where his mouth was.

Just as she took the first sip of her coffee, there was a knock at the door. Probably a disgruntled local wanting to complain about Logan's plans. Well, she couldn't blame them. She sighed and put her coffee down, and went to see who it was.

Avery's face when she opened the door told Logan everything he needed to know. She'd seen the report, and she wasn't happy. Carter had been right.

"Hey," he said cautiously. "Uh...I missed a call from you."

Ace came to the door, his tail lashing around in happy

welcome, but Avery put a hand on his back with a quiet admonishment and he sat down next to her. "How did you get here so quickly?" she asked. "Have you upgraded from jet travel to some kind of millionaire teleportation now?"

The sarcasm in her tone bit hard. "No. I got to town a few hours ago."

"I thought you had things to do in San Francisco," she said, her eyes narrowing.

"Well, I was worried about you, with this situation with my father..."

"Really." She leaned against the door jamb, her arms folded across her chest. "Not some other reason? Something else you forgot to tell me about?"

There was no getting around it. She was pissed. Time to fall on his sword. "You watched the report about the development."

"I did. It was very interesting. So interesting, in fact, that I can't understand why you didn't tell me about it in the *five days* I was with you in San Francisco."

This really wasn't going well. "Did Carter tell you about it?"

"I don't think that's relevant. But yes, he told me I should watch the show."

Logan felt his fists clenching involuntarily. "Of course he did. He was the one who set the whole report in motion."

"Look," she said sharply. "I don't care if it was Carter or the Pillsbury freaking Doughboy. The point is, this development can't go ahead. That land is my backyard. It's the whole town's backyard. It's a precious, irreplaceable ecosystem, and destroying it for some hulking development would completely change Austen forever. You know that."

"It wouldn't be *hulking*," he said. "It would be very sympathetic to the environment."

"Okay, however you want to justify it," she said.

"The aim is to give the town an attractive new asset," he said, adopting his best business tone in an effort to sound reasonable and not argumentative. "Something that will benefit everyone. It would bring in more visitors and boost local businesses. Barbara said that more tourists are starting to come to town, and that's making a difference to the local economy. Look how many people came to the Jane Austen festival. More accommodation like this would be a big boost to the community."

She scoffed. "Oh, come on. Any fool can see that you're doing this for profit. Even Carter."

He laughed at the implication that Carter was a fool, but immediately wished he hadn't as her expression darkened. "There's more to it than that. I told you."

"Yeah, I heard you." She tipped her head, seemingly considering something. "That land doesn't belong to you any more than this house belongs to me. How are you getting around that?" She paused, and he could see the moment when everything fell into place. "Ohhh. *That's* why you hired a private investigator to find him."

This was getting more complicated than he'd envisaged. But he'd never stumbled at this stage of a project before, and he wasn't about to start now.

"I don't get why you're even messing around with a project like this," she continued before he could say anything. "If you're such a big hitter, this should be too small for you to even bother with."

The way she said "big hitter" left him in no doubt that it wasn't a compliment.

"The focus would be on quality, not quantity," he said.

"I have a suggestion," she said, as though he hadn't spoken. "I think the whole thing is a way for you to get back at your father. Prove to him that you can take his land, and make something better than he ever could. Show the town that you're the good Wagner. But you picked a crappy way of going about it."

As her words sank in, he realized that she was close to something he hadn't even seen himself. Close, but not quite correct.

"I didn't want to get back at him," he muttered.

"What?" she said. "What then?"

He made a vaguely dismissive gesture, not wanting to say out loud what he'd only just admitted to himself. She stared at him, frustration on her face, but then her expression changed.

"Oh," she said softly. "I see it now. You wanted a way to *get* him back."

He shook his head. "No."

"That land was your only physical connection to Jeff. The only excuse you'd have for reaching out to him."

"I didn't need an excuse. I could have gotten in touch with him any time."

"But this way, if he said no, you could call it business and move on. He'd never need to know the real reason you reached out."

He stared at her, processing her all-too-real words in real time. It was impressive, and kind of scary, that even ten years on she still understood him well enough to figure out things he couldn't put together himself. Things he didn't want to accept.

"Is he here?" he asked.

"No." She shook her head. "I think he and Mom are at the A-OK. I'm not waiting up for them." She took a step back into the house.

"Okay. I'll go then." He waited for her to suggest otherwise, but she didn't. "I'm sorry about him doing that, by the way. I honestly never thought that would happen."

"I pretty much hate it," she said. Then she shrugged. "But it takes two."

Her hand was on the door handle. He took the hint. He nodded, then turned and crossed the porch and started down the steps.

Halfway down, he turned and looked back. She and Ace were framed in the doorway, lit from above by the porch light. He stared at them for a moment, imprinting the image on his memory. Then he walked down the steps and away, yet again. This time, he had no idea if he'd ever be back. Second chances were a dime a dozen, even for guys who didn't qualify as romantic heroes. But third chances really were the stuff of fiction.

Avery closed the front door, then took Ace into the backyard for a before-bed bathroom stop. She sat on the porch swing in the sweet night air and watched him roam the big yard, checking and rechecking all his usual spots. Luckily there was no sign of the cat.

Over the fence, the river ran smoothly on its winding path to the sea, about a mile downstream. The untamed country on the opposite shore sat silently in the moonlight. It looked constant and enduring, but now she knew it was vulnerable too. It was unthinkable that the danger would come from Logan.

After a while, Ace came and sat next to her, looking out at the view that was as familiar as her own face in the mirror. Then a mosquito buzzed around her ear, and she flapped it away.

"Let's go to bed," she said to the dog. "Nothing good will come from sitting here thinking about him anyway."

As they went inside, she remembered their conversation at the beach cleanup, when she'd talked about pieces of bad luck coming in threes. She'd never imagined that Logan himself would bring the fourth.

Chapter 40

The A-OK Motel looked exactly as it had when Logan was a kid—a row of eight A-frame cabins, straight out of the sixties. The office building was a bigger A-frame structure, with "A-OK" in huge neon-lit letters at the peak of the triangle. It was the kind of place Instagrammers would go wild for, if they even knew it existed out here.

He had called his father before driving over to the motel. There was no reply, but he figured it was a safe bet that Jeff would be there now, at nine on a Sunday morning. Probably not much chance of him and Cathleen rushing off to church together. Now he pulled his rental car into a parking space and turned off the engine. There was only one cabin with a vehicle parked outside, so he got out of the car and headed for it.

He only paused for a moment outside the door before knocking firmly. There was a long wait, then just as he was about to knock again, Jeff opened the door wearing boxer shorts and a white T-shirt. When he saw Logan there, his expression flicked through surprise, guilt, and worry before settling on "cool as a cucumber."

"Morning," he drawled. "This is a surprise visit."

Logan was struck silent for a moment. It had been so long since he saw his father in person that he'd almost forgotten the presence he had. He'd always been confident, Logan remembered that, but there was a charisma about him that made him slightly larger than life, even though he wasn't a big man.

"What are you doing here?" his father added.

Logan refocused. He was here for a reason. "The bigger question is, what are *you* doing here?" he replied. "More specifically, what are you doing here with Avery's mom?"

Just then, Cathleen came to the door. "Oh! Logan." She pulled her robe closer at the front, her cheeks pink. "How are you?"

"I'm fine thanks, Mrs. Robinson. You?"

At the sound of her married name, she looked even more flustered. "Good, good. I'll just..." She gestured back into the cabin.

"Of course," Logan said, feeling the heat of his father's glare. "Nice to see you."

"You too." She turned and disappeared inside.

"That was a cheap shot," his father growled when she was gone.

Logan shrugged. "This whole thing seems pretty cheap to me."

Jeff stepped outside and pulled the door closed behind him. "We're in business. That doesn't give you the right to dictate my personal life."

"You already wrecked Avery's family once. Don't play fast and loose with it again, just when they have a chance to heal."

"Who says I'm playing fast and loose? Cathleen is a great lady. We might really have something."

There was no way Logan was letting this happen. For Avery's sake, and for Cathleen's sake too. "Actually, I don't think you have anything," he said. "Not if you want to be a part of this development." Having learned a little about Jeff's knife-edge financial situation, he guessed that money might be the only leverage he'd have.

But his father rolled his eyes. "You need me," he said. "You need that land. And now I know what it's worth. If you have a problem with me, I have no problem walking away. There are plenty of other people who'd like a piece of it."

Logan felt adrenaline pumping through him. He was this close to shoving his father up against the cabin wall and giving him a piece of something else. Why had he ever thought any of this would work?

"We seem to have skipped over the part where you lovingly greet your long-lost son with open arms."

"And the part where you show your father some respect," Jeff shot back.

"Respect is earned, not owed," Logan said. "And ten years of silence doesn't entitle you to anything."

"Seems to me you think having money entitles you to all kinds of things. You're not the only goddamn millionaire around, you know."

They stood for a moment looking at each other. Logan could feel a burning tension in his chest, hear his pulse pounding in his head. Unfortunately, Avery had been right—he had wanted his father back. But now that the man was standing in front of him, he wished he'd left well enough alone.

With an immense effort, he took a step back. "I'll be in touch." Then, without waiting for a reply, he turned and walked away.

Halfway across the parking lot, he heard the cabin door close. He got in the rental car, pulled out his phone, and made a call. "Rick, Logan Wagner here. I need you to dig a little deeper."

Avery walked into the community hall that afternoon to find it almost full. Birdie had called to let her know that Ellen Allsopp had announced an impromptu crisis meeting about the development at church that morning. Judging by the rows of people seated in the hall, word must have flown around town.

Seeing her aunts sitting with Claudia and Freya, she went over and joined them. They all sent her carefully sympathetic looks.

"Did you know anything about this?" Claudia asked as she sat down.

"Nope. Nothing."

Claudia made a face. "So awkward."

"You're telling me," Avery replied. She hadn't heard from Logan yet today, and she wasn't expecting to. She didn't even know if he was still in town, or if he'd gone back to the city. She looked around, but Barbara wasn't there to ask.

"I'm only here as a representative of the town," Freya said apologetically. "Just to be informed."

"It's okay," Avery told her. "I'm not exactly thrilled about the whole thing myself."

Cece reached across and took Avery's hand. "I'm sure he'll do the right thing."

Avery wasn't so sure. Especially as Jeff was in on the project too.

Ellen went up onto the stage and tapped the microphone, then blew into it. The resulting noise made everyone in the audience flinch and put their hands over their ears.

"Terry!" she said loudly, sending a speaker screech through the hall. "Can you deal with this please?"

Everyone watched as Terry scrambled toward the stage. He adjusted something on a control panel, and gave Ellen a nod. She returned her attention to the audience.

"Thank you for coming today. I won't keep you long. You will all have heard about the development being planned by the Wagner family on the other side of the river." She waited while a general sound of confirmation went around the hall. "Good. I've discussed it with the mayor, and although he can't be here today he feels that the first step is to gauge public reaction to the proposal. So, I would like to have a show of hands."

Claudia, Freya, and the aunts all looked at Avery, and she put a hand to her forehead. "Oh, great." Nothing like being put on the spot in public.

"Everyone who is opposed to the development, please

raise your hands," Ellen said.

A forest of arms went up, but Avery, Claudia, Freya, and the aunts sat awkwardly unmoving.

Ellen looked around, assessing, then nodded. "Now, everyone who is in favor of the development, please raise *your* hands."

A few people tentatively put their hands halfway up, looking anxiously around for reassurance that they weren't alone. Again, Avery's team sat still.

Ellen pursed her lips. "Alright, thank you everybody. I think that's a conclusive result." Then she turned in their direction, her laser-beam focus fixing on Avery.

"Avery," she said. "Are you for this development, or against it?"

Every pair of eyes in the hall turned to her. She shifted in her seat, wishing she hadn't come. Wishing Logan hadn't given her—any of them—a reason to be here. But she knew what she had to do. She took a deep breath.

"I'm against it."

Chapter 41

L ogan had made very few missteps in his career so far, thanks to a number of rules he always followed. There were three in his motto, of course: Keep moving. Do the next thing. Don't look back. The other main one was to always keep things as simple as possible. Somehow, with the Austen development, he'd found himself breaking them all. Not to mention making an almighty mess of things with Avery.

After the Statewide Scoop revelations on Saturday night, and her startlingly accurate doorstep diagnosis of his subconscious motives, he knew one thing for sure—if he asked her straight out now whether she regretted their last night in San Francisco, she wouldn't hesitate to say yes.

And he shouldn't have let her go so easily the morning after. What he *should* have done by the car was sweep her up and bowl her over with a passionate, supercharged kiss, and tell her exactly how he felt, making it impossible for her to leave.

In short, he was an idiot. Spectacularly successful in business and investment, an incompetent dunce in romance.

Now, after a few days back in San Francisco, he'd returned to Austen and was staying in one of the rooms above the Clover. The vacation rental hadn't been available, but staying with Patrick felt comfortable—more like being home again.

It was weird how he'd started liking that feeling more lately.

Once Patrick made sure the staff were handling the Thursday lunch rush, he came over and joined Logan at the bar.

"Penny for 'em," he said, going around behind the bar.

Logan grimaced. "You don't want to know."

"I think I already do." He passed Logan a pale ale. "Jeff. The development. Avery."

Logan accepted it gratefully and took a mouthful. "Does *everyone* in town know what's going on?"

"Probably. That's small-town life for you."

Of course. It made him cringe inside knowing that everyone was talking about him again. That was why he'd left in the first place. That, and because Avery hadn't wanted him anymore. Or so he'd thought. Now he knew that hadn't been completely true, but it all seemed even more complicated now than it was then. "I need to talk to her," he said. "In person."

Patrick nodded. "Cece told me that Avery said she was going to the mayor's office at two o'clock this afternoon, to talk about your development."

"Really?" He checked his watch. One forty-five. "Maybe I'll go and talk to them too. See if we can't come to an understanding."

Patrick looked doubtful. "I don't know if that's a good idea. It sounds like the town is very against it." He hesitated. "Are you sure you want to go ahead?"

"You're a businessman. Don't you think it would be an asset to the town? To the local economy?"

"Honestly?" Patrick took his time polishing a glass, then set it on the bar. "I think there must be a better way."

Logan rotated his own glass on the bar top, thinking. "Patrick, what would you do if you were me?"

He laughed. "I'd take my money and buy one of those trips into space. I always wanted to see the stars for real.

And I'm so single no one would miss me if it all went pear-shaped."

"For starters, that's not true." Logan pointed a finger at him. "This town wouldn't be the same without you and your Dublin coddle."

"Ah, leave off," he said, busily wiping away an invisible mark on the counter.

"Secondly," Logan said, "if I went interstellar, I think Avery would wave me off without a tear."

"Don't be so sure," Patrick said. "Until you've done every last thing to win her over, there's still a chance."

"I don't know. I've made too much of a mess of it. All this crap with my father, and now the development."

"I think you can fix that."

"Part of it, maybe." In his time back in San Francisco, he'd had some very productive discussions with Rick Miller. The private investigator had uncovered illuminating details about Jeff's tax situation and his private life. The latter wasn't something Logan had relished learning, knowing it would hurt Avery's mom all over again. But the financial stuff was gold.

"Good," Patrick said. "Then you can move forward."

"It's not as simple as that though. I've lost her trust by not telling her stuff I should have. More than once."

"Hmm," Patrick said thoughtfully, straightening some bottles next to the bar sink. "Have you tried telling her the most important thing of all?"

Logan stared at him as two and two made its way toward four in his mind.

"You're a smart guy." Patrick smiled. "I think you can figure something out."

Mayor Whittaker's office was a throwback to the eighties, with beige décor shot through with shades of teal and pink. It had obviously been decorated long before he was first elected, and never changed since. Looking around, Avery thought his lack of interest in redecorating showed how dedicated he was to the town itself. His priorities were in the right place.

"Avery, hello," he said, coming to give her a kiss on the cheek. Then he gestured to a comfortable chair in front of his desk. "Please, sit down."

"Thanks," she said as she took a seat. "You're looking well."

"I am well," he said with a smile. As he took his own seat behind the desk, he looked more somber. "Your father's farewell was wonderful—a fitting send-off for a great man. We all miss him very much."

A wave of emotion came over her. "Thank you. I do too."

"Well, you know our thoughts are with you. How are you coping?"

She shrugged. "Not too bad. I have my moments."

"I heard your mom is back in town."

She waited for him to say something about Jeff, but he either didn't know or was kind enough not to mention it. "Uh…yes. That's been interesting for us both."

Interesting didn't go anywhere near to describing the last few days, but she couldn't think of an adjective that would sum it up. On Sunday night, her mom had finally come back to the house—with Jeff in tow. She had seemed hesitant, mousy; Jeff had been self-assured, pleased with himself. Ace had stiffened on seeing him, his hackles rising, but Jeff bowled on through like he owned the place. Apparently he was even bolder when fully dressed.

And now it was Thursday, and neither of them seemed inclined to move on. Avery and Ace had been sleeping in a bedroom at the far end of the upstairs, and she'd been spending a lot of time in town. Luckily everyone knew and loved Ace, thanks to Owen taking him everywhere too, and he was welcomed wherever she went for breakfast, lunch, and dinner. He'd even gone with her to the appointment with the lawyer, who confirmed that everything her mom had said was true.

She knew they couldn't go on this way, but she didn't want to leave town until the issue of the development was sorted. Logan hadn't tried to contact her. She'd been so sure he would change his mind. Clearly, she'd been wrong.

Now she changed the subject. "I thought Ellen might have made you come to the community meeting on Sunday."

The mayor gave a wry smile. "She tried. But I didn't go to the meeting because it's important to maintain some distance in cases like this—remain neutral until all the facts are in."

She nodded. "I can see that. And are all the facts in?"

"Well..." He shuffled through some papers. "I've followed up with the county, and they tell me the applications are progressing. The proposal is the maximum size allowed for the location, but it is allowed. As long as the owner of the land wants to go ahead, there's nothing we can legally do to stop it."

Discouragement sank into her. She knew that the town had been lucky to have access to the land all this time, and it wouldn't be right to prevent Jeff and Logan from realizing the value of it, but—

A light bulb went off in her head. "Is there any way the town could buy the land? Like years ago, when they bought the last lots on this side of the river?"

The mayor shook his head. "That would be an excellent solution, Avery, but there's no way we could afford it. Property prices have shot up around here, and we'd also have to pay enough to compensate for the loss of the development income."

It seemed like between them, Logan and Jeff had everything in their favor. She thought about the untouched land on the other side of the river. The Wagner lot was only a piece of it, but it was the most visible and accessible part. That area was the relief valve for everyone in town—a retreat for hiking, biking, dog-walking, or just getting away and breathing a little easier. She'd escaped over there countless times herself over the years, running her fingers along the handrails on each side of the little footbridge as she went.

Then something else occurred to her. That footbridge was no more than an arm's width wide, and there was no road access. Any major project on that side of the river would need to be accessed via water from Austen. Without the support of the town, it would be almost impossible to function.

"Did it say anything in the paperwork about access to the site?" she asked. "How will they get all the equipment and materials over there?"

The mayor sat up straighter. "Ah. Good question." He flicked through the papers again. "Yes, there will need to be a headquarters on this side, and some kind of wharf built to facilitate shipping. That would require permission from the town itself."

They looked at each other.

"That falls under your jurisdiction, right?" she said.

"It does."

"And are you still maintaining a neutral position?"

He tapped his chin. "I believe I will be announcing an official opinion on the matter very shortly—one that you will find satisfactory." Then he leaned forward, his tone changing from kingly to kindly. "I understand this is a difficult position for you to be in."

"Me? No, I'm fine."

He clucked his tongue in sympathy. "My granddaughter Meg told me about you and Logan almost getting back together. Everyone remembers the two of you in high school. I know this can't be easy for you."

She opened her mouth to protest, but no words came out. She kept forgetting how quickly news spread in a small town. If even the mayor was in on the gossip, there would be no escaping it.

"This is something important for the town," she said, getting up. "Logan and I will just have to see what happens."

And right now, what looked most likely to happen was nothing at all.

Chapter 42

L ogan made his way from the Clover toward City Hall. The building itself hardly carried the weight of the name—it was a modest two-story brick structure that looked more like someone's house. But it had done honest duty for the town since before he was born, and would probably continue long after he was gone. He wouldn't be surprised if Mayor Whittaker outlasted him too—the man had been mayor for as long as Logan could remember, and apparently showed no sign of wanting to retire.

Patrick had convinced him not to barge in on Avery's meeting with the mayor, and after some protest he'd realized the Irishman was probably right. He'd been concerned about looking like a needy boyfriend; "heavy-handed developer" wasn't somewhere he wanted to go either. But hopefully he'd catch her on the way out, and they could talk properly. He passed the Riverbend Café. Maybe he could take her there, and they could talk over coffee and something sweet.

Then he saw Avery on the other side of the street, coming out of City Hall and starting down the steps. He stopped to watch her. Damn, she was beautiful. She looked so at home here, like she belonged. But then she'd seemed the same way in San Francisco too. There was something about her that glowed, no matter where she was. He waited by the café as she checked for traffic then crossed the street and walked in his direction. She was wearing jeans, a pastel print blouse, and gold sandals, and her blonde hair was pulled up in a ponytail. Then she stopped outside her aunts' gift store, her lips pressed together, and he realized he was staring. He raised his hand and started toward her.

"Hey," he said as he reached her.

"Hi," she said, but she didn't sound pleased to see him.

Well, it was a start. At least she hadn't turned and walked away.

"No Ace today?" he asked.

"He's with Claudia. She's looking after her nieces this afternoon, and they love him."

"Ah." No canine backup for him today then. "How have you been?"

She looked straight at him. "You've got my number. You could have asked me that any time since Saturday night."

"Yeah." He cleared his throat. "And your mom?"

"Still here. Still with Jeff."

"At the motel?"

"Nope. In my house. *Her* house."

"Ah. That's not ideal," he said. "Is he treating her right? Is she happy?"

"Actually, I don't know," she replied, her worry showing even as she kept her distance. "It feels like she's walking on eggshells. But he's completely at home. I asked him when he'll be leaving, and he just laughed and said he'll leave when he's ready."

At that, Logan felt a familiar anger radiate through him. "If your mom is unhappy, maybe she'll ask him to go."

Avery gave him a dark look. "I don't think so. She said he's her weakness. And from what I can tell, he knows it."

"I'll talk to him," Logan said. "I'll fix this."

"Oh my God, would you just stop?" she said. "You made this mess in the first place. You opened Pandora's box. There are actual people involved now—you can't just stride in and fix it." Then she looked over his shoulder and stiffened. "Oh, damn it."

He turned around to see Jeff and Cathleen right behind him.

Cathleen gave a little circle wave. "Hello."

"Hi, Mom," Avery said. Then she shot a glare at Jeff.

"Afternoon," he said blithely.

"Don't they need you back at work in Pahrump?" Logan said to him.

He shook his head. "My second-in-command is holding the fort."

"Second-in-command? Is that what they're calling it in Nevada now?"

In an instant, his father switched from nonchalant to quietly dangerous. "Excuse me?"

Logan turned to Cathleen. "I'm sorry for what you're about to hear, Mrs. Robinson."

Her face went pink. "What?"

He turned back to Jeff. "Donna-Marie Norman. Your second-in-command. Your assistant manager. Your girlfriend."

"You don't know what the hell you're talking about," Jeff snarled.

Cathleen took hold of his sleeve. "Jeff, is this true?"

"Of course it's not true," he told her impatiently. "I work with a lot of women, doesn't mean there's anything going on."

"There won't be *now*," Logan said. "Not since Donna-Marie found out about you and Cathleen."

Cathleen put her hands over her mouth and made a strangled noise. "Not again."

Logan wished he hadn't had to break that particular piece of news to her, but he knew Jeff would never come clean himself.

Just then the door of the gift store opened, and Birdie came out and took in the sidewalk tableau. Logan knew it didn't look good—Cathleen distraught, Jeff glowering, Avery glaring between father and son. As a local couple walked past, their curiosity obvious as they slowed down,

Birdie made a quick assessment and took action.

"Cathleen," she said. "You must come in and see our latest delivery." She tucked her arm through Cathleen's, then looked at Avery. "Will you join us, Avery?"

"You go ahead," she replied. "I'll be there in a minute."

Cathleen let Birdie steer her inside to where Logan could see Cece waiting, then the three women disappeared toward the back of the store. He was impressed by their kindness to the woman who'd left their brother so many years before. That was the kind of family they were. Unlike his.

As if to prove his thoughts true, Jeff stepped forward and placed a heavy finger in the center of his chest. "What the hell are you playing at?"

Logan glanced down at the finger, and stood his ground. "You're the one who's been playing, Jeff. And not just with Donna-Marie. The IRS might be interested in some of your creative financial games."

The finger dropped. "Nice try," he scoffed. "Donna-Marie doesn't know anything about my personal finances."

"I didn't need to ask Donna-Marie," Logan replied. "Your accountant was very helpful when we pointed out some discrepancies that he might be held...*accountable* for."

Jeff stepped back, his face twisted in a scowl. "What do you want?"

Now they were talking. "I want you to sell me the land at current market value. I'll give you a fair price, nothing more. And I want you to go back to Pahrump—or anywhere else you choose—and let Cathleen and Avery get on with their lives."

"And the taxes?"

"That's between you and your accountant and your conscience. Unless you don't sell me the land. Then it's between you and the IRS."

Logan waited for his father's reply. Jeff seemed to be hovering on the verge of an outburst, his shoulders raised and his jaw clenched. But then he shook his head.

"My lawyer will be in touch," he said, and turned and

walked away down the street.

Logan let him go without replying. There was nothing to say anyway. He watched him go, feeling years of hope slide away. But there was something else too—a new freedom. Letting go.

He turned to Avery. Only minutes before, he'd promised to fix things. Would she thank him for getting rid of Jeff, or see it as another secret kept, another blow to her mom?

Before either of them could speak, Birdie came out again. "Avery?"

"I'm coming," she said. She glanced at Logan, unreadable, then went in.

But he didn't plan to let her walk away. He followed them into the store. The bell tinkled as he went through the door, and he found himself in a home décor cocoon— pillows and throws, fragrant candles, fake plants, and wall signs with cutesy inspirational sayings. His nose twitched and he leaned down to read the label on the nearest candle. Ylang ylang? Right then he knew this wasn't his territory.

The faces of the four women looking at him from near the sales counter confirmed it. For a moment all five of them stood in silence as shopping-friendly background music played. Michael Bublé, maybe, or Harry Connick Jr. He guessed they were waiting to see what he'd say. And he knew what that would be.

Chapter 43

"Avery," Logan said. "We need to talk."

"Not now," she said, gesturing to Cathleen, who was sitting on a stool by the counter clutching a handful of tissues.

"I'm alright," Cathleen said, mopping her face. "I brought it on myself. And I messed up my chance to reconnect with you, Avery."

"That's okay," Avery replied, but it was obvious to Logan, and probably everyone else, that it wasn't really.

"No, it's not," Cathleen said. "And it's not the first time I've ruined everything. I'm sorry, Avery. For back then, and for now." Her face crumpled. "I'm a terrible mother."

"Oh, Mom," Avery said. "Only kind of terrible."

Cathleen snorted out a laugh, and Logan watched as a half smile crept onto Avery's face. Maybe they would be okay after all.

Then Cathleen looked to Cece and Birdie. "I know how much you loved Owen. I owe you both an apology, too."

The aunts murmured noises that sounded like they were both agreeing and disagreeing at the same time.

Then the bell over the door tinkled again as two

women came in, talking loudly to each other. Cathleen turned on her stool to hide her red eyes, and Avery put a tentative hand on her shoulder. Logan could see that it was the start of something. And he wanted to get back to the start with Avery too.

He looked to Cece and Birdie. "Is there anywhere Avery and I could talk? Just for a minute?"

Avery frowned in his direction, her brows knitted, but Cece nodded. "Come on," she said to Avery, coming over and taking her arm. "You two need to get this sorted out."

"There's nothing to sort out," Avery protested as Cece towed her toward a door in the back wall. Logan followed close behind, thanking his lucky stars for interfering relatives.

Cece saw them in, then closed the door. They were in a tiny, dimly lit stockroom that was just one corridor lined with ceiling-height shelves, all packed with boxes. Avery stood by the end wall, as far away from him as she could get, but he noticed that her eyes raked over his body before she crossed her arms and fixed him with a rebellious look.

"Let's do this," he said.

"We've done all our talking already," she told him.

But he shook his head. "I don't think so. I get the impression you have more to say. You look like you're holding in a *lot* more."

"It's probably indigestion," she said. "I had a big lunch."

He raised an eyebrow, and she rolled her eyes. "Okay. I thought we could just leave this be, but sure. I have a question."

"Shoot," he said, happy at least that they were talking.

"If you wanted to reconnect with your father, you should have just gone and done it in Nevada. Did you have to drag Austen into it? Did you have to drag *me* into it?"

"I didn't—" He stopped, looking at her beautiful, conflicted face.

They were very good questions, and all of a sudden, he knew the answer.

He thought about his very first days back in town.

Seeing her at Owen's funeral, then on the river path the next morning, he had known straight away that their chemistry was still there. And through all their interactions, that had been constant, even when things were going wrong. But it wasn't just physical chemistry for him. It was the heart connection—the simple knowledge that they were meant to be, just like they'd known as kids.

She had only been partly right when she told him the Austen development was just an excuse—a front for trying to get his father back. There was another reason.

Her.

He'd come back to Oregon for her. And she was so much more important than Jeff Wagner.

But she was so damn stubborn, so ready to pick up the old anger. If he was going to have any chance, he had to break through, even if he risked pushing her away even more. At this point, he had nothing to lose...and everything to lose.

"You told me something about myself on Saturday night," he said. "Now I have some armchair analysis for *you*."

She laughed. "Oh, really. This I have to hear. Lay it on me."

She watched as Logan shoved his hands through his hair and blew out a breath.

"I'm ready," she said. "Tell me *all* about myself." This ought to be good, coming from a guy who had been entirely clueless about his own motivations.

"Okay. I didn't come back here for the land, or for my father. I came back here looking for you."

That didn't even make sense. "You said you came for Dad's funeral." Then a realization hit her. "Did you really? Or did you actually come to get started on your development?"

"Well...both, to be honest," he said. "But I didn't know I was looking for you too. I was skirting around the edges, picking up the threads—"

"You're sewing now?" She shook her head and started toward the door. "I think we're done here. You've caused enough extra trouble for me and Mom. I'm going to go."

But he put an arm out sideways to block her way, and she stopped. "Seriously?"

"Avery. You told me to let it go, but I don't think you want that, not really. And I don't want to let us go. Just the bad stuff."

"You can't separate it out," she said. "It's all tangled up."

"You can separate it if you want to. You seemed to manage it when *we* got tangled up."

She shot him a death glare. Damn him for being right—she had totally let go of everything, including her inhibitions. She noticed just a hint of a self-satisfied smile lurking on his lips as he watched her.

"That's not even funny," she said, grit in her voice. "Don't use my own emotions against me."

"And now you're mad at me again," he said calmly. "I get it. All the ways you've been mad at me since I came back are tangled up with your original anger about me leaving. But you were the one who pulled away, remember? You told me to leave you alone, and then when I did, you regretted it. But it was easier to blame me than accept you'd made a mistake."

His words cut through all the noise to something she'd never been willing to consider or examine. Automatically, she fell into defensive mode. "It's more complicated than that."

"It doesn't have to be complicated. It could be just you and me, a simple, easy love, same as it used to be."

"Love?" She backed up, her heart pounding. "Oh, no. I can't go there."

"Can't, or won't?"

He came closer, his eyes dark, the width of his shoulders almost filling the space between the shelves. Her pulse picked up even more.

"Listen," she said, working to keep her voice steady. "The best thing you can do for all of us is take yourself back

to San Francisco. But don't worry, I'll still think of you—
every time I step outside or look out my window and see
whatever monstrosity you build over the river. And you'll
be fine—you'll find some other woman who values
ambition more than heritage."

As the words "some other woman" left her lips, she felt
sick to her stomach. But that would be better for both of
them. Really, it would. Eventually.

"You say *ambition* like it's a bad thing," he said,
ignoring her suggestion about the other woman. "But you
had ambition. You wanted to work in radio, and you made
that happen."

"Yeah, and look where it got me. Outsmarted by a guy
who didn't care about me at all. Someone who was always
looking for the next, better chance. Someone whose career
was more important than me."

"I'm not like him, you know."

"I didn't say you were."

"You didn't need to say it in so many words."

"Okay, fine, if you want to identify with that, go right
ahead. You, Carter, Jeff...you're all as bad as each other."

He shook his head. "I know you don't mean that."

"I just watched you win a dirty contest with your
father, so you can line your own pockets at the expense of
this town."

"I already told you it would be something that benefits
the town. You must know I wouldn't harm this place. It
was my home too."

She noted the past tense. It wasn't his home anymore.
But in the last few weeks she'd found herself getting even
more attached to this little town, reconnecting in a way she
hadn't expected. She wasn't going to let him ruin it. She
wasn't going to let him distract her from what was really
important.

"What I know is that I'm going to look after our
environment."

He looked directly at her. "And who's going to look
after you?"

"I don't need anyone to look after me. I plan to look

after myself, in work and relationships," she said. "No one is going to be my weakness."

"It's not a question of weakness," he said, his voice soft. "It's about letting someone in. Being weak and letting yourself be vulnerable are two different things."

A panicky feeling started to overcome her, and she shook her head. "Wagners and Robinsons aren't good for each other. It's a multigenerational thing, there's no point fighting it. We should just accept that and move on." She swallowed. "And now I want you to let me pass."

She brushed past him. He didn't try to prevent her from going, but he didn't get out of her way either, and she felt the heat of his body as she went by, couldn't stop herself breathing in his warm scent.

She opened the door and burst out into the store, the heady combination of vanilla bean and ylang ylang and French pear knocking her away from him and back to reality. Her aunts and her mom turned and looked at her expectantly, and she went over to join them.

"Let's go, Mom," she said.

But now they weren't looking at her. She swiveled to see what they'd focused their attention on. Logan was coming out of the stockroom, a dark frustration hanging over him.

"Ladies," he said with a nod. He met her eye, and she felt an unspoken promise in his steady gaze—*this isn't over.* Then he went out the door, and was gone.

The others turned to her again, but she shook her head.

Wagners and Robinsons weren't good for each other. Everyone knew that. Development or not, there was no way they could ever go back to a simple, easy kind of love.

Her heart would accept it…eventually.

Chapter 44

Logan stood between the trees on the riverbank in the last of the Saturday afternoon sun, his nerves raw. Despite his outfit, and his grand plan, he'd never felt less like a romantic hero.

"Do you think this has any chance of working?" he asked Patrick.

Patrick looked him up and down. "Well, your boots could be shinier."

On edge, he bent down to check them. Then he heard Patrick's laugh, and straightened up.

"She's not even going to see them up close, Mr. Darcy," Patrick said.

"Oh. Yeah." Damn, he was a wreck and she hadn't even come out of the house yet. He squinted across the river, looking for the waving dish towel on the porch that would be Cece's signal. Nothing. It felt like he and Patrick had been standing there for hours.

He ran a hand through his hair and adjusted the neck cloth Birdie had tied for him earlier, at the rambling, cat-filled house she and Cece shared. The sisters had fussed around until his Regency costume was tweaked to their satisfaction, then stood back to assess his reflection in the mirror.

"If you can't make this work, looking the way you do, no man in the world would stand a chance," Cece had said.

One of their enormous, shaggy cats curled around his legs, its tail held high. He bent down and stroked its fur, and it butted its head against him.

"Even Gloria agrees," said Birdie. "And she's *very* hard to please."

"I'll take that endorsement," he'd replied.

Now he paced the clearing where he and Patrick were waiting, running over in his mind what he wanted to say.

"It doesn't matter if you don't remember all the flowery words," Patrick reminded him, "as long as you tell her the most important thing of all."

Logan stopped pacing. Patrick was right. He just had to keep it simple. It was one of the rules, after all. He thought of the others: Keep moving. Do the next thing. Don't look back. They'd served him well in business, but they could apply equally well to finding love with Avery. He wanted to follow the rules with her by his side—looking forward to a future together. If she would have him.

Avery pulled into the driveway at home and stopped the car, then turned to Claudia. "Thanks for coming with me to drop Mom off."

"Any time," Claudia said. "You know me, I love a trip to the airport. Shame you didn't lend her your jet though." She grinned.

Avery rolled her eyes. "Ha-ha."

"Seriously though, I'm glad you guys were in a better place by the time she left."

"Me too." Avery undid her seat belt and reached into the back for her purse. "We have a way to go, but at least Jeff Wagner is history. Again."

"I guess you can thank Logan for that."

Avery made a noncommittal noise. "I guess."

After the incident on the street when Jeff and Logan had their showdown, and Logan broke the news about Donna-Marie, Cathleen had been thoroughly shaken. But she had regrouped surprisingly quickly, almost as though she was relieved that her temptation was gone.

"I thought she seemed happier," Claudia said. "Like he'd been weighing her down."

"Yeah. And she said she was looking forward to going back to sea. I think she likes that life."

"Maybe you can go cruise with her one day."

Avery nodded. "That's what she said too. I'm planning on it."

Theirs would never be a traditional mother–daughter relationship—too much water had gone under the bridge—but Avery hoped they could figure out a way to make it work. For now, knowing that her mom wasn't going to sell the house from under her was a huge relief. If her podcast plan came to fruition—and she was determined to make it happen—she could be based anywhere. And if she did well enough, she could give her mom some substantial financial help, ensuring the house would remain in the Robinson family for years to come.

As they got out of the car, she saw her aunts arriving too. She and Claudia went over to join them as they came up the path.

"Is book club finished already?" she asked.

"Yes, all done," Cece said breathlessly.

"All finished," Birdie added.

They went up the steps and Avery felt in her purse for her keys. The three women seemed to be hovering very close to her. "So…would you like to come in?"

They all nodded and smiled in agreement, so Avery opened the door and waved them in. Ace was right there, acting as a solo welcoming committee as usual. He jigged around in excitement, stepping on her feet and whining.

Between him, Claudia, and the aunts, Avery was feeling very crowded. She broke through and headed for the kitchen. "Coffee?"

"Yes," said Claudia.

"No," said the aunts.

"Actually, we should take Ace for a walk," Claudia said as they all reached the kitchen. "He's been in here all afternoon." She went and took his leash from the hook and held it out.

Avery's shoulders slumped. "Can't we have coffee first? We only just got home."

Cece was over by the counter, a dish towel in her hand. "Birdie and I will make coffee," she said. "You girls give Ace a quick run along the river path." She went and opened the back door, and waved the dish towel violently around. "Shoo, fly! Shoo!"

Avery hadn't noticed a fly. Both Birdie and Cece seemed very on edge—maybe Lori and Debra-Ann had eaten all the book club cake again. Or maybe they were just being their usual eccentric selves. She clipped the leash onto Ace's collar.

"Off you go," Birdie said, hustling them out the door. Avery had little choice but to obey.

"They seem tense today," she commented to Claudia as they went down the steps.

Claudia shrugged. "I didn't notice anything out of the ordinary."

"Huh. Maybe I'm just tired. Mom and I stayed up really late last night, talking." They reached the bottom of the backyard, and she stopped and closed her eyes for a moment, enjoying the warm sun on her face. "What a gorgeous day."

Ace tugged on his leash, looking at her expectantly, and she crouched down and put her arms around his neck. "Okay, mister impatient. I'm just going to let you have a run in the yard."

"But we were supposed to take him for a walk," Claudia said, frowning.

"It's okay." Avery unclipped the leash. "He can stretch his legs in here for now, and I'll take him later. I'm more interested in that coffee right now." But Claudia had turned away, and was unlatching the gate. "Where are you going?"

She turned around, a grin on her face. "To show you something you might find more interesting than coffee. Come on."

"What?" Avery went to join her.

Claudia opened the gate, then pointed over the river.

Logan was standing on the opposite shore. And— Avery's heart did a traitorous flip in her chest—he was dressed as Mr. Darcy once more. What on earth was he doing?

"Go," Cece said from right behind her.

She turned to see her aunts standing shoulder to shoulder, smiling. Suddenly their insistence that Ace needed a walk made sense.

"You had something to do with this," she accused them.

Birdie waved a hand. "Not at all."

"Just a little," Cece said.

Avery raised an eyebrow at their mismatched denials, but she couldn't be mad at them. Then Claudia pulled her through the gate, before standing back with the aunts. Ace had noticed Logan now too, and sent a volley of woofs across the river, his tail whipping from side to side.

Logan gave a slightly sheepish grin and raised his hand in greeting. Avery's own hand went up automatically in return, but she was distracted by what he was wearing. There was something ridiculously dashing about him in that outfit. As she watched, he bent down and pulled off one boot, then the other. Then his long coat was off, and he started to unbutton his waistcoat.

Ohhh. She knew what was coming next. With that realization, she felt an anticipatory blush heat her cheeks. She glanced over her shoulder. The others were riveted to the scene on the opposite bank. Looking back, she saw that Logan had finished unbuttoning the waistcoat and was taking it off. He dropped the garment on the ground and began loosening the neck cloth, a tantalizing replay of his actions at the festival.

Within moments the cloth was undone, and the neck of his shirt fell open. He paused for a moment on the riverbank, then carefully made a long, flat dive into the water. As a splash went up, Ace woofed again, an increased urgency in his tone.

The water was flowing faster than usual today, and Logan came up slightly downstream from where they were standing. Then he started swimming back toward them. Ace was beside himself now, rushing back and forth on the shore, barking. Avery wasn't sure if it was excitement or worry.

"Calm down," she told him. "He'll be here shortly."

But Ace couldn't calm down. Taking a flying leap, he threw himself into the water and started paddling desperately for Logan.

"Ace!" Avery shouted. "Ace, no!"

Ignoring her, Ace continued his mission to reach Logan, who was making his way back upriver. They met midstream, and Ace tried to clamber up on Logan's shoulders, pushing him half underwater. Avery put a hand to her forehead as a struggle ensued, with Logan trying to grab a proper hold of Ace, and Ace doing his level best to protect the object of his affection but repeatedly submerging him in the process.

Finally Logan gave up and made a break for it, swimming against the current with Ace in pursuit. Avery held her breath, but they were both good swimmers, and every now and then Logan reached back and pulled Ace along. He reached the shore first and hauled Ace out, depositing the dog half on the bank. Ace scrambled the rest of the way up then stopped and shook himself vigorously, sending a spray of river water in all directions.

"Ace!" Avery exclaimed, ducking away. "Stop that!"

But he took his time, shaking himself at length until there were only a few drops flying. Then he danced around them, wiggling and lolling, ready for petting and praise. He was clearly thrilled with the whole situation, and his very helpful "rescue."

Logan gave her a rueful smile. "That didn't go how I planned."

She took in the man standing before her—tall, dark, and dripping wet, the white shirt outlining his torso, the pale-colored pants clinging to his strong thighs. Canine drama aside, she didn't think the outcome could have been much better.

But she wasn't going to tell him that.

Instead, she waited to see what he had to say this time.

Chapter 45

J ust as Logan had hoped, Mr. Darcy wasn't letting him down.

He stood on the grassy riverbank, cold drips of water running down his neck, his wet clothes plastered to his body. He was pretty sure Ace had scratched his shoulder through the shirt, but he didn't move to check. Not while Avery's eyes were sweeping over him, and she had that flush in her cheeks.

Then she seemed to realize he was watching her and looked quickly away, pointing over the river. "You know there won't be any forest left to make an entrance from, by the time you're finished over there," she said tartly.

He shook his head, scattering water droplets, then swiped his wet hair away from his forehead. "There's been a change of plans," he said.

"Really." The word was heavy with skepticism. "What kind of change?"

He smiled. "Something I think you'll like."

"Great! You're canceling the development."

He should have seen that coming. "No. But I promise it's something good."

"Can't be that good if you had to reprise your Mr. Darcy act to tell me about it." She gestured to his soaking attire.

"Don't you like it anymore?" he asked, standing straight and broad in front of her. He looked over her shoulder to the other women, and she followed his gaze. All three of them were lit up like it was Christmas. "Some people do," he pointed out.

She frowned in their direction. "Some people can't resist meddling in other people's lives."

But they just laughed, and Ace joined in with a jovial woof. The dog was sitting between him and Avery, exactly as he had that day on the river path. Not for the first time, Logan was grateful to have a friend on the inside.

Then he nodded to Birdie, and she came over and handed him an envelope, as planned. He thanked her, then she stood back again and he passed it to Avery.

"Here's the change of plans," he said. "Open it and tell me if you like them."

"I'm not going to like them," she said stubbornly.

He smiled. "Sometimes you don't know what you'll like until you give it a chance."

"I wish you would just forget this tragically misguided attempt to 'help' the town," she said, making air quotes with the envelope in one hand.

"Just take a look," he insisted.

After their discussion in the stock room at the aunts' store, he'd had a brainwave. Something he was pretty sure Avery would approve of. And now he couldn't wait for her to see it.

She sighed. "Alright, fine, if it will get this over with." She opened the envelope, then pulled out the papers inside and unfolded them. "Oh."

He watched her face transform as she realized what she was looking at. They were artist's impressions of the Wagner land, from different angles and elevations. And up in the trees, like something out of a fantasy realm, were tree houses. Not big, ungainly structures, not sleek contemporary accommodation, but natural-looking dwellings, each one hugging the trunk like an extension of the tree itself.

She looked up, entranced but puzzled. "This isn't what I expected."

"They're only concepts," he said. "But I gave the artist the best description I could at short notice."

"You can build these?" She held up the illustrations.

"We'll need experts in the field, but yes. They'd be ecofriendly, with solar power and other technologies to minimize the impact on the environment. And if you want to, you can be involved in the design, so they blend in perfectly. I managed to get it completely wrong last time...as you know."

"You want *me* to help?"

He nodded. "If you're interested. I need someone on my side, since I created enough of a crisis to make Ellen mobilize the town against me."

Avery laughed. "Yeah, it's not a good idea to cross her."

"She wasn't my biggest fan to start with," he said. Then he gestured to the illustrations. "Do you think something like this will be good for Austen?"

She looked at them again, then over the river and back to him. "If you really can do something like this, then yes, I do."

"Good." He stepped a little closer. "You know, I never did fill that garbage bag. Does this prove that I do care about the town after all?"

Her smile lit a fuse of hope in his heart. "I think maybe it does."

Avery clutched the papers in her hand, her mind racing at Logan's turnaround. She had been totally against the idea of any development over the river, no matter what, but this was magical. Even Ellen and Mayor Whittaker would have to agree that it could be an amazing asset for Austen.

Now Logan cleared his throat. "There's something else I care about," he said. "*Someone* else."

A warm anticipation rose in her as she met his brown eyes. "There is?"

He nodded, and pushed his wet hair away from his forehead again. She'd never seen him look so nervous.

"It is a truth universally acknowledged," he began, echoing the famous first words of Pride and Prejudice, "that I have made a royal mess of our second chance. So this is me, calling on the power of your Mr. Darcy for support, standing here asking for a *third* chance."

She heard an *ahh* from behind her, and turned to see Claudia, Cece, and Birdie all looking enraptured by Logan's declaration. They had been joined by Patrick, who was holding Logan's discarded clothes and boots, puffing slightly. He gave her a wink, and she smiled and turned back to Logan again.

"Third time lucky?" she suggested.

"That's my plan."

He shifted on the spot, a hopeful, uncertain expression on his handsome face. In that moment, she could see through the confident, successful businessman to the eager, unruly teenager she remembered from so long ago. He was so different now, in so many ways, but that boy was still there. A regular hometown guy who'd taken his heartache out into the world and done something amazing. And standing in front of him, she felt like the Avery of long ago too. The Avery who'd wanted him in so many ways, but had to wait ten years before she knew him completely.

And what she knew now changed everything.

She looked over her shoulder again to Cece and Birdie, just one question in her heart. They didn't need her to say it aloud.

"Your dad would approve," Birdie said softly, giving her a nod.

"He would," Cece confirmed. "And we do too."

It was all Avery needed to hear. She turned back to Logan and gestured to his Regency attire, which was still distractingly plastered to his body. "Aren't you going to tell me how—"

"Ardently I admire and love you?"

She laughed. He was getting pretty slick with his Darcy quotes. "I was actually going to say, how you planned all this."

"Oh," he said, looking discouraged.

"But that works too," she added hurriedly.

"Good." He pulled her into his arms and held her close. She slipped her arms around him, feeling the heat of his body radiating through his wet clothes. If they didn't have company, she would have dragged him through the gate, into the house, and straight into her bed to warm up properly. Looking into his eyes, she knew he was having the same kind of thoughts.

"You're getting me all wet," she said, but she didn't move away.

He grinned. "So you *do* like it."

"I'll admit it. Colin Firth had nothing on you."

He raised an eyebrow. "Wow. High praise indeed." Then he became serious again. "Avery, this is where I tell you that I do admire you. And I do love you. I loved you back then, and I love you now. And if we were pulled back in time to eighteen-whenever, I would love you then too. Mr. Darcy would have a fight on his hands."

She laughed. "No fighting necessary. I know who I love now."

"Took you long enough," he teased.

"Well, you didn't make it easy," she told him, but she was smiling. Then she shook her head. "When we were kids, we never doubted we were meant to be. I might be older now, but I think I was wiser then."

"And do you doubt us now?" he said. "Because I don't."

Standing in his arms on the riverbank, with their past all around her, friends and family behind her, and their future ahead, one thing was finally clear. She looked at the cool, clean river, the green palette of forest on the opposite side, and the clear Oregon sky, then at the man who was home to her just as much as any place could be.

"I have no doubt that you're the person I want," she said, smiling as she saw the happiness in his eyes. "And that you were the right person all along. I'm glad you came back."

"Back to where we began," he said.

She nodded. "And where we began again."

Thanks for reading *Where We Began!*
Continue the Austen, Oregon series with *Say We Will*
and *Like We Used To*, coming soon.

Also by Serena Clarke

One Distant Summer
A North So True
The Same But Different
All Over the Place

About the Author

Serena Clarke writes escapist romantic fiction set all over the world. Readers have described her books as engaging page-turners, with sigh-worthy happy endings that will leave you smiling.

Her own story? She's lived in thirty-nine houses, in seven cities, in four countries. She's been a riding instructor, edited a medical journal, worked at a London law firm, and taught English as a second language to wayward teenagers. And now she's found her own happy ending—living near the beach in beautiful New Zealand with her family, writing the kind of feel-good books she loves to read. She hopes you'll love them too!

Find her online at www.serenaclarke.com.